T0129416

Praise for *Open for Murder*

"When you add up a fun setting, characters who would make excellent friends, and an engaging mystery you get Angela's *Open for Murder!*"
—**Lynn Cahoon, *New York Times* bestselling author of the Kitchen Witch series**

"*Open for Murder* is an absolute delight! You'll adore your visit to the charming Spirit Canyon, where nothing is quite as it seems. The very talented Mary Angela has created a gorgeous setting, a lively cast of characters, and a tremendously satisfying mystery that will keep readers happily guessing."
—**Cynthia Kuhn, author of the Agatha-award-winning Lila Maclean Academic Mysteries**

"A great start to the Happy Camper series. *Open for Murder* features a strong protagonist, likable secondary characters and a compelling mystery with the gorgeous backdrop of the Black Hills."
—**Catherine Bruns, *USA Today* bestselling author and Daphne du Maurier award winner**

Also by Mary Angela

Happy Camper Mysteries
Open for Murder

Professor Prather Mysteries
An Act of Murder
Passport to Murder
A Very Merry Murder
Coming Up Murder

Midnight Spells Murder

Mary Angela

LYRICAL UNDERGROUND
Kensington Publishing Corp.
www.kensingtonbooks.com

LYRICAL UNDERGROUND BOOKS are published by

Kensington Publishing Corp.
119 West 40th Street
New York, NY 10018

All Kensington titles, imprints, and distributed lines are available at special quantity discounts for bulk purchases for sales promotion, premiums, fundraising, educational, or institutional use.

Special book excerpts or customized printings can also be created to fit specific needs. For details, write or phone the office of the Kensington Sales Manager: Kensington Publishing Corp., 119 West 40th Street, New York, NY 10018. Attn. Sales Department. Phone: 1-800-221-2647.

Lyrical Underground and Lyrical Underground logo Reg. US Pat. & TM Off.

First Electronic Edition: July 2021
ISBN-13: 978-1-5161-1070-4 (ebook)
ISBN-10: 1-5161-1070-6 (ebook)

First Print Edition: July 2021
ISBN-13: 978-1-5161-1073-5
ISBN-10: 1-5161-1073-0

Printed in the United States of America

To my sisters Tammy, Sandy, and Penny, the good witches in my life.

Chapter One

"Of course I believe in witches." Jules squared her shoulders. "I am one."
Harley paused decorating mid-cobweb, but Zo continued tacking up the orange and white twinkle lights at Happy Camper gift store. Marianne Morgan's book talk was in an hour, and she needed to finish getting ready. Besides, she knew what was coming next. She and Julia Parker had been friends since grade school.

"Seriously? You're a witch?" asked Harley, Zo's employee. A dedicated accounting student, she was puzzled by Jules's revelation. If Harley couldn't add, subtract, or multiply it, it didn't make sense.

Jules placed the cauldron on the table, her sleeve brushing the gossamer webs surrounding the pot. "I come from a long line of witches. My great-aunt was a witch, her daughter was a witch, and I have several cousins who practice. If you need a spell, I can hook you up. Just let me know before the end of October. I'm running a sale."

At Spirits & Spirits, there was always a sale. Jules not only communicated with spirits, she sold spirits of the alcohol variety. Zo admired her entrepreneurial spirit. Since they were kids, Jules had been making money off the town's name, Spirit Canyon. She was glad Jules had volunteered to help with the book event.

Zo stepped down from the ladder. "Marianne's talk is 'Embracing Your Inner Witch.' It isn't about spells or magic. It's about reclaiming your power as a woman. Her book is really good." Zo had ordered twenty copies for today's talk. She hoped it was enough. With Halloween on the way, she had a feeling it would be popular.

"I dig all this witch stuff, though." Jules motioned to the table of food set up in front of the folding chairs.

Zo smiled. It was a witchy smorgasbord. The cupcakes, or Cackle Cakes, as she liked to call them, resembled witches' hats with green frosting, a chocolate cookie, and a candy kiss. The cauldron was filled with lime punch, and the snack mix was arranged in individual green and purple paper cones. The scene screamed Halloween.

"It fits this weekend's festivities, that's for sure," said Zo. Spirit Spooktacular was one of Spirit Canyon's busiest weekends. The town had several events that led up to Halloween, including a pumpkin-carving contest, a parade, and a costume party, which Zo was hosting. Tourists flocked to Spirit Canyon not only for the events but also for the fall foliage in Black Hills National Forest. Right now the canyon was a menagerie of yellow, red, and russet trees, and the crisp autumn air made the weather perfect for sightseeing. Zo inhaled. Her store smelled like pumpkin spice. *Yum!*

"Do you think we have enough chairs?" asked Harley. The dark purple streaks in her black pixie cut flickered as her head bobbed, counting the seats.

"I hope so," said Zo. "Those are all the chairs I have." Happy Camper was a gift store, not a bookshop, but Zo Jones sold books and hosted events that fit her store's positive vibe. For October, she'd ordered merchandise that said EAT, DRINK, AND BE SCARY and shirts with the phrase TRUST YOUR MAGIC on them.

"If you need more folding chairs, I can run back to Spirits & Spirits," Jules offered. "I have at least five. I'd like to check on Duncan anyway. Do you know I caught him handing out punch cards? Buy five music lessons get one free? I told him to peddle his music on his dime, not mine."

"Who cares what he does?" Harley arranged the orange napkins emblazoned with DRINK UP, WITCHES next to the punch. "Duncan Hall is hot."

"Evil Woman" filled the void left by the pause in conversation. The song hummed from the antique record player in the corner. Nobody could argue with Harley's declaration. Duncan was definitely hot. He was also a musician who gave guitar lessons. Zo guessed the classes didn't pay the bills because he was working at Spirits & Spirits part-time now.

"Being good looking doesn't give him a free pass," said Jules. "Though, I have noticed an uptick in my female customers."

When the door opened, Zo assumed it was the author, but it was Max Harrington, a local forest ranger. "Hey, Max. We were just talking about your roommate."

"What'd he do now?" Max stopped in front of the book display. "This is nice."

"Thank you." Zo smiled.

"He's handing out punch cards for guitar lessons to my customers," Jules explained, joining Max. She was almost as tall as him, and Harley was close behind. In their company, Zo's five-feet-five felt short.

"I found some in my jacket pocket the other day," said Max. "He's not getting much business lately. The college didn't hand out his flyer this year."

"Change in curriculum?" asked Harley.

"Change in dating status." Max's sky-blue eyes sparkled. "Duncan dumped the president's daughter."

"Bad career move." Zo chuckled. When Max picked up one of Marianne's books, she added, "Are you here to embrace your inner witch?"

"No, I'm on good terms with her. I want to sign up for the Harvest Hike on Sunday."

Harley flinched. Jules gave Zo a sideways glance.

Zo counted to five and silently recited the mantra on her witch t-shirt: KEEP CALM AND FLY ON. Max had opinions about her guided tours, opinions she didn't share. He claimed they were unsafe. She knew they were a good source of revenue, especially for tourists who didn't want the rugged outdoor experience. In the Black Hills, visitors could climb, raft, or bungee jump. They could see Mount Rushmore by helicopter and Crazy Horse by paraglide. But many didn't want to. Lots of people wanted a brief walking tour of the area and a little history of the canyon. That's what Zo provided.

"I'll see if there's room." Zo walked to the counter, where she kept her event log.

He followed her. "I'm sure you could make room for one extra person."

A six-foot ranger with the subtleness of a mountain lion? She wasn't so sure. She opened the planner, smoothing the pages. She ran her finger down the list of names.

Max leaned over the counter and pointed to the number ten. It had an empty space behind it. "Lucky me. One spot left."

"Jules, didn't you mention coming?" Zo hoped her friend would catch the hint.

"Nature's your thing, not mine," said Jules. "I hate bugs."

"I thought witches were in tune with Mother Earth," said Harley.

Jules picked her fingernail. "I use herbs all the time."

Max pulled his wallet out of his green uniform pants. "Great. That means I can come. How much do I owe you?"

"So you can spy on me?" asked Zo.

"Why do I need a reason?"

"Because you hike this area all the time." Zo tapped her pen. "Why would you want to go with a bunch of tourists?"

"You'll be there, too," said Max.

"Exactly." Zo nodded.

"Exactly."

Jules looked up from her nail.

Zo scribbled his name in the book. "Fine, thirty-five dollars. But not one word of ranger talk. This is a fun, casual event."

He handed her the money. "That's kind of expensive for a one-hour hike."

She put the bills in the register and smiled her sweetest smile. "Don't worry. It includes the nature scrapbook we'll be using."

"What do you mean, 'scrapbook?'" Max's eyes widened.

"The things we find on the hike?" said Zo. "We'll be putting them into a scrapbook. You know how to use a glue gun, don't you?"

Max's brow wrinkled in confusion. "On second thought, maybe I'll sit this one out."

"Sorry," Zo apologized, still smiling. "No refunds."

Chapter Two

After Max left, customers began to file in for the book event. Zo checked the time. The talk was twenty minutes away, but the moment she put out the sidewalk sign, people took notice. Though it was Thursday, plenty of tourists were already in town for Spirit Spooktacular. They didn't want to miss any of the festivities, and the fun started early tomorrow. Customers mingled in the store, commenting on the fun quotes and cute space. Zo was helping a woman select a bison postcard when Marianne Morgan breezed in the door, wearing a long dress, blue headscarf, and black shoes with gold buckles. A young woman, maybe her daughter, was close behind.

"I thought she wasn't *that* type of witch," Jules muttered.

"I stand corrected," whispered Zo. Though Marianne lived in Spirit Canyon, Zo had never heard of her until she read an article about her new book. The feature was in *Canyon Views* and described the local author making it big. The book was a *USA Today* bestseller, and Zo downloaded it after reading the article. She loved it and knew her customers would, too. That's when she reached out to Marianne, who generously agreed to come to the store.

Zo greeted Marianne with an outstretched hand. "You must be Marianne. I'm Zo Jones. It's so good to meet you in person. I feel like I already know you from reading your book."

Marianne handed the young woman her tabbed book and planner. She shook Zo's hand. "It's good to meet you. Thanks for having me. I *need* that sign on the door."

Zo pointed to the display of signs: NOT ALL WITCHES LIVE IN SALEM. "That one? I just happen to have some left."

"Perfect," said Marianne. "I'm buying one when we're finished. By the way, this is my daughter, Emily. She's been a dear to do these events with me, even with her busy year as a freshman at Black Mountain College."

"Hi." Unlike her mom, Emily wore jeans and a simple white cable-knit sweater. Her hair was as light as her mom's was dark, but their brown eyes were the same, serious and sincere. Carrying postcards, bookmarks, and pens, she displayed the maturity of a well-organized adult, and without Marianne's information, Zo would have taken her for a college graduate.

"Hi, Emily," said Zo. "This is my friend Jules. She'll be helping me today, along with my employee, Harley. If you need anything during the event, just ask one of us."

Marianne paused on Jules's face. "I think you used to date my boyfriend, Roberto Salvo."

Jules nodded. "It's been awhile. How's he doing?"

"Good," said Marianne. "He'll be here today. Any minute."

"Cool." Jules pulled her long fishtail braid over one shoulder. It was a dazzling mix of blond layers and pink ends. "We can catch up."

"If there's time," added Marianne. "As you know, he's a very busy guy."

Jules smiled but said nothing.

Zo needed to ask Jules about Roberto, but now wasn't the time. She didn't recognize the name, which didn't mean much. They both had dating failures they didn't bring up. A boyfriend had to become newsworthy before they exchanged details. She motioned Marianne to the area of the book talk. "In a few minutes, we'll get started. I'll introduce you, you'll talk, and then sign books and enjoy treats afterward."

Marianne smiled at the display. "I've never been to an event *this* witchy. I love it."

"It's the eve of Spirit Spooktacular." Zo shrugged. "It can't be witchy enough, in my opinion."

"I agree," said Jules. "You're bound to make a fortune on Halloween décor alone."

Zo chuckled. For Jules, it was all about the bottom line, but for Zo it was about getting together with friends, making food, and planning for the holidays. Her customers were like family, her store an extension of her home. Some people were born into large families; others made their own. Upstairs were her living quarters, the second story of the cabin. It sure made the commute easy. All she had to do was walk downstairs to open the doors of Happy Camper.

Marianne followed Zo to the vintage music stand that she used as a speaker podium for events. The stand had two candleholders on each side of the music holder, and Zo had placed black candles in them for the occasion. Emily touched Marianne's shoulder. "Shouldn't we wait for Roberto?" "Like I said, he'll be here any minute." She put her hands on her daughter's shoulders. "The first step in embracing your power is to set your own schedule. Don't wait on others."

"Funny how my schedule is your schedule," mumbled Emily.

Marianne didn't hear the remark or if she did, she ignored it. Getting ready to speak, she was busy arranging her notes on the podium.

A single chair was available, so when the door opened and the bell rang out, Zo worried she'd need to find another guest seat, perhaps the stool behind the counter. Apparently, it was Marianne's boyfriend and a young man Zo assumed was his son. Marianne gave them a wave, and they joined the group. Roberto took the open chair, but his son hung back near the wall. He didn't appear excited to be there, so Zo skipped grabbing the stool.

"Readers, friends...witches," Marianne began her talk.

With the candles flickering and black tendrils of hair escaping her blue headscarf, Marianne looked like a witch, the traditional kind. While reading Marianne's book, Zo learned witches were once considered wise women and healers, and hags were nonconformists. They were called on for help, remedies, and contacting the dead. It was modern society that labeled them undesirable and ugly. Hence the green face, warts, and hunched-back people identified with witches today.

Marianne didn't give the full history lesson from her book, though. Instead she told participants how to recall their inner witch: the powerful, passionate, magical person they'd been told was unattractive and unladylike. It might feel like waking or a memory, something dismissed or buried. All that they needed was within them. They just needed to find and trust it. Approval came from within, not from others. Zo liked that idea.

"I invite you to invoke your power now," said Marianne. "Say it with me. 'I take back my power'. Feel it returning from all the places you've left it: jobs, boyfriends, family members. Let's try it together."

"I take back my power," the group murmured, Zo along with them. As a child, she'd survived foster care by adhering to the belief that she had power over her own destiny. She might not have been able to choose what house she lived in or what clothes she wore, but she could plan for her future. And with a lot of determination, here she was.

"Again." Marianne closed her eyes.

The group repeated the words louder, liking the idea of becoming stronger and more whole.

From the back of the room, Roberto's son snickered. The moment was broken.

Marianne's eyes flew open. "Seek from within, friends. Pay no attention to small-minded people who thrive on greed and lies. They have no idea about real power or happiness. You can't buy it. It's not for sale."

The words were meant as an assault on Roberto's son. Clearly, Roberto could tell, and so could Zo. Short and stocky, the boy walked away, fists clenched at his sides. Zo was glad Roberto didn't go after him. She had a feeling his son would make a bigger scene if given the opportunity. Instead, Roberto stared straight ahead, listening to the rest of Marianne's talk with respect and perhaps even reverence. He obviously admired her a great deal.

When she finished speaking, Marianne asked if readers had questions. A few hands went up, and Zo joined her at the podium to moderate the remainder of the event.

"Nikki Ainsworth." Marianne smiled at a woman clad in red. "For those of you who don't know her, this woman is responsible for single-handedly renovating Spirit Canyon's opera house."

The audience members turned their heads and clapped.

Standing, Nikki took a little bow. Tall and slender, she was the managing theater director but could have been a model or an actress. She had the bones for it—and the clothes. Her red blouse looked expensive, and her posture was picture perfect. "Thank you, Marianne, but you're the one who deserves the applause. I really enjoyed the book and recommend it to everyone here. It has practical advice for obtaining goals, which I appreciate."

Marianne beamed. "Thank you, Nikki. That means a lot. You've never been afraid to go after what you want, and I admire that." She pointed to another participant. "Yes, in the blue shirt?"

The woman in blue opened up her well-thumbed copy of the text. "In the book, you say readers need to identify the negative energy and negative people weighing them down. Are the examples based on personal experiences?"

"They are." Marianne paused thoughtfully. Maybe she was deciding how much personal information to divulge. "My ex-husband, for one. He told me I wasn't good enough, and after being told it enough times, I believed it." She glanced at Emily, who was staring into her lap. "But I don't want to get into that here. The point is to recognize the negative people in your life. They will drain your power if you let them. Don't let them. Don't try to change them. Let them go."

The woman in the blue shirt nodded, and the room fell quiet.

"Any other questions for Marianne?" Zo asked.

Tiffany Snow, a town volunteer and do-gooder, stepped forward. She must have come in late because Zo hadn't seen her. With her fall sweater, skinny jeans, and ankle boots, she looked as if she was ready to lead a PTA meeting or school cheer. Her loose ringlets were tied into a girlish ponytail. Zo didn't think she went anywhere without curling her hair.

"First, I just want to let you all know that I'm taking orders for holiday wreaths." She smiled at the group, showing off ultra-white teeth. "You know how beautiful they are, and they're for a good cause."

Zo sighed. Tiffany was here to hawk her kids' holiday wreaths.

"Second, to the author, your book needs an adult rating so that it doesn't get into the wrong hands," continued Tiffany. "My daughter picked it up at the bookstore, probably because of the witch on the cover. Before I could stop her, she was reading a spell—out loud!"

"There are no 'spells' in the book," explained Marianne. "Even if there were, I don't believe in censorship. This book is for everyone, especially young girls."

Tiffany crossed her arms. "I'm going to assert my power and say that I heartily disagree."

"That's your right," said Marianne. "Good for you."

With no other questions, Zo decided this was a good time to mention the snacks. Her customers expected an upbeat atmosphere, and Marianne had turned Tiffany's complaint into a positive. It was a nice place to conclude. "If there are no other questions, help yourself to a treat while Marianne signs books. Thanks so much for coming out, and don't forget. I'll be giving away apple cider to trick-or-treaters and their parents on Halloween. Stop by and warm up."

Zo pointed to the table near the podium, and Marianne and her daughter situated themselves near the stack of books. A line formed quickly, and shoppers munched on snacks while talking or waiting to purchase books. Zo stayed with Marianne and Emily to help with pictures while Harley rang up sales and Jules managed the food table. Zo noticed Roberto sneaking out the front door, perhaps to retrieve his son. When he came back alone, she realized the attempt was unsuccessful. His son must have been put out by Marianne's comments, and Zo wondered what she'd meant by them.

Jules touched Zo's elbow. "Miss Priss is peddling her wreath order form near the snack table. What do you want me to do about it?"

"I'll take care of it," said Zo. "Would you mind staying with Marianne?"

"No problem."

Zo handed Jules the camera and walked toward Tiffany, smiling at customers who were enjoying the food. She had to say something to Tiffany. She didn't want her wreath campaign cannibalizing Marianne's book sales. Despite Happy Camper being a small local gift shop, Marianne agreed to come, speak, and sign books. Zo knew she had bigger signings she could have attended, and Zo wanted to show her appreciation with decent book sales. Tiffany was jeopardizing that.

With a leg propped up like a table, Tiffany was writing out a receipt for a wreath. She exchanged the paper for a customer's check and tucked it in with the many others in her accordion folder. She clicked her pen as Zo approached. "Last year you bought a wreath, so you know how wonderful they look and smell. What about two this year? One for the store and one for your home?"

"You're right," Zo agreed. "They are beautiful, and I'd be happy to make a purchase. But I need to ask you to sell the wreaths on your own time. This event is part of Marianne's book launch, not a fund-raising event."

Tiffany snapped shut her folder with a huff. "Fine. I'll come back."

"Perfect," said Zo. "Thanks so much."

Her curly ponytail swung back and forth as she marched out. Zo joined Harley at the register. "Do you know where Roberto's son went?"

"His name is Alex," said Harley.

"How do you know him?"

"I'm a math tutor at his high school. He claims he's going to an Ivy League school next year." Harley rolled her eyes, expertly outlined in black liner. Her heavy bangs, which came to a point on her forehead, emphasized her dramatic look.

"He must be smart," said Zo.

"Not even close." Harley took a purchase from a customer, scanning the bar code. "He has the attitude but not the aptitude. He'd be lucky to get into Black Mountain."

Black Mountain was the college Harley attended in Spirit Canyon. It was a favorite of outdoorspeople, but expensive. Still, it was cheaper than most colleges in Colorado. "Did you see where he went?"

She nodded toward the door. "I think he's waiting in his dad's car."

"Oh boy," said Zo. "I'd better move things along." When she returned to the book signing table, the line had dwindled to one person, Roberto. Marianne was finishing with Nikki, who handed her tickets to *Phantom of the Opera*. The musical opened tomorrow night, and Nikki was papering the theater. Marianne thanked her, promising to spread the word, and passed the tickets to Emily. She turned to Roberto with a frustrated look. "Where's Alex?" asked Marianne, peeking around him. "If he's going to act like a child, don't bring him. I don't need him making fun of me or the people at my events." Roberto calmly kissed the top of her headscarf. "He *is* a child. Don't expect too much of him."

"You need to stop making excuses for him," Marianne insisted. "You're not doing him any favors by protecting him."

"And you're not doing him any favors by calling him out in front of two dozen women." Roberto turned his warm brown eyes on Zo, giving her a kind smile. Obviously, he didn't want to argue with his girlfriend in public. "I enjoyed the event. It was the best one I've been to. Thank you."

"I agree." Emily was seated next to her mom. "I could live in this store." Marianne stood. "When I get back to town, I'm coming here to do some more shopping."

"I'd love that," said Zo. "Are you traveling for your book tour?"

"Five states starting Monday." Marianne pushed in her chair. "I've done the surrounding area, but I'm taking on the East Coast next week. I need to get everything packed this weekend."

"Don't forget this, Mom." Emily handed her the witch sign as they walked past the display.

That girl doesn't miss a thing. If Emily weren't working for Marianne, Zo would've recruited her to work at the store. She needed more organization in her life.

"Thanks, honey." Marianne took a detour toward the register. Harley rang up the sale, and Marianne wrote a check for the purchase.

When they were finished, Zo walked them to the front entrance. "Good luck with your book tour, and thanks so much for coming. I know you'll do great."

Roberto stopped short of the door. "What's Jake doing here?"

Zo assumed he was referring to the large man in the wool flat cap. He was leaning against a sedan, smoking a cigarette. He waved at them.

"I told Dad to pick me up," Emily explained. "I hope that's okay. We're going out for dinner."

"Of course it's okay." Marianne gave Emily's arm a squeeze. "Have a good time. Thanks again, Zo. It was a lovely day."

Roberto was too distracted to say goodbye. He was busy glaring at Emily's dad, who was as sloppily dressed as Roberto was tidy. From their shirts to their shoes, they were opposites. Perhaps that had been Marianne's intention with the new relationship.

"You're so welcome," said Zo.

With a loud noise from the muffler and a puff of smoke, Emily and her dad were gone, leaving a hubcap turning in the parking lot. Roberto and Marianne joined Alex in a Lexus, shaking their heads at Jake's eventful departure.

Watching them from the window, Jules muttered, "I'm not sorry to be out of *that* relationship."

"I was going to ask you about Roberto," said Zo. "I didn't know you dated him."

"I don't know if you'd call it dating." Jules shook off the description. "We were together a few months, but I hardly saw him. He's a workaholic."

"*You're* a workaholic," Zo pointed out. "It sounds like a perfect match."

Jules followed her to the food table, where Zo started picking up. "That's what I thought. He built his business from the ground up, and I admired his work ethic. But he was too intense for me. He couldn't enjoy a glass of wine without checking his email fifteen times."

"Yuck." Zo made a face.

"Exactly." Jules threw away scattered cupcake wrappers. "I'm surprised Marianne even knew our brief history."

"I suppose they discussed their recent relationships." Zo wiped the table with a disinfectant wipe. "If her ex-husband is the guy in the book, he sounds like a real bum. She wouldn't want to date another one."

"That explains it," said Jules. "Roberto's anything but a bum."

Zo wrinkled her nose. "His kid, though."

"I don't know anything about him," said Jules. "I knew Roberto had a son but we didn't date long enough for me to meet him."

"You didn't miss anything." Harley joined them. She and Zo took down the table. "Alex is a conceited jerk. He called me a nerd for trying to help him with his algebra. All his friends chimed in."

"What a bully," said Jules.

"Agreed," Zo added.

Harley waved away their concern. "I'm a big girl. It's fine."

"Let's recite Marianne's mantra," said Zo, with a smile. "Just to make sure."

Chapter Three

After putting away the table and podium, Zo zipped upstairs for a late afternoon pick-me-up. Since school was in session, Harley would close Happy Camper, as she did most nights during the school year. The bulk of her hours were put in on evenings and weekends, allowing Zo to break for tea. She had the perfect autumn blend waiting for her, a mixture of cinnamon, clove, and orange peel. It was exactly what she needed after all the sweet cupcakes.

She opened the door to a loud meow. Her cat, George, was angry at being trapped upstairs, but with so many people coming and going for the event, Zo didn't want him trampled. Looking at the large, orange tomcat, she admitted the possibility was slim. With his long hair and fluffy tail, he was hard to miss. George (or St. George, as her neighbor called him) was a Maine Coon she'd adopted from the humane society last year. The living arrangement had been an adjustment for both of them.

She knelt down, and he ducked her pet. Okay, the challenge was mainly hers. He preferred to spend most of his days outdoors. But they were closer than they used to be, and she couldn't imagine life without him, which made her kind of clingy, a wholly new feeling for her. They'd both have to get used to it.

George darted outside, and she followed him to her large cedar deck and turned on the outdoor fireplace. Then she went back inside to make her tea. When she returned with her mug, her neighbor was crossing her small backyard.

Russell Cunningham was an English professor at Black Mountain College, and this time of year was hard for him. He had lots of papers to grade and did what he could to avoid them. That usually meant long philosophical talks about anything but student essays. She called down to him before she sat. "Can I get you a cup of tea, Cunningham?"

"No thank you," answered Cunningham, coming up the deck stairs. "I wanted to see how the book event went. I'm sorry I couldn't attend." She sat down on her L-shaped sofa in front of the fireplace and motioned for him to join her. Dressed in thick corduroy pants and a button-up sweater, he settled into the chair next to her. His were the kind eyes of a teacher who put others' concerns above his own, and it was hard not to look at him and remember a teacher or mentor who had once made a difference.

"No worries," said Zo. "It went really well. We sold out of books."

He nodded. "That's what I thought. I saw a lot of cars in the parking lot."

Zo sipped her cinnamon tea, relishing the hint of clove. This time of year was the best—for her anyway. "How are the papers coming?"

"The papers are not coming." Cunningham scowled. "The stack is at a standstill." He leaned over his knees, warming his snow-white hair and beard in the firelight. "I have a feeling my students didn't read the novel. Nobody reads books anymore."

"They're reading Marianne's book," said Zo. "Maybe you should try integrating it into your class next year." His open mouth told Zo the idea was scandalous. "Just for a change of pace," she added.

"Thank you, but no." Cunningham lifted his chin. "The day students can't get through *Main Street* is the day I retire, move to Hawaii, and drink mai tais all day."

Zo stretched out her legs on the elongated lounge of the sofa. She remembered Sinclair Lewis's classic *Main Street*. She had to read it in one of the English classes she'd taken while getting her degree in communications. She'd been a journalist for almost ten years before starting Happy Camper. Now she wrote the weekly Happy Camper column for *Canyon Views*, which was creative and fun and so much better than the news. "Isn't *Main Street* five-hundred-something pages?"

Cunningham bristled. "That isn't long."

To students who were used to absorbing information at warp speed, Zo had a feeling it was but didn't say anything. She liked reading and writing. It was why she wrote the column. "Maybe you need a break from grading. Why don't you come with me to Wine and Waterfalls? Jules is hosting a tasting at Spirits & Spirits."

"I'd love to." Cunningham stood. "But I can't. No matter how bad, the essays need to be read—and graded."

"If you change your mind…"

"I know where you live," said Cunningham.

Finishing her last sips of tea, she watched him return to his house. He waved from his deck, and she held up her mug.

Zo stood and flicked off the fireplace. She could relax the rest of the afternoon, watching the quiet smoke waft up from new nighttime campfires, but needed to get ready for Jules's event. A local tour group was visiting area waterfalls and wineries. The Black Hills had several gorgeous waterfalls, but Spirit Canyon's was the most well known and the last stop on the tour. With its sixty-foot plunge and lace-like cascade, the waterfall attracted lots of tourists to the canyon.

Zo exchanged her witch t-shirt for a burgundy sweater. Like it or not—and actually, she did like it—the evenings were getting colder, and she was walking to tonight's gathering. She didn't want to worry about driving home, and Jules's store was only a few blocks away. After giving her edgy bob a tousle, she slipped on her tennis shoes and grabbed her keys, locking the deck door behind her.

On the eve of Spirit Spooktacular, downtown Spirit Canyon was a sight to behold. Store windows were decked out with goblins, ghouls, and ghosts, and doors were decorated with haystacks and pumpkins. The opera house had costumes from *Phantom of the Opera* on display, complete with the Phantom's signature mask. Even the old-fashioned lampposts, just beginning to glow yellow, were adorned with miniature ghosts, swaying spookily in the autumn breeze.

The tour bus was in the parking lot of Spirts & Spirits when Zo arrived, and she quickened her pace. Jules assured her she didn't need any help, but after hearing about Duncan's missteps at work, Zo worried he wouldn't be the support Jules needed for the event. Since Spirit Canyon didn't have a winery, tour participants were enjoying a glass of wine at Jules's super-spirited store, and from the size of the caravan, Zo guessed many participants were inside, not to mention several locals, who looked forward to the evening every year.

For the occasion, Jules had created wine glasses etched with Spirit Canyon's signature waterfall. She was filling them with a rich-looking cabernet while Duncan stood by with a bottle of white, several ladies opting into his line. Maybe they preferred white, or maybe they preferred his dark wavy hair, killer smile, and honey-smooth voice.

Zo made a beeline toward Jules. "Can I help?"

"I'm good." Jules shooed her away. "You go mingle. There's a guy in a red shirt who looks like he could use some company."

Zo turned around. The guy in the red shirt was Max. It always surprised her to see him out of his park ranger uniform. Though he looked the same, a sandy crew cut and broad shoulders, he seemed less ready to rescue a trapped animal or put out a rogue campfire. Seeing her glance, he gave her an easy smile.

Jules gave her a glass of red wine. "Here, take this."

"Are you sure?" asked Zo.

"If I need you, I'll holler." Jules was certain. "Go."

A skeleton in a coffin sat up as Zo walked by a table, startling her. She laughed at herself for being spooked by the decoration.

Max laughed, too. "That guy is creepy, right?"

"I get the feeling the whole place is full of spirits, and not just the alcohol kind," said Zo. While Happy Camper was filled with cutesy Halloween décor and quotes, Jules's store had a different feeling. Behind a fringe curtain, Jules did tarot-card and palm readings. She also held séances. The store was filled with a variety of ghost beads, dream catchers, and voodoo dolls for sale. Zo was wearing the mood ring she'd bought here last year. It was one of her favorite pieces of jewelry.

"I bet she makes a killing at these events," Max observed. "I saw one woman order half a dozen of those wine glasses."

"She's always had an eye for business," said Zo with admiration. "She knows what people want." A customer chuckled at something Duncan said, catching Zo's attention. He seemed to be doing fine. Better than fine. She decided to ask Max. "How's Duncan? Are you here to check up on him?"

"Believe it or not, I don't spend my evenings policing the world." Max took a drink of his beer, a local cream ale that left a soft foam on his top lip. Spirit Canyon's brewery was very popular in the tristate area, and Jules sold gallons of it by the growler.

Zo sipped her wine, saying nothing. She knew him too well to believe he was here for the wine event. He was drinking beer, for goodness' sake.

"Fine," Max admitted. "I'm *sort of* checking up on him. After what Jules said about him handing out business cards, I'm worried about his job. I don't want him to do something stupid and lose it. I figured I could help out if he needed it."

Zo noticed Max's short beard, a handsome outline of his jawline. It was new, or perhaps a change for fall. His hair was mussed and a bit longer on top. Was he more worried about his friend than he let on? "Is Duncan in trouble?"

Max eased her worry with a quick smile. "Duncan's *always* in trouble." He closed the space between them, talking quieter. "To be honest, he's driving me crazy. Since he's been out of work, he's been writing his own songs, and they're terrible."

Zo choked on a laugh.

"Don't get me wrong," added Max. "He's a great musician, and you know he's my friend. But he's been experimenting with country." He shook his head. "It's just not his thing."

It wasn't Zo's thing either. "I thought he was more of a rock-and-roll guy."

"He is," said Max. "But he thinks country might be more marketable." *Maybe Jules is already rubbing off on him.* People dug the Wild West, and that meant country music. But Spirit Canyon was eclectic, a mesh of thrill-seekers, nature-lovers, and cowboys. There was room for all kinds of music and musicians.

"He's been writing songs about pickup trucks," Max explained. "He drives a *Camaro*."

Zo held back another bout of laughter. Max was a good guy, maybe too good sometimes. She wondered if he was having a hard time being honest with Duncan. "Have you tried talking to him?"

He furrowed his brow, his blue eyes darker in the shadows. "What am I supposed to say? Your songs suck?" He shook his head. "That's not going to inspire him, and despite appearances, he's a sensitive guy. If this job doesn't work out, he might be living with me permanently."

Duncan moved in after his music lessons disrupted neighbors in his apartment complex. The arrangement was supposed to be temporary, and it sounded as if it was time for him to move on, but how was he supposed to do that without a steadier income? Maybe Zo could mention something to Jules. She was walking in their direction right now, her floor-length sweater floating behind her like a cape of a sorceress.

"Do me a favor, will you?" Jules asked. "Watch the store while I run home to get more wine glasses."

"Of course," said Zo.

"I have a woman who wants to get her Christmas shopping done early." Jules lowered her voice. "She wants two dozen."

"Can I help you grab them?" asked Max.

Jules laughed, taking off her Spirits & Spirits apron and putting it over Zo's head. "Do I look like the kind of women who needs help carrying wine glasses?" Strong to the core, with arms to match, Jules could handle wine glasses—or anything else that came her way.

"I'm just offering." Max raised both hands in surrender.

"And I'm just kidding," answered Jules. "You can help Zo. You never know when Duncan will find a better offer and dash off with one of my patrons."

While Jules ran home, Zo and Max mingled with customers, who were enjoying the event. Duncan was enjoying himself, too, chatting with a group of young women. Whatever he said must have been hilarious, because every one of them was either laughing or smiling.

Not one for group attention, Max struck up a conversation with a couple about their upcoming visit to Wind Cave. He told them about the different formations they could spot inside. Meanwhile, Zo refilled the bowls of snack mix at the counter, listening in to his informative tidbits. She loved his quiet passion for nature and was fully engaged in his descriptions when the door chimed, and Tiffany Snow walked in. With a quick sweep of the room, Tiffany grimaced. The event was obviously not her cup of tea—or glass of wine, for that matter.

"Can I help you?" asked Zo.

"Thank god, it's you," said Tiffany. "All the downtown stores are buying wreaths to display on their doors. I'm here to collect Jules's payment."

Zo frowned. Jules hadn't said anything about a wreath. "Does she know you're coming?"

"No." Tiffany blinked. "Why would she?"

The woman wouldn't give up the ghost. She was doggedly persistent, but this was taking it too far. "I admire your zeal," Zo said. "I really do. But aren't your kids supposed to be selling the wreaths? It seems like they're missing out on an opportunity."

"My children are at home, asleep." Tiffany flicked a blond curl over her shoulder. "Do you think I'd let them come in here? With this…this *sorcery*? It's a devil's workshop."

"Only if you want it to be." Duncan appeared at Zo's elbow as if by magic.

Zo swallowed a laugh. Tiffany turned on her heel and stomped out of the store.

Duncan raised a dark eyebrow. "Usually my lines have better results."

"I can imagine," said Zo.

"Should I try again?" Duncan leveled the question at her.

It was tempting. Duncan appealed to her in more ways than one—well, primarily just one. He had a reputation for being a playboy, but she'd gotten to know him through Max, and he was a nice guy. Jules must have agreed, otherwise she wouldn't have hired him.

The door reopened, and Jules walked in with a box of glasses. She slid it on the counter. "I saw Tiffany leave in a huff. What was that about?"

"Take a guess." Zo took off her Spirits & Spirits apron and laid it on the counter.

"Christmas wreaths?" answered Jules.

"I stand corrected." A smile played on Duncan's lips. "You *do* have psychic powers, Jules."

Jules wasn't amused. Unlike most women, she wasn't smitten with his good looks and handled him like a well-used pilsner glass. "Help me wrap these."

While they packaged stemware, Zo chatted with Melissa Morris, who worked at the Visitor Center. She was excited about the costume party at Zo's house on Halloween night. Zo was excited, too. It was fun to get together and celebrate the successes of the weekend. She'd begun the tradition at her original store and kept it up after changing addresses. It felt great being part of the local community.

"What if I'm not a business owner?" asked Max, who'd overheard her conversation with Melissa. "Can I still come?"

"Only if you dress like Smokey the Bear," said Zo.

He rubbed his light beard. "That can be arranged."

"Jules and I are going to dress like Bonnie and Clyde." Finished packaging the glasses, Duncan handed the customer the box.

Jules thanked the customer again for the purchase then joined the conversation. "Says who? You're not a business owner."

Duncan pointed to Max. "He gets to come, and *I* work here."

Jules turned her brown eyes on Zo. "Is flirting and working the same thing? What do you think?"

"If it results in a sale, I think so." Zo chuckled. "But I have to tell you, he struck out with Tiffany a few minutes ago. She gave him the biggest brush-off I've ever seen."

"Maybe you're losing your touch," Max teased.

"At least I have a touch," countered Duncan.

"*I* have a touch," said Max. "A big old effective touch."

Zo winced. The way he described it didn't sound very effective.

Jules put her hand on Max's shoulder. "In this one specific case, Duncan is right. You got no game."

Max looked pleadingly at Zo. "Tell them, Zo."

Tell them what? How they had gone from sparring partners to speaking acquaintances after solving a murder together on Memorial Day? A couple of times over the last five months, she thought they were growing closer, and then she'd wonder if she imagined the entire idea. He would say something about her tours or her kayaks or her motorcycle, and they'd be back to square one. "Max has game—the long game."

Jules and Duncan laughed at that.

"Very funny," said Max, but he was laughing, too. "That comment earned you a little rangerly advice during your Harvest Hike on Sunday. You know I'm signed up."

"Try it, and I'll clog your glue gun," warned Zo.

Duncan gave Jules a confused look.

"You don't even want to know," said Jules. "Come on. Help me clean up, guys."

The bus was gone and so were most of the customers. A young couple sat at a pub table, finishing a glass of wine. Wiping the counter, Zo thought they made it look easy. But from experience, she knew relationships took more than a good cabernet. Wine could only do so much to smooth the bumps in a relationship. Unfortunately, in her case, it didn't do enough. Her boyfriends would say or do something that got up her guard, and she would break up with them before they really hurt her feelings. She saved herself a lot of headaches that way. Still, it would be nice to share a private moment with someone special at the end of the day.

Zo placed her cleaning cloth on the bar. "I'm finished, Jules."

"Thanks for your help," she said. "I'll see you at the parade?"

Zo nodded. "I'll look for a woman smoking a cigar."

"I'll be in a fedora," said Duncan.

"And I'll be in a felt cap," added Max.

"See you tomorrow, guys." They gave her a wave, and Zo started for home, the warm feeling of friendship fading fast.

Outside, the wind had picked up, scattering curled leaves down the sidewalks. Somewhere a campfire burned, and the sweet smoke lingered in the air. With a fresh gust of wind at her back, Zo crossed under the yellow-blinking streetlight. Maybe it was the full moon, or maybe it was the myth of the canyon coming to life for Halloween. Whatever it was, something hastened her step, telling her to hurry.

She focused on the charming downtown storefronts, trying not to let her imagination get away from her. It didn't take much for it to invent an alternate story. The Cut Hut was running a sale on black hair dye, and Honey Buns was selling orange bread. Its iconic beehive was colored orange and black for the weekend, and the bees wore miniature ghost costumes. Spirit Canyon's bookstore, the Cracked Spine, was decorated like a haunted house. The windows were flecked with black paint, cobwebs netting the corners. Inside, books were stacked into a staircase that led to the ceiling, and a skeleton read *Bag of Bones* while lounging in a rickety coffin. Pop and Shop, the gourmet popcorn store, was small but not to be outdone by the larger stores. It had the longest string of gold, orange, and brown popcorn she'd ever seen. It festooned the store in beautiful autumn colors. As cute as the decorations were, Zo didn't relax until she came upon her own block. The night had grown cold, and she was glad to be home. In a few minutes, she would be tucked inside her warm bed with a book and maybe even her cat. Nothing sounded better.

She noticed a life-sized witch propped up near the bales of hay on the sidewalk. Her face was hidden by her hat, but she was very lifelike. She even had shoes. Harley must have found the decoration in the forgotten box of décor Zo recently unearthed. Zo just hoped the witch didn't cackle as she passed. Zo breathed a sigh of relief when she didn't.

Zo took a couple more steps, then stopped. A sense of familiarity or déjà vu wouldn't let her continue. She turned around. Despite her desire to pile into bed, she sensed something was wrong. She studied the decoration. That was it—the shoes. *They were Marianne's.* She remembered the buckles. *It couldn't be.*

Zo bent down for a closer look. The long black skirt was the same, too. Zo's hand shook as she reached out to lift up the hat. Marianne's lifeless eyes peered back at her.

She dropped the hat and screamed.

Chapter Four

Zo scanned the area for help. Buffalo Bill's bar and grill was hopping, and she yelled out, but no one heard. A country band was blaring, and partiers were dancing under the patio warmers to the twangy beat. Cunningham was nowhere to be seen. Zo pulled out her phone, her hands trembling. She dialed 9-1-1, and the operator assured her the police would be there right away.

Zo tucked her phone in her pocket and waited. She knew Marianne was dead, but something pulled her back to the body, a feeling she had to obey. She glanced at the vacant eyes, pointed toward heaven. Shivering, she touched her wrist, hoping she was wrong. If Marianne could be resuscitated, she would try. She felt no pulse. Her fingers still on her wrist, Zo noticed a mark on her head. "You must have fallen..."

I didn't fall. I was hit.

It was as if Marianne had said the words aloud. Zo's eyes flew to hers, but they showed no signs of life. Zo must have imagined it. She shook off the voice, squinting at the patrol lights in the distance. She noted the sound of the sirens, thankful they were close. She was starting to doubt whether Marianne was dead. Giving her a quick once-over, Zo saw scratches on her arm. It looked as if she'd been in a tussle with someone. So she *was* hit. But who would hurt Marianne?

Zo followed the scratch down to Marianne's fist and swore it relaxed, revealing a piece of information. A paper was tucked inside. Shudders rocked Zo's spine, but she took a deep breath and uncurled the fingers. It was a scrap of blue paper with a number, maybe a check. She didn't have time to examine it, but something—or someone—told her it was important. A squad car squealed into a parking spot, and Zo snapped a quick picture and tucked her phone into her pocket. Standing, she waved to the officer to notify him of her location.

She stopped mid-wave. It was Brady Merrigan, chief of police. His black leather cowboy hat was as recognizable as the sign outside of town. They'd tangled last Memorial Day when a local business owner was found dead at Spirit Canyon Lodge, the resort owned by her friend Beth. Now here was Zo with another body. He was going to kill her, and then he'd have two dead people to haul to the morgue.

"Zo Jones? Is that you?" Brady's dark hair blended into his hat, but his green eyes stood out like emeralds in a diamond mine. His concern was clear, and not all for the victim of the crime.

"Yes," answered Zo. "I was walking home from Spirits & Spirits when I found Marianne Morgan. I assumed it was a new decoration, but then I recognized her shoes. I think she's dead."

"It's okay, we'll take it from here," said Brady. "Don't go far."

She did as she was told, watching the scene unfold like a horror film. The ambulance arrived at the same time as Max. She would recognize his mint-and-white pickup anywhere. It was at least fifty years old.

He jumped out to help, but seeing the EMTs surrounding the body and her at the curb, he veered in her direction.

"Are you okay?" asked Max. "What happened?"

"I…it's…Marianne Morgan." Zo felt a little dizzy. "I'm sorry. I think I need to sit down."

Max took her hand and helped her to the bench near her doorway. "Just a second." He ran into the sea of blinking lights and came back with a blanket. He placed it over her shoulders and sat down beside her. "Better?"

"Much." Zo pulled the material closer. "Thank you." She tried telling her story again. "I was walking home from Jules's place when I saw Marianne. I thought she was a decoration. Recently, I'd found a box of forgotten Halloween décor, and I figured Harley had put it out to surprise me for Spirit Spooktacular. Then I recognized the shoes—and everything else." She took a deep breath. "Marianne's dead, and I think somebody killed her."

Max tilted his head to one side. "What makes you say that?"

"She had scratches on her arm and a mark on her head," Zo explained, tucking a lock behind her ear. "I think someone hit her."

"Maybe she fell," Max said.

"I thought so, too, but…" Zo let her sentence trail off. She didn't know if she should tell him about hearing Marianne's voice. Instead, she tried appealing to his logical side. "It doesn't make sense. If she fell, she wouldn't be propped up like a Halloween decoration. Somebody disguised her to look like a witch. Isn't that cruel?"

"Cruel and ironic," agreed Max. "Wasn't she a witch?"

Zo shook her head. "Not the type you're thinking of. Her book is about empowerment. There are no spells or witchcraft in it. My customers loved her talk."

"I bet she had her enemies, though," said Max. "Some people can be pretty close-minded."

Zo recalled Tiffany Snow. She was one of those people. "Tiffany told Marianne she should have an adult rating on the book. She implied if it got into the wrong hands, it could warp children's minds. Obviously, she hadn't read the book. If she had, she would have realized it wasn't what she believed it was."

"Tiffany has opinions about everything and everyone." Max put a warm hand over hers. "Even people not buying Christmas wreaths."

She gave him a rueful smile. It was comforting having him close. He was an excellent listener, and not just because he was an officer, though she admired his work, too.

"Anything else you remember?" asked Max.

Zo wondered if she should tell him about the paper in Marianne's hand. She didn't want him to think she was tampering with evidence, but she wasn't certain Brady would share the information with him. Brady thought of Max as a forest ranger, and not much else. Because Spirit Canyon was small and didn't have a lot of crime, Max spent most of his time in the Black Hills National Forest, which suited both him and Brady. Still, the relationship was fraught with tension, and Zo sympathized with Max's situation. She decided to tell him about it. "Marianne had a tiny scrap of paper in her hand, part of a check I think. It might have something to do with her death. I took a picture." She started to pull out her phone, but Max stopped her.

"Later," said Max. "If Brady thinks you tampered with his crime scene, the next few hours will be miserable for you."

Zo felt a new appreciation for Max. She'd trusted him with the information, and he returned the trust. It was nice.

Max glanced toward the crime scene. "Will you be okay alone?"

"Of course." Zo nodded. "You go ahead. I'll be right here."

Watching him walk away, she pulled the blanket around her shoulders, thankful for its warmth. The night was growing colder, and despite the activity, she felt alone. A wispy cloud flickered across the moon, darkening the bright circle for a moment. A shadow fell over Spirit Canyon, distorting the Halloween decorations into hideous shapes. Zo blinked, and the cloud was gone. Her town looked normal again.

Her eyes were playing tricks on her. It was hard not to see Marianne's dead eyes staring back at her, a desperate plea for help. *Not help.* She was beyond help. *Justice.* Marianne had written a new chapter of her life, a book that described her journey back to self-sufficiency after hardship and divorce. According to her story, the confidence she displayed now was hard won. She'd been vulnerable most of her life and had only recently discovered her power. Now someone had taken it again, permanently. Zo was determined to find out whom.

Another shadow fell, but this time, it was Brady Merrigan's. He was standing beside her, the outline of his hat clear in the street light. Looking over her shoulder, she confirmed her guess. It was Officer Merrigan all right, his look a mixture of curiosity and annoyance. He didn't like trouble in his town; he took any violence as a personal jab. While she didn't always agree with his methods, she had to admire his commitment. She, too, felt a deep loyalty to Spirit Canyon. It was her home, and she'd do anything to protect it.

"There you are, Ms. Jones," said Brady. "I see someone found you a blanket."

Zo stood. "Max Harrington brought it to me. I had a chill."

"Finding a dead body will do that to a person," said Brady. "Why don't you tell me about it?"

She relayed the last hour in detail. Brady drilled down on her answers, prodding for more information. When she explained that Marianne did an author talk at Happy Camper earlier in the day, he wanted a play-by-play of the event. By the time she was finished, she was exhausted from talking.

"Let me get this straight." Brady tapped his notebook. "She *wanted* to be called a witch?" Obviously, he was still sorting out the last fifteen minutes in his head.

"If you look at the history of the word, it's not a bad thing," said Zo. "Witches were powerful sources of healing and knowledge. She wanted women to embrace that power."

"It sounds like a lot of hocus-pocus to me."

"I imagine it does," Zo agreed. "You were born into power and privilege. The Merrigans are one of the wealthiest families in town. Some of us weren't that lucky."

He raised his dark eyebrows. They, like his hair, matched his black hat. "You seem to be doing all right to me. Your store is always busy."

"I am," said Zo. "That's not the point. The point is Marianne's message was very empowering, especially to women who feel marginalized."

"Ah, I get it." Brady clicked his pen and tucked it in his shirt pocket. "Feminist stuff."

Zo let out a breath. She could tell how he felt about the topic—and Marianne Morgan.

"Don't get huffy with me, young lady," warned Brady. "You're the one who found her. Pretty convenient if you ask me, right by your store."

Zo crossed her arms. She was done talking to this cowboy. She admired Marianne. That's why she invited her to speak at Happy Camper. Why would he insinuate she'd hurt her? Maybe he was searching for more information, but there were kinder ways of asking.

Brady hooked his thumbs through his belt loops. "The silent treatment might work on Max, but it won't work on me. You can cooperate, and we can finish our discussion here. Or I can haul you down to the station, and we can finish our conversation there."

The downtown clock tower struck twelve, each chime an answer to the real question on his mind—and hers. Who killed Marianne? Darkness cloaked the despicable deed, but it couldn't hide the truth. It was the eve of Spirit Spooktacular in Spirit Canyon, and someone seized the opportunity to commit a deplorable act of violence. In this town, on this night, midnight spelled murder.

Chapter Five

The next morning, Zo opened Happy Camper. She tried not to stare at the crime scene tape as she unlocked the door, but it was hard not to imagine Marianne's dead body lying where it had been hours before. With a final look, she opened the door and turned on the lights. It was a busy weekend, and she had a lot of work to do. The sooner she got to it, the sooner she could quit replaying last evening's tragedy.

The thought lasted about thirty seconds, until she found Marianne's day planner lying on the counter, next to the cash register. An eerie feeling came over her, and she stopped and glanced over her shoulder. Nothing but sunshine and merchandise. The planner was another grim reminder of Marianne's death. Was it something else? No. Marianne must have set it down when she purchased the witch sign. Still, wouldn't Zo have noticed it before now? Like when she left for the night? The idea that Marianne wanted her to find it hit her hard. It might hold a clue to her death. Zo opened it, and two tickets to tonight's performance of *Phantom of the Opera* fell out.

Zo glanced up. Twenty-four hours ago, Marianne was alive and planned to go to the musical. With the sun glinting off the store windows, Zo struggled to reconcile the death with her surroundings. Outside, the sweet smell of hickory lingered in the yellow leaves, stirred by visitors pouring in for Spirit Spooktacular. The downtown was buzzing with people—and life. Despite the tragedy, the festive feeling of fall was in the air. Buffalo Bill's was smoking meat for barbeque sandwiches, and Honey Buns was baking fresh bread. The O.K. Coffee Corral was brewing its fall blend, and Happy Camper had its own part in the festivities. Though Zo wasn't making food, she was making memorable experiences for her customers. She had to keep that in mind as she started her day.

With new determination, Zo checked Marianne's planner for a phone number or address. She had her contact information in an email, but many times, planners had a return address. This one didn't. It had all kinds of quotes and stickers, but no address.

Zo glanced through the month of October, a punch of guilt hitting her stomach. She hated invading Marianne's privacy, but Marianne was dead, and something told her Marianne wanted her to investigate. Whether it was a feeling or a hunch or a sign didn't matter. What did was getting her justice. Investigating the last few days of her life might help Zo figure out who would hurt her.

She stopped on today's date. That was interesting. Marianne had an appointment with a lawyer at ten a.m. She checked the clock. If Marianne were alive, she'd be there right now. Zo wondered if she was having legal problems. Was it possible that someone killed her to keep her from the appointment?

Two customers walked in, and so did her cat. Zo tucked the planner under the counter. She would call Marianne's daughter to retrieve it. When she came, Zo would ask her about the appointment. Maybe she knew what it was in regard to. If so, it might lend insight into her death.

"Sorry!" the customer exclaimed. "That cat just pushed right past me."

"No worries," said Zo. George sauntered in as if he owned the place. "He's mine."

"He's beautiful," said the other customer. Both women had orange and black Spirit Spooktacular canvas shopping bags. One of the hotels was giving them out with weekend stays. It was a cute idea.

"Thank you," said Zo. "He's a Maine Coon." Swerving against the back of her legs, George came behind the counter. He knew it was where she kept the tuna fish. "Can I help you find anything?"

"Maybe a bigger bag," laughed the customer.

Zo assured her that could be arranged while she dished up George's breakfast. As he tore into his food, she counted out money for the drawer. When he was finished eating, George joined her at the counter, using his favorite stack of books as a bed. His paws hung off the edge like two orange popsicles as his eyes followed the customers, who were overjoyed with the selection of used books. Spirit Canyon had two fine bookshops, but when the used bookstore went out of business, Zo picked up a lot of selections. Reading made her happy, and it made her customers happy, too. It was the only purchase she knew of that came with its own personal escape. No wonder it was said that people who read lived longer.

With more customers filing in and Harley not coming until later, Zo decided to give Marianne's daughter a call before things got too busy. Emily answered on the third ring. Her voice was ragged, and her sentences were disjointed. She started and stopped talking a few times. After telling her how sorry she was about her mother's death, Zo mentioned the planner. Would Emily like her to drop it in the mail, or would she stop by the store? Thankfully, Emily said she would come. She was in the area anyway. Zo could ask her then about her mom's appointment with the lawyer.

Zo was wrapping a bird print for a customer when Emily arrived. Zo was shocked by the change since yesterday. Her brown eyes were red and swollen, all efficiency and intelligence drained. With her blond hair pulled back in a ponytail, the dark roots framed her face in a circle of grief. She looked nothing like the bright woman who accompanied her mother yesterday. It was as if the news had wrecked her instantly.

After finishing with the customer, Zo came out from behind the counter and gave Emily a hug. "I'm so sorry about your mom. Is there anything I can do to help?"

Emily sniffled. "No, thank you. The funeral director has been very kind to me. I was on my way there when you called."

Zo motioned to the carafe of apple cider on the antique sideboard. She was offering free hot drinks to her shoppers. They loved stepping inside the store to warm up. "Can I get you some cider?"

She attempted a smile. "No thanks."

Zo retrieved Marianne's planner and stepped into a vacant nook filled with discounted camping accessories. Though she didn't stock many, she had a few cute décor items for RVs and campers. "Your mom left this here yesterday. I knew you'd want it back."

Emily took the planner, thumbing through the pages. "She took this thing everywhere. I tried to talk her into using the calendar on her phone, but she was very old school that way."

"I understand. Paper doesn't run out of batteries. Phones do." The hum of the store filled the lull in conversation. Though Zo dreaded bringing up last night, she knew she had to if she was going to be any help to Marianne or Emily. "I don't know if the police told you, but I was the one who found her."

"They mentioned the store. I saw the crime scene tape outside." Emily swallowed hard.

"Did they tell you how she died?" asked Zo.

Emily shook her head. "They said she might have been in a fight, which doesn't make sense. You knew my mom. She wasn't a fighter, not in the physical sense. She wouldn't hurt a fly."

Zo agreed. Though she didn't know Marianne well, her book was against violence.

"The police said the medical examiner will determine the cause of death." Emily scrunched up her nose as if smelling something foul. "If she had a bump on her head, like they said, I have to think someone put it there on purpose. Unless she fell..."

"I don't think so," said Zo. "She was disguised when I found her. She had a hat on. It would have fallen off if she stumbled."

"A hat?" questioned Emily. "What kind of hat?"

Zo swallowed. "A witch hat."

Emily's swollen eyes changed. They were no longer empty, they were angry. "*Someone did this to her.* Someone did this to her because she was a witch. The hat was a sign...an indictment against her."

"I agree," said Zo. "I think someone hit her on purpose. I'm just not sure why. Maybe you can help me?"

"Anything."

"When I was looking for a phone number in the planner, I noticed she had an appointment with a lawyer today. Do you know what that was about?"

"Her will," said Emily. "Now that I'm eighteen, she was changing me to the sole beneficiary. We talked about it last week."

"Who's the current beneficiary?" Zo asked.

She responded in a rush. "My dad, but he had nothing to do with this. They didn't get along, but he would never kill her."

A shopper approached the counter, and Zo excused herself. "I'll be right back."

She rang up the sale, a used vinyl record, while the customer gushed about the selection of items in the store. Despite being preoccupied, Zo was glad for the compliment. She worked very hard at finding unique and diverse items for the store. She attended auctions and yard sales for this very reason.

"Sorry about that." Zo returned to Emily. "It's going to be a busy weekend."

Emily didn't acknowledge the disruption. Obviously, she was still thinking about her dad. "I was with him last night, so he couldn't have done this. We went to dinner at Lotsa Pasta then a movie. He didn't drop me off until ten."

That didn't help her dad's case as far as Zo was concerned. She found Marianne just before midnight, and even though she hadn't seen a lot of dead bodies, she didn't think Marianne had been deceased very long. He could have killed her after dropping off Emily. But why? From what Zo knew, Marianne wasn't wealthy. How much money would he really inherit? Zo put the question to Emily.

"I don't have an exact amount," said Emily. "But from our talk last week, I understood it to be a lot. Her book went to auction, and she ended up with an advance of one hundred thousand dollars. Plus she was writing a second book."

Zo was speechless. One hundred thousand dollars was a lot of money. She had no idea Marianne had secured that kind of deal. Zo respected her for not bragging or making it an issue. Being a local author from a rural state, she could have done so very easily. Zo only knew one author, and it was Marianne. Yet when Zo invited her to speak at the store, she was gracious and even grateful. Her humility made Zo more determined than ever to find her killer.

"We will figure out what happened last night," said Zo. "I promise. If there's one thing I'm good at, it's piecing together a story."

For the first time since arriving, Emily's face brightened. She looked a little bit more like a college freshman. She opened Marianne's planner and took out the *Phantom of the Opera* tickets. "She would want you to have these. I won't be going, obviously, and Nikki was her good friend. Mom papered the theater for her, handing out additional tickets to friends and family. She was a lifelong patron and would want the show to be a success."

Zo took the tickets. "Thank you. That's so nice of you."

Emily turned to leave.

"Keep in touch, okay?" said Zo. "If you need anything, just give me a call."

"Sure," said Emily. "I will. And thanks for looking into this. I wish I could do more."

"You have enough to do right now," said Zo. "Leave it to me."

After Emily left, Zo scanned the tickets. They were very nice seats, row B. Zo loved the theater. Going would give her an opportunity to talk to Nikki about Marianne's death and the theater's plans for the holidays. Zo's Happy Camper column this week was titled "Spirit of the Season." It would showcase the upcoming charity events taking place during November and December.

She noticed a customer looking for a price on a candlestick and went over to assist her. She'd be busy with customers until Harley got there, which left her very little time to find a friend or date to go with her to the theater. The bell on the door jingled, signaling the entrance of a new customer, and Max strode in. Maybe she wouldn't have to find a date after all. Maybe a date had found her.

She had to admit, Max's forest ranger uniform was becoming more attractive every time she saw it. Tangling with authorities a time or two when she was young, she never thought she'd be one of those girls who fell for a man in uniform, but maybe it was a universal thing. Maybe she could only deny its appeal for so long before she became beguiled by the creases in his shirt. They accentuated his biceps just right. Nor could she deny his smile, which was so kind that she was starting to believe it. He might *be* as good as he seemed.

"You're just the guy I wanted to see," greeted Zo.

He turned and looked over his shoulder. "Me?"

Zo smiled.

"Even with this?" From his back pocket, he pulled out a folded piece of paper.

His uniform suddenly looked less appealing. "What is it?"

He handed her the paper. "It's a Trip Plan. I'd like you to use it for your nature hikes. It approximates the times and lengths of the hikes. You leave it with an emergency contact."

Zo scanned the form: emergency contacts, equipment carried, length of trail. "Harley has all this information."

"I'd like to have the information as well," said Max. "Just to be safe."

"I'm really glad you're coming with us on Sunday," said Zo. "Then you'll see for yourself that these hikes are not like yours. They're not even hikes. They're nature walks."

"Nature is unpredictable," said Max. "It's good to plan ahead."

Even though Zo didn't want or need more paperwork, she tucked the form under her counter. The man was obstinate on the point, and she had other things to discuss, like Marianne's death. But first she needed to take care of tonight. "Fine. I'll use the form if you go to the *Phantom of the Opera* with me tonight."

His eyes crinkled when he smiled. "I'm flattered you think you need to bribe me to go out with you."

"It's not a date," Zo quickly replied. "Emily gave me two tickets, and I want to use them to talk to Nikki. She and Marianne were friends, and she might have another perspective on Emily's dad. He stood to inherit a lot of money." Zo told Max about Marianne's book advance and her appointment to change her will.

"It's a possibility," agreed Max. "The medical examiner just determined Marianne died from blunt force trauma to the head."

Zo knew it. Someone hit Marianne and left her to die in the dark of night, the bewitching hour. "Does Brady have any idea who might have done this?"

"If he did, he wouldn't tell me," Max muttered. He straightened his shoulders and changed his response. "We're working on it."

"Last night, he acted as if I had something to do with Marianne's death. Do you think I'm in danger? Or my store?"

Max didn't have time to answer. A customer approached to purchase a birdfeeder.

"That's a lovely feeder, Mrs. Bixby," Zo said. Mrs. Bixby was one of her regular customers. She was seventy-five, which was surprising since she still shopped like she was eighteen. Snow, rain, or wind didn't stop her from making her weekly trek in from the canyon. "The Mountain Blue Bird is sure to visit this winter."

"Splendid." Mrs. Bixby turned over her wallet in her wrinkled hands. "I need more visitors this time of year."

Max received a call over his radio. "I need to check on this. What time is the show?"

Mrs. Bixby raised her sparse eyebrows at Zo. "He's cute," she mouthed.

"The performance starts at seven. I'll pick you up." Zo put the feeder in a brown paper bag with the Happy Camper logo on it. "Thank you, Mrs. Bixby. Stop in again."

"I'll be ready," said Max. "Can I carry your package to the car, ma'am?"

"And a gentleman, too," whispered Mrs. Bixby. "He's a keeper."

Zo smiled. She was starting to agree.

Chapter Six

That night, Zo wondered what to wear to the theater. She was a casual dresser and loved jeans and sweatshirts, but the opera house meant a nice dress. Though the theater was on the small side, tourists and locals turned out in their finery. Despite the opera house being located in the heart of the Black Hills, Nikki Ainsworth brought in talented theater troupes and big-name shows. She wasn't afraid to take on *Phantom* or any other musical, and the newly renovated theater would only help attract larger companies.

Originally built in 1906, the Spirit Canyon Opera House was home to many popular productions, but at the end of the decade, motion pictures competed for its business. The theater fell into disrepair until a group of Black Mountain College students took renewed interest in the opera house. When they graduated, however, the interest was lost. It would take a local graduate like Nikki to stay for the vision of a thriving theater to be fulfilled. She'd worked tirelessly on the opera house, and after several years, the renovations were finally complete. Zo couldn't wait to see the finished product. *Phantom of the Opera* was the first production in the remodeled theater.

She checked her outfit in the full-length mirror. Dark green on the top and black on the bottom, the dress was lovely. It was short and had a cute ruffle. She had the perfect green earrings to match. They added a bohemian touch and made her feel more comfortable. Plus they turned her green eyes a little greener. She touched her silver necklace. A half-moon, it didn't really go with the outfit, but she never took it off. It was the only gift she had from her birth parents. Engraved with the name Zo, it was with her when she was found at the police station, and her adopted parents kept the name, unique as it was.

Hopping into her Outback, she noted Happy Camper was still busy. It was open until ten during Spirit Spooktacular, but Harley was managing just fine. With any luck, she could spend the last hour doing homework. Harley was a committed employee, and if Zo could keep her at least until she graduated, she would be thrilled. Hopefully, she would keep working long after.

Dressed in a black jacket and looking very handsome, Max was waiting for her on the porch of his bungalow. He opened the front door, hollered something inside, and walked to the car.

She rolled down her window. "You ready?"

"For so many reasons, yes," he grumbled.

A screech came from the house. It sounded like a cross between a hurt cat and a caged bird. Max upped his speed.

"Are you sure?" Zo asked. "It sounds like someone needs your help in there."

He shut the car door, his eyes like blue crystals against his dark shirt. "I'm the one who needs help. Duncan's decided to take up the fiddle."

"The fiddle?" asked Zo. "I'm no musician, but I don't think it has much in common with the guitar besides the strings."

"I guess he didn't notice, because he's playing that thing like he's Charlie Daniels." He turned to Zo, his face a puzzle of emotions. "I don't know what I'm going to do."

Zo backed out of the driveway. "Maybe you could take up the drums. Start a real band."

"I'm serious," said Max. "If this job at Spirits & Spirits doesn't pan out, I don't know what I'm going to do." He faced her. "Could you talk to Jules? Make sure she understands my predicament? With a steady paycheck, he could move out—permanently."

"I can talk to her, but when it comes to business, she makes her own rules. My advice to Duncan would be to toe the line."

"Ha!" Max laughed. "That guy has never toed the line a day in his life. He reminds me of my brothers."

"How's that?" Zo pulled into an open spot near the opera house.

"They never listened," explained Max. "They expected things to just 'turn out.' The future was a vague place to them, but not to me. I'm the oldest, and when our dad left, I had no choice but to work and plan for it."

She turned off the ignition. "I didn't realize."

He shrugged.

"Your dad—"

"—left when I was five. I hardly remember him." Max buttoned his jacket. "Do you have the tickets? It's almost seven."

He reached for the door handle. Zo guessed he didn't want to go into detail right now, and it was almost showtime. Still, being an oldest child explained a few of his behaviors. She probably even shared a few. She better understood his need for rules and organization. He needed them while helping his mother raise his younger brothers. "Yes, I have them in my purse."

While she turned to the backseat to find her purse, he ran around to her side of the car and opened the door. *This is a first.* "I guess Mrs. Bixby was right."

"Why?" said Max.

"You *are* a gentleman."

They walked into the bustling opera house, and Zo gave the usher their tickets. The renovations were better than she imagined. Instead of industrial carpet, refurbished oak floors gleamed under the light of the new crystal chandelier. The ratty seat cushions were replaced with plush burgundy fabric that matched the burgundy walls and stage curtains. The ornate, cream-colored woodwork was a nice contrast to the dark walls, and Zo found herself admiring the stage boxes and ceiling paintings anew as she scooted into her seat.

From the looks of the audience, it would be a packed house. A meet-and-greet with the cast was scheduled for after the performance, which might have had something to do with the large crowd. Then again, *Phantom* was known for its beautiful costumes and singing, and it *was* Spirit Spooktacular. Lots of visitors were in town. Zo sneaked a glance at Max. She just hoped he was in the mood for music after Duncan's jam session.

The lights flickered, and Max leaned over and whispered, "Let's find Nikki after the performance."

Zo nodded. It was hard to concentrate with him this close. He smelled of pine needles and cold air, an intoxicating combination that reminded Zo of Christmas, his blue eyes bright like snow in the moonlight.

The show began, and Zo lost herself in the drama. From the time she was little, Zo loved the theater. Stories were the reason she went into journalism in the first place. She liked nothing better than to take a book into the canyon and disappear. Unlike most of the foster houses she lived in, nature was serene, and books made sense. They had beginnings, middles, and endings. There was a certain order to them that she found attractive. She checked Max, who was enjoying the show as much as she was. Maybe they were more alike than she realized.

After the performance, they went to the lobby to meet the cast. The actors paraded in, still dressed in elaborate costumes. The Phantom was especially haunting. With his burned face and white half-mask, it was hard to remember he was playing a role. He looked so *real*.

Nikki was congratulating him on his performance. Standing next to him in a black suit, she was as strong as she was beautiful, not only physically, though she was that, but mentally. Her willpower to transform the opera house was palpable, and the cast revered her. It was as if she, too, had a little theater magic up her sleeve. She could draw performers and patrons and locals into something bigger than themselves, if only for a night. Zo admired her commitment to the arts. The world needed more people like her.

Max peeked into the room adjacent to the lobby. "Did you see this?" She followed his gaze.

"They put some of the memorabilia they found during the renovation into display cases," said Max.

It looked as if Nikki would be awhile. She had not only actors to congratulate but donors to talk to, so Zo followed Max. She scanned the newspaper clippings from past productions, framed on the walls. "What a great idea. I wonder where they found them?"

"Hey, look at this," said Max. "*Phantom of the Opera* performed at the opera house before."

Zo noticed tonight's performance harkened to the original. The actors wore similar colorful attire and dress. Even Christine's wig looked identical. "Nikki got tonight's performance perfect. Just think, this place might have been demolished years ago if it weren't for her. Can you imagine?"

"I can't imagine not having an opera house in Spirit Canyon," said Max. "Where would *our* phantom live?"

Max was referring to the woman in white who was said to haunt the opera house, the upper left balcony specifically. Zo hadn't seen her, but she believed the story. Spirit Canyon was home to many legends, including the woman in white. According to the accounts, she wasn't an actress but a patron who owned the box in the early 1900s. Apparently she didn't enjoy sharing it, because people who occupied it complained of noise, cold air, and a general feeling of ill-ease. Since the 1980s, the box had been kept vacant for these reasons. A yellow cord blocked access to patrons and ghost hunters.

Stepping back into the lobby, Zo noticed Nikki was finished talking to the Phantom and quickly called out her name before she was accosted by the next actor. "Hi Nikki. Great show."

"Thank you…"

Zo wondered if she remembered who she was. Everyone in town knew who Nikki was, but it would be impossible for her to remember every name. "I'm Zo. We met at the book signing at Happy Camper." Max appeared at her side. "And this is Max Harrington. He's a forest ranger."

"Of course I remember you." Nikki greeted her warmly. "Your event was fantastic. Were you there, Max? I don't recall."

"No," said Max. "But I'm assisting with the investigation into Marianne's death. I'm sorry for your loss. I understand you were friends."

"I'm sorry, too," added Zo.

"Thank you." Nikki's eyes flicked around the area. "She was supposed to be here tonight, you know. Hers was the box in the right balcony. She wouldn't have missed it, and she would have invited everyone she knew. I can't believe she's gone." A tear slipped down her cheek, and she dabbed it away quickly. "It's not just a loss to me, but a loss to the entire theater community."

"You were good friends?" asked Zo.

"Yes," Nikki answered. "We were both into theater, art, books—obviously." She smiled a sad smile. "We raised our kids together. My Hannah and her Emily are the same age."

"I didn't realize you had a daughter," said Zo.

Nikki pointed to a younger version of herself, who was talking to an actor. With her fair hair and tall frame, there was no mistaking the connection, though Hannah's attire was more relaxed. While her mom's hair was carefully coiffed, hers was secured in a messy bun.

"She's pretty," said Zo.

"Thank you." Nikki turned to Max. "You said you are with the police. Do you know what happened? It didn't really say on the news."

"We don't know for certain, but it looks as if she took a blow to the head," explained Max. "She died of blunt force trauma."

Nikki's hand flew to her mouth. "From the news report, I figured she tripped or…or fell. Her house is just a block away from Happy Camper."

That explained why Marianne was found near her store.

"But that's not the case?" prodded Nikki, looking between Zo and Max. "She didn't die of a fall?"

"I'm not at liberty to say," Max said.

Spoken like a true officer. Zo shared what she knew. "It didn't appear that way to me. I was the one who found her."

"I'm so sorry," Nikki apologized. "That must have been terrible for you."

"It was." Zo shook off the memory and focused on finding justice for Marianne. "What do you know about Marianne's relationship with her husband?"

"*Ex-husband*," Nikki corrected. "The divorce was recently finalized. He's a lazy bum. Hasn't worked for years. She was right to get rid of him." She blinked, her lashes thick with mascara. "You don't think he hurt her, do you?"

"We don't think anything yet," cautioned Max. "The police are still gathering facts."

"If that slob did something to her, he'll have to answer to me." Nikki crossed her arms. "I know he's Emily's father, but I never liked him."

"Emily told me he is Marianne's sole beneficiary," said Zo. "He'll inherit everything, including her book advance."

Nikki was silent for a moment, digesting the implication. A patron called to her from across the lobby, and her face changed with a smile. She waved before returning to the conversation. "If you're asking me if he would have killed her for the money, my answer is absolutely," said Nikki. "He would do anything for a handout." She pulled down her suit jacket. "If you'll excuse me, I have to see a couple people before they leave. But please catch me again before you go."

Nikki turned, a black streak walking in the opposite direction.

Zo looked at Max. "It sounds as if she really hates Marianne's ex-husband."

Max shrugged. "With good reason, maybe. I'll be right back."

While Max used the restroom, Zo perused the memorabilia in the next room. She loved history, anything old, really. She was fascinated with Spirit Canyon's past, and the opera house was finally clearing out. She could get to the display cases along the wall, filled with treasures recovered during the remodel.

Stopping at a display of sheet music, she perused the musical numbers, happy that Nikki had brought back not only the theater, but also the orchestra. The ensemble was a luxury in a small town like Spirit Canyon.

With Max still gone, she moved on to another display case of costume jewelry, hairpins, and makeup. Zo moved closer, her face near the case. Not all the jewelry was costume. Some was gold or silver, albeit tarnished. She squinted at a necklace that resembled her own. She blinked. It had the same intricate silver inlay and same chain but was shaped like a sun. Zo's hand flew to her throat. Sun and moon. Could it be a matching set?

Max said her name, and she jumped.

"Sorry," Max apologized. "Did I startle you?" His smile vanished. "What's wrong?"

Zo swallowed. She didn't know if she could tell him what she saw in the case. What if it turned out to me nothing? She was thirty-three years old. She wasn't a kid anymore. But suddenly she felt like one, vulnerable and shy.

Max was looking at the case. He tapped the glass. "It's your necklace. The one you always wear."

"I don't know."

"I'm going to get someone to open the case." It wasn't a question. He was gone before she could she could answer yes or no.

After a few minutes, Nikki returned with a puzzled look on her face. She had a key in her hand. "Max says a piece of jewelry in here belongs to you."

"I don't know." Zo felt like a broken record. Confronted with the match, she couldn't allow herself to hope it was hers. She'd wished for a clue for so many years. Now one was here, and she was afraid.

Nikki opened the case and took out the necklace. "It's beautiful." She turned it over in her hands, reading the engraving on the back. "Elle. What does that mean?"

Zo took the necklace and shakily placed it next to her own. The crescent moon fit perfectly around the sun, the "Zo" and "elle" making one word. "I think it's the other half of my name."

Chapter Seven

To find out her name was not her name was surreal. She'd always wondered about the spelling. She assumed whoever had given her the necklace didn't want Zo pronounced with the long *e*. She'd always felt as if a part of her was missing; now she realized it wasn't just her parents. It was her name.

"Zoelle," said Max. "That's pretty."

They locked eyes. It was the first time she'd heard her full name, and in his voice, she liked the way it sounded. How it rhymed with Noël. She was glad he was there to share the news with her.

Zo explained to Nikki, who was confused by the revelation. "I was given away. This necklace was the only possession I had on me when the police found me at the station."

"Keep it, of course." Nikki nodded to the jewelry. "It's obviously yours."

Or Zo's mother's. There were two chains, two necklaces. Two people were meant to wear them. Why was this one in the opera house? Zo asked Nikki.

"I don't know the details," said Nikki. "You could ask the construction workers where they found it. Would that help? A few will be here tomorrow and more on Monday. They're just finishing up the balcony."

Zo appreciated Nikki's cooperative attitude. Nikki could've made her jump through hoops to get the necklace back, but she didn't. It made a big difference. "That's a great idea. I'll do that. Thank you."

An actor drew closer, waiting to talk to Nikki. She gave him a nod of acknowledgment. "Let me know if you need anything else, and Max? Will you let me know if you find out anything about Marianne?"

Max agreed before leading them to the coat check, where he retrieved their jackets and tipped the employee. Zo moved in a fog, thinking about the possibilities. Her mother—or father—had worked in or attended the theater. Did they live in Spirit Canyon? Impossible. The couple who adopted her kept the name Zo. Even when she was put in foster care, it would have been easy to find her.

The old doubt started creeping in, a rip in an umbrella of hope. Maybe they didn't want to be found. Even after all these years, they might not need the headache. Which was fine. She didn't begrudge them. She had a good life, a nice home, and a thriving business. She was grateful to have been raised in Spirit Canyon and loved the Black Hills. Growing up as she did made her resilient. She wouldn't change the past even if she could.

Max held open the door, and the blast of cool wind brought her back to the present moment. It was fall, and the nights were growing darker earlier. Soon the snow boots would come out and remain a staple for the winter, when the Black Hills received five to fifteen inches of snow a month.

"What are you thinking about?" asked Max.

"Snow," said Zo.

He paused on the sidewalk. "What are you *really* thinking about?"

"*Snow,*" she said with a laugh. "And everything else. It's a lot to take in."

"I bet," said Max. "Where do you think the necklace came from?"

They were standing in front of the wine bar, Canyon Vines. The tables were lighted with candles that made a happy glow against the dark night. It was the perfect atmosphere for a private conversation. "Do you want to go in for a glass of wine?" she asked.

"That's a good idea," said Max. "I want to hear your thoughts on what Nikki said."

They chose a table near the crackling stone fireplace. The two facing couches in front of it were already taken. However, the chairs were plush and comfortable, and the entire room was cozy, designed to look like a wine cellar, with bottles lining the walls.

When the waiter came, they ordered glasses of pinot noir and a cheese plate. He returned with the wine, and Zo admired the canyon etched on the bowl of the goblet, appreciating the small detail. She took a sip of wine, the liquid warming her insides while the fire warmed her outsides. Glad for the detour, she was too edgy to think about sleep.

"Zoelle is a unique name." Max took a large drink of his wine, swigging it like a beer. "I wonder if you're named after someone."

"Like a famous person?" The thought had also crossed her mind.

"Right," said Max. "Unless it's French or something." He tilted his head. "Are the French stubborn? Maybe that's where you get it."

She smiled, despite his remark. Max made it easy to talk about her name. She didn't know how, but he was making it seem normal.

"Ask Hattie," Max suggested. "If there's a Zoelle out there, she'll find her."

It was a good idea. Hattie Fines was the town librarian and a very dear friend. She knew everything, and if she didn't know something, she knew how to find it. "I will. I'm also going to ask the construction crew where they found the necklace. Maybe that will give me a place to start."

The cheese plate came, and Max stabbed a piece of Gouda with his toothpick, holding it mid-air. "Have you ever searched for your birth parents before?"

Zo spread a cracker with hummus. "Vaguely, when I was eighteen. It was the early internet days, though, and I wasn't successful."

"You should have your DNA tested." Max pointed the now-empty toothpick at her. "A lot of cases have been cracked with those ancestry sites."

"True," agreed Zo. "But I don't want to waste time yearning for something I might never have. I wasted a lot of time that way in my twenties. I told myself I'd never go there again."

"You might be right," said Max. "Even if you did find them, it might not be the reunion you'd hoped for."

"Thanks for your encouragement." Zo selected a piece of cheese.

"Seriously, though. Reunions can be disappointing."

Zo had a feeling he wasn't talking about her anymore. "I know you went to college in Montana, but did you grow up there?"

He took a sip of his wine before answering. "Born and raised, which is probably why I love the mountains so much."

"Theirs are much bigger than ours."

"But the company here is better." His lips twitched with a smile.

A piece of her melted. She, too, loved her little mountain town. It had a thriving downtown, arts community, and picturesque canyon, not to mention nearby waterfalls, streams, and lakes. It didn't have the jagged peaks of the Rockies, but it didn't need them either. "Do you get home often?"

He leaned back in his chair, crossing a shoe over his knee. It was shiny black from rare use. "Sometimes I forget you were a journalist. I could tell you my life story without realizing it. But yes, I do go home, quite a bit. It was one of the reasons Spirit Canyon worked. It's not too far away."

She took in the information. "I've been told I'm a good listener."

"And investigator," added Max. "What did you make of Nikki's comments about Jake Morgan?"

"Marianne's ex-husband?" asked Zo. "I think Nikki's right. Emily loves her dad, but she admitted he was out of work. If someone killed Marianne for money, it was probably him."

"It would have been his last chance to cash in before she changed her will," said Max.

"And she had a check in her hand." Zo took out her phone and pulled up the picture. "At least I think it's a check. Which would also imply money." They studied the picture, their heads together.

"Can you zoom in any closer?" asked Max.

"This is as far as it goes without getting blurry," said Zo.

"It looks like a check to me, but it's hard to say." Max drew back from the phone. "Did you tell Brady about Marianne's appointment with her lawyer?"

Zo raised her eyebrows. "What do you think?"

"Brady cares about getting justice for Marianne as much as we do," argued Max. "He just goes about it a different way. You need to tell him."

"I know, but the guy drives me crazy." She popped a grape in her mouth, reviewing all the ways Brady drove her mad. First was their history. She hadn't been the most obedient kid in Spirit Canyon, and he was always there to remind her. Second was his brother Patrick. He wouldn't renew the lease on her original store, sending her packing after one year of business so that he could open up his own sporting goods store. She had to start over at her new location, which wouldn't have been so bad except she hated moving. She'd done too much of it as a kid. Third was his attitude, righteous and stubborn. He'd been a pain in the neck when a murder occurred last summer at her friend Beth's lodge. Finally, there was his last name, Merrigan. It was all over everything. Their family practically owned the town, and his father had been the police chief before him. But Max was right. It was probably one of the reasons Brady cared so much.

"When we talked the night of the murder, he brought up Marianne being a witch," Zo recalled. "Do you think that makes him superstitious?"

"The entire *town* is superstitious," said Max. "This time of year, it's even worse."

"With good reason," said Zo. "I swear Marianne's been giving me signals, clues. First the check. Then her planner shows up on my counter, out of nowhere."

"What? Like haunting you?"

"Like giving me signs."

"If only it were that easy." Max pointed with his finger. "This way to catch a killer."

"This way to stay out of jail," Zo added.

"Brady isn't going to put you in jail," promised Max.

"I hope not," said Zo. "Finding Marianne near Happy Camper was bad luck for me."

"Or good luck for Marianne," said Max.

Zo liked his way of thinking better.

Chapter Eight

Zo slept poorly, partly because of the necklace and partly because of her cat. She and George were used to sleeping alone, which meant when they invaded each other's space, a proper rumpus followed. She wasn't complaining, but George was big—twenty pounds big. When he turned, she felt it.

She reached around him for the clock on her nightstand. It was a little after seven. George moved to the end of the bed, circling once before going back to sleep. He might not be a morning cat, but she had lots to do before opening Happy Camper. Today was Halloween, which meant the Spirit Canyon Pumpkin-Carving Contest, not to mention her costume party. The shops in Spirit Canyon were carving jack-o-lanterns to enter into the contest, and the winner would be announced by the mayor before tonight's parade. This year, a customer had given Zo an enormous pumpkin to carve. Standing three feet tall and weighing a hundred pounds, the pumpkin was prize worthy. She and Harley would be carving it together, but Zo needed to gut it this morning. Throwing on a sweatshirt and sweatpants, she wasn't looking forward to the sticky work, but it would be worth it if they won. The winning entry received five hundred dollars and a free ad in a popular visitor's guide.

She opened the deck door, coffee mug in hand, and George shot out of bed like an orange bullet. He wasn't going to miss an opportunity to get outside for the remaining days of nice weather. Gazing at the canyon, a blaze of red, orange, and gold, she shared his enthusiasm. She would miss the campfires and crisp perfume of fall, yet the changing of seasons meant new adventures. Winter brought snow, skiers, and hot cocoa. Terry Peak was a popular skiing destination in the Black Hills and just thirty miles away. Life was never dull in a tourist town like Spirit Canyon.

Spotting Cunningham on his deck, Zo waved. His shoulders were perpetually hunched, as if always in the middle of reading a book, and he was gazing over his railing, his hair a white bush atop his head. He hadn't noticed her, which was odd. With their side-by-side lawns, it was impossible not to hear what the other was doing.

"Morning, Cunningham," she called. "You're up early."

It was all the encouragement he needed to pad down the steps in his worn moccasins. Over his flannel pajamas, he wore a tightly tied knit robe with the monogram RMC. They met on her lawn. "I couldn't sleep."

"Again?"

"Again," he repeated.

"You need to take a sleeping pill." Zo set down her coffee, knife, and trowel on the picnic table. Beside it, the extra-large pumpkin waited to be carved.

"I'd take a sleeping pill, but I'd rather not raid the refrigerator while I'm asleep, thank you very much. That's one of the side effects, you know."

"It's starting to sound like the safer alternative, if you ask me." Zo knew how he felt about pills. He didn't trust them, but he needed rest. She pointed to the initials on his robe. "What does the M stand for?"

"Meriwether," answered Cunningham. "My mother wanted me to be an explorer. Unfortunately, reading *Moby-Dick* was as close as I ever got."

"That's interesting," said Zo. "My birth parents wanted me to be Zoelle." She picked up the second necklace, still around her neck, and flipped it over to show him the inscription. "We came across this last night at the theater. It was found during the renovation."

Without his reading glasses, he had to squint to read the engravings. "Sun and moon. It explains your fascination for astronomy—and astrology."

At the Zodiac Club, a hobby group made up of amateurs and astronomy professor Dr. Linwood, Zo learned the sun and moon were powerful forces. The sun indicates personality, and the moon represents emotions. Together they determine mood and outlook.

Cunningham let go of the necklaces. "They're a perfect fit, a clue."

"After all these years looking, I finally found one." She grabbed the knife.

"What are you going to do?"

She stabbed the pumpkin. "About the necklace? I'm going to stop by the theater, ask the renovation crew if they remember where they found it."

"Once an investigator, always an investigator."

She couldn't deny it. She loved the thrill of chasing a lead and getting to the truth behind a story. "I need to check on the theater's holiday plans anyway, for my column. With all the commotion, I forgot to ask Nikki last night."

"Right, *for your column.*"

They'd talked enough about her for one morning. She turned the questions on him. "Why couldn't you sleep?"

He let out a breath. "My students' papers, of course. Their errors always keep me up."

He averted his eyes, and she knew there was something else. "*And...*"

"And I worry my classes aren't useful anymore," he added reluctantly.

"Of course they are," said Zo. "I've learned a lot just living next door to you. I can't imagine what it's like to be in one of your classes."

"Boring, according to their evaluations." Cunningham picked up the trowel, then set it back down on the picnic table. "I think I have something better than this in my shed."

She gave him the most enthusiastic smile she was capable of this early in the morning. He needed a break from his troubles, which meant his papers. A little physical activity and fresh air would do him good. It was the best thing for improving your mood. "Yes, grab your shovel, and we'll make it a pumpkin party. I could use the help. Besides, I want to talk to you about Marianne. I have some new information."

Cunningham returned with a tool, and even with both of them digging, it took over an hour to gut the pumpkin. However, they'd talked as much as they'd scooped, about the necklace, Marianne, and her ex-husband. When they were finished, she had a stack of seeds a foot high and was more than ready for a shower.

She turned to go inside, excited to don her catsuit costume. "Don't forget to vote for Happy Camper's pumpkin. The ballots have to be in before the parade."

"I hope you know our friendship won't influence my decision," Cunningham proclaimed. "I'll need to peruse the competition before I cast my vote."

She laughed all the way up the stairs, glad he was feeling like his old self again.

An hour later, Zo and Harley hauled the supersized pumpkin to Happy Camper together. Like all the hip ideas, the design was Harley's. She'd watched a show on master pumpkin carvers and ordered special stencils and knives for the project. Zo loved the picture, which was a combination of leaves, acorns, and the words FALL IN LOVE WITH YOUR LIFE. She just hoped they could finish in time.

Spirit Canyon Carving Contest's rules were very specific. Store owners had to place their pumpkins outside their doors by ten a.m. for inspection, to ensure nobody started carving early. They were given until five p.m. to finish, at which time townspeople had to start voting for their favorite pumpkin. The mayor would announce the results before the Spirit Spooktacular parade, a mix of locals, tourists, and floats traversing Main Street.

After being given the okay to start, Zo and Harley finagled the pumpkin inside. Several curious customers followed them to see what they were going to do with it. Zo set up a little carving station near the front window so that passersby could see their progress. Dressed appropriately in a Superwoman costume and cape, Harley took up the task. Her chin was set in a way that told Zo she meant business. She was determined like that, especially when it came to a project.

"Relax, okay?" said Zo. "It's sort of our store motto."

Her winged eyeliner lifted, so Zo understood she was smiling, but she didn't take her eyes off the pumpkin. After watching her for a few minutes, Zo wasn't sure she wanted to take turns carving. Harley was *that* good. She decided to leave the artwork to her.

The bell chimed, and Zo refocused on her customers. She meandered to the door. It was Officer Merrigan. He was either dressed as a cop for Halloween or here on official police business. She was pretty sure it was the latter.

He indicated the pumpkin. "That's a big piece of fruit. You think you'll finish in time?"

"I hope so," said Zo. Harley threw her a glance, and she adjusted her answer. "Yes, we will."

Brady Merrigan looked around. "This isn't a camping store." He picked up a yellow coffee mug that read BEE HAPPY, a bee chasing the words. "I always thought it was."

"No, it's a gift shop."

"That makes sense," said Brady. "A book signing probably wouldn't go over so hot in a camping store."

"It depends on the book, I guess," Zo said.

"True." Brady put down the mug. "I need to ask you a few questions about Marianne's book signing, if you have time."

Anyone with eyeballs could see she didn't have time. At least ten shoppers were in the store, and Harley was busy carving the pumpkin, but she wasn't going to *not* talk to him. He was the chief of police. She didn't want her customers to think she had something to hide. "Of course, as long as you can ask me in between guests. I don't have any other employees to ring purchases."

"Not a problem." He followed her to the counter, the serious sound of his boots interrupting the quiet hum of Simon & Garfunkel playing on the record player.

"What can I help you with?" Zo readjusted her cat-ears headband. She couldn't wait for George to see her costume. He was going to be jealous of her jet-black fur.

"Just a little town gossip," he said. "I was talking to Tiffany Snow—do you know her? She sells those holiday wreaths?"

"Yes, I know her."

"She said Julia Parker used to date Marianne's boyfriend..." Brady checked his notebook. "Roberto. Were they still close?"

Zo was surprised by the question. "I don't think they were ever close. Jules never mentioned him to me, and we're good friends. I didn't know they dated until the day of the book signing."

"That's interesting," Brady mused.

"Why is that interesting?"

"Because she was keeping it a secret." Brady paused the conversation, moving aside to let a customer through. Zo rang up her purchase.

"Love your costume," the customer said as Zo handed her the bag. Then she gave Brady a smile. "Yours, too."

Zo noticed Brady's face flush as the woman walked out the door. "That lady was hitting on you."

He made a noise like a cough. "She was joking."

Zo didn't think so. Brady was a nice-looking man, with dark hair, intelligent eyes, and a broad smile. If he didn't have an oversized attitude to match, he would be Spirit Canyon's most eligible middle-aged bachelor. Then again, some women liked attitude—and uniforms.

"Anyway, a woman like Julia Parker wouldn't take well to another woman stealing her boyfriend," argued Brady. "She's been tough since she was knee-high to a grasshopper."

Zo tilted her head to one side. "I don't know why people say that. I don't think grasshoppers have knees."

"It's an idiom," said Brady. "The point is, Julia might have argued with Marianne about Roberto. Maybe that's how Marianne landed on the street with a knot on her forehead. Julia is strong enough to put it there."

"Impossible," Zo insisted. "First, Roberto wasn't her boyfriend anymore, and second, I was with her the night of the murder. I can vouch for her whereabouts. Spirits & Spirits was the last stop on the Wine and Waterfalls tour. She was there until close."

"Tiffany Snow said she wasn't at the store when she came in," Brady refuted.

"That's a lie." A few customers glanced in her direction, and she lowered her voice. "She was there all night."

He raised an eyebrow. "All night?"

"Yes, she—wait." Zo recalled the evening. "She left for a few minutes to get more wine glasses. A customer was interested in purchasing them for Christmas presents."

Brady crossed his arms.

"Come on," said Zo. "There's no way she could have retrieved the boxes and killed Marianne in the ten minutes she was gone. That's ridiculous."

"Ridiculous, maybe." Brady's eyes narrowed. "Impossible, no."

"Is this a new thing you do?" asked Zo. "Accuse my friends of killing people?"

"It's called an investigation," Brady said. "I'm sure you're familiar with the concept, being a former journalist."

"Then ask yourself why Tiffany is pointing the finger at Jules," said Zo. "Maybe she's the one with something to hide."

A woman touched Zo's arm. "I'm voting for your pumpkin, sweetie. I know it's going to be the best."

"Thank you." Zo smiled. "I appreciate it."

"Plus Marianne and Jules are both witches," continued Brady after the customer left. "It might have been a turf thing."

Brady had no idea what he was talking about. He was thinking about witches that cast spells and flew on brooms. The witches in *The Wizard of Oz* had turf wars; Marianne and Jules did not.

"Before you pigeonhole Jules, I think you should talk to Marianne's daughter," said Zo. "She said Marianne had an appointment to change her will. Her ex-husband stands to inherit a lot of money."

He bristled at the information. "When did you talk to Emily Morgan?"

"Yesterday," Zo informed him. "Marianne left her planner at the store, and Emily stopped by to pick it up."

"Anything else you'd like to tell me?"

So many things, she thought, but none she could say out loud.

"I know you've lived here a long time, Zo, and I know you care about the town." He adjusted his hat. "But you're not a teenager anymore, making your own rules."

What next? Was he going to bring up her old curfew violations?

"There are proper channels to follow," said Brady. "Next time you have information on a crime, call me. Can you do that? All evidence regarding a death investigation belongs at the police station."

She really hoped there wouldn't be a next time.

Chapter Nine

On her lunch break, Zo scooted down the street to the opera house. It was after two o'clock, and traffic in the store had finally slowed. The pumpkin was nearing completion and looked better than she imagined. Different sized and shaped leaves covered the surface, and the inspirational message was beautifully scripted. She didn't see how another store could have a pumpkin as festive as Happy Camper's. The jack-o-lantern at the opera house was neat, with two theater masks on it. But the carving wasn't as intricate as Harley's. Zo was hopeful Happy Camper might win.

The theater lobby was empty, except for the will-call booth, where an employee was selling tickets for tonight's show. Zo asked about the construction crew as a noise came from the auditorium.

The employee, a young man with a pockmarked face, pointed in the same direction. "In there."

Entering the auditorium, she saw where the noise was coming from. One of the workers on the main floor was attaching a light switch cover. The others were on the balcony, touching up. She went upstairs, figuring the more people she could talk to, the better. One of them might remember her necklace and where they found it.

"I'm sorry to bother you," said Zo, when she reached the balcony. "Nikki said I could stop by and ask you a couple questions?"

"Sure. How can we help?" The young woman wore overalls and a backward hat. Two red pigtails peeked out underneath the cap.

Zo reached for the necklaces, tucked under the neckline of her cat costume. "I was at the theater last night when I saw the match to my necklace. Nikki said it was found during the renovation. I'm wondering if anyone remembers where. It might tell me something about my birth parents. They gave me the other half when I was born."

The woman's hands were streaked with ivory paint, so she leaned close to the necklace but didn't touch it. "That's cool. I don't recognize it though." She hollered over her shoulder. "Chaska, Sean—have you seen this necklace before?"

One of the men walked over, shoving a tool in his tool belt. He squinted at the piece of jewelry and shook his head. "Never. Chaska, come look at this."

When Chaska didn't respond, Sean walked over to him and gave him a nudge. Chaska had headphones on and took them off. Zo could hear the music blaring from the earbuds as they dangled around his neck.

"Sorry, what was that?" asked Chaska.

"This lady wants to know if you've seen a necklace," said Sean.

"If I find anything, I bring it to Nikki." Chaska stood. A long black braid hung down his back. "Where did you lose it?"

"I didn't lose anything," Zo clarified. "I want to know where the match to my necklace was found." She extended the chains so that he could see both necklaces.

"Look at that." He admired the sun and moon combination. "It's a match. I found it in the dressing room about a month ago."

Zo's breath caught in her throat. "Men's or women's?"

"Women's," answered Chaska. His eyes were still on the pendant. "It's yours?"

"I think it's my mother's," said Zo. "I never met her. I can only guess she lost it while working here. You didn't find anything else, did you?"

Chaska shook his head. "Nothing memorable."

"Your mom must have been an actress," said Sean. "Right, Carrie?" He turned to Zo. "Carrie's our theater expert."

"I'm not an *expert*," Carrie clarified. "I majored in it in college, a thousand years ago."

Zo had the feeling it was five at most.

"But if I had to guess, I'd say it belonged to an actress," said Carrie. "Theater personnel might go into the dressing rooms, but they don't take things off, like jewelry. Only an actress would do that."

The notion made sense to Zo. If her mom had to change for a part, she couldn't keep the necklace on. It was large enough to attract notice. But Zo was thirty-three, so the necklace had to be at least as old. *What was my mom doing in the theater thirty-three years ago?*

My mom. For the first time the words didn't sound foreign. They were attached to a necklace and place. Her mom seemed like a real person now; she even had a job, actress. A flutter of excitement washed over her. *My mom was an actress.* That was a cool occupation. Plus, Zo loved the arts, and her mom must have, too.

She noticed the crew members staring at her and stopped her imagination mid-flight. "You all have been so helpful. I'm on my way to lunch. What can I bring you?"

"Thanks," said Chaska. "But we've already eaten."

"How about dessert?" Zo asked.

"That's so nice of you," said Carrie. "But we're almost finished. We have one more job site to visit before we're done for the day."

After thanking them again, Zo decided to drop off Happy Camper gift cards on Monday. They'd done something kind for her, and they were restoring the theater back to its original splendor. It was the least she could do as a token of appreciation.

Pumpkins graced all the downtown storefronts now, and some business owners were passing out ballots and pencils, asking for customers' votes. Honey Buns' pumpkin looked like a large cinnamon roll with a bee in the middle. The Chipped Cup, her favorite tea spot, had a beautiful teacup with a noticeable crack painted on their pumpkin. The swirling brown liquid was too much to resist. Zo had to pop in for a mug.

She ordered black pecan tea, a chicken salad sandwich, and chips. The employee working the counter offered her a ballot, but Zo said she'd already cast her vote. Obviously Happy Camper was getting her support, but if she could vote twice, The Chipped Cup would come in a close second. It was one of Zo's favorite places to grab lunch or a snack because of its wide variety of loose-leaf teas. While they had a few expensive tea sets, most of the mugs and accessories were moderately priced, and the store was inviting and comfortable.

Zo chose a seat close to the window to people-watch. Spirit Spooktacular brought out the crowds, and as she paused to relax and re-energize, she enjoyed surveying the costumes. Everyone wore one, adults and children alike. As the evening drew closer, the kids would become more excited. Not only were there parade floats but downtown stores offered candy bars and prizes. A boy walking past the window in a Batman costume already had a hard time holding his mother's hand. Then again, the mom was carrying several shopping bags.

The scene brought Zo back to her own childhood, which wasn't without its good memories. The Jones family, who adopted her as a baby, tried very hard to make a good life for their children. But ten kids proved too many, and she was put into foster care. Many of the homes had been decent. She would have stayed at any of them. It was the moving she hated. She'd think a home was *the one* only to find out it wasn't. Maybe that's why she was so mad when Patrick Merrigan forced her to move out of her first store. It brought up all those old feelings of here-I-go-again. Finding the necklace was the first time in a long time that she had looked back. But this time, it wasn't painful. It was even kind of nice.

Her order was called, and she picked up her food and brought it back to the table. The warm smell of pecan tea filled her senses, and she cupped the mug to warm her hands and enjoy the scent. Zo wondered if the theater brought her mother to Spirit Canyon, or if she had been here all along? If she had the other half of the necklace, it meant Zo had been born at the time her mother was an actress at the playhouse. Zo was good at research, but Hattie was better. She'd know where to begin.

But first Zo needed to see Jules. She wanted to tell her about Brady and his witch hunt. *Literal witch hunt.* What was it about Spirit Canyon that brought out superstition in people this time of year? *The ghosts dangling from the lampposts?* She finished the last bite of her sandwich and placed the empty tray near the garbage.

Ten minutes later, Zo arrived at Spirits & Spirits, where she found Jules and Duncan arguing. Duncan must have won their earlier contest because they were dressed like Bonnie and Clyde, at least that was Zo's guess. Jules had her long blond hair pinned under, the pink layer invisible, and wore a close-fitting cap. Duncan wore a pinstriped suit and gray fedora. Thankfully, the guns were fake. From the looks of the argument, Jules might have been tempted to use hers. She was just the gal to do it, too. Now that Zo thought about it, Jules would have made an excellent Calamity Jane.

"A tasting is a taste, not half a glass," fumed Jules.

Duncan gave Jules a wicked smile. It was the smile that made most women tremble. "They bought a bottle, didn't they?"

Jules was steadfast. Obviously, the look didn't affect her. "They were going to buy it anyway. Don't do it again."

Duncan turned to Zo. "I think we need couple's therapy. What do you think?"

"I think you'd better zip it before she beats you with her rubber gun."

Duncan lowered his felt hat over one eyebrow. "She wouldn't do that. She adores me."

"I think he would make a better Casanova," Zo said to Jules.

"He would make a better *anything* than employee." Jules walked over to Zo and gave her a spontaneous hug. "I'm sorry about Marianne."

"Thanks," said Zo, her voiced muffled. "I've been meaning to stop by, but you know what this weekend is like."

"Same."

Zo stepped back and readjusted her cat ears, which were crooked after the embrace. "Brady Merrigan came by Happy Camper today. I wanted to warn you before he comes here."

"Too late," said Jules. "He dropped in about an hour ago."

"You're kidding." Zo guessed he didn't break for lunch.

"Afraid not," Jules answered. "I was right in the middle of the lunch rush." She nodded toward Duncan. "Clyde here offered him a glass of wine."

"What?" Duncan shrugged. "I thought he was in costume."

"Anyway," continued Jules, "he asked me about my relationship with Roberto. I said what relationship? The guy and I exchanged a dozen words. Did you tell him Roberto and I dated?"

"No," said Zo. "I just found out myself, if you recall."

Jules didn't like being reminded of the omission. She flicked her brown eyes in another direction. "Then who did?" she asked.

"Tiffany Snow."

"The lady with the wreaths again?" said Duncan. He was trying unsuccessfully to remove packaging tape from a box. "The woman is everywhere you *don't* want to be."

Zo laughed. That pretty much described it.

"It doesn't surprise me," Jules mused. "Tiffany hates everything about me, including my store."

"She called it the 'devil's workshop,'" added Duncan.

Jules rolled her eyes.

"Brady asked about your whereabouts the night of the murder," Zo informed her.

"I hope you told him we were here," said Duncan.

"I did, but Tiffany told him Jules was gone when she arrived," explained Zo. "You'd left to get more glasses. Remember?"

"Give me a break." Jules grabbed a box cutter from her back pocket. She opened the box Duncan was struggling with. "I was gone fifteen minutes. Who commits murder in fifteen minutes?"

"Do you want me to have Max talk to him?" Duncan asked Jules. "Max can fix anything."

Zo agreed. Max was pretty good at fixing problems—*although Duncan was one problem that had gotten worse, not better.* "I don't know if that would help. Brady and Max aren't exactly simpatico when it comes to official police business."

"Why is that, anyway?" asked Duncan.

"Brady thinks Max's work is in the forest," Zo explained. "He doesn't like him encroaching on his turf." She groaned. "Which reminds me. That's the other reason he suspects you, Jules. You and Marianne both practice witchcraft."

Jules put her hands on her wide hips. "It's a really bad time to be a witch, you know that?"

"Or a guitar instructor," Duncan added.

Zo chuckled. For once, they were both right.

Chapter Ten

After he finished unboxing wine bottles, Duncan left. His shift was done, and Zo was relieved. She needed to tell Jules about the necklace, but Jules was cleaning beer taps. Zo didn't know if it was the right time. Although it might be the only chance she had before the after-work crowd bombarded the store for Halloween spirts. Time was in short supply from now until the first of the year.

In her tan suit, Jules swiftly turned around, pink hairs coming loose from her makeshift bob. Maybe she *was* psychic. She seemed to sense the predicament. "Spit it out, Zo. We both have stores to run. Is it about Duncan?"

Zo frowned. "Duncan? No, why?"

"Max?"

"No…it's not about a guy. It's about my mom." She uncovered the necklaces, hidden beneath her cat costume. "Max and I went to *Phantom of the Opera* last night and found the match to my necklace."

Jules released the tap and rushed over to where she was standing. Grabbing the charms, Jules closed her eyes and rubbed them. "She was an actress. Nice cheekbones, light hair. A bit of a hippie."

Zo rolled her eyes. Except for the actress part, that could describe her. "Read the inscription."

Jules opened her eyes and flipped over the sun and moon. "*Zoelle.*" Her brown eyes shimmered with tears.

"Oh no," Zo warned. "Don't start that. Like you said, we don't have time to go there. I need to get back to the store, preferably with an unblotchy face."

Jules hugged her tightly. "It's perfect. It's you."

"Thanks," said Zo. "I like it, too."

Jules stepped back. "What are you going to do?"

"See what I can dig up, I guess. I know a few people who can help me."

"Hattie?" Jules asked.

Zo nodded.

"Be careful." Jules clasped Zo's hands. "I don't want you getting hurt."

Zo knew she meant emotionally hurt and wanted to save that discussion for another day. It was a conversation they'd had many times before, but it'd been a while. She was older and more mature. That didn't make it less difficult, however. She buttoned her coat and slipped on her black Ray-Ban sunglasses. "I will."

"Before you go, I have the posters for the Zodiac Club." Jules retrieved a stack of printouts from beneath the counter. "Give them to Hattie, and hang one at the store, will you?"

"Will do." The Zodiac Club met once a month. In the summer, they met at the observatory at Black Mountain College. When it grew colder, they met in the library or at a member's house and had guest speakers and discussed books. Next week, they were meeting at Zo's house. "Don't forget," added Zo. "Tonight's party starts at eight. You're signed up for drinks."

"I'll be there," Jules promised.

Zo started for Happy Camper, checking the ballot box on the corner. If the overstuffed container was any indication, many people had already cast their votes. The rest would vote before the Halloween parade, which started in two hours. She needed to get her candy ready. Hundreds of children would trick-or-treat before the parade. Seeing little ghosts and goblins visit the store was her favorite part of the night. The older ghouls she could do without. A year didn't go by without a few teens racing by, grabbing candy or smashing pumpkins. Which reminded her: she needed to get George inside for the night. She didn't want anyone playing tricks on her cat.

A block away, she spotted Happy Camper's pumpkin lighting up the store window. It was that big. Zo was amazed by the final product. She didn't know a pumpkin could be a work of art. But with the intricate leaves and scrolled letters, now glowing with candlelight, it was nothing short of beautiful. She poked her head inside to thank Harley. Because of her, they had a real shot at winning the contest.

"It's perfect," Zo gushed. "I don't know how you did it."

"Mathematical preciseness," proclaimed Harley. "I mapped the leaves by grid numbers."

"Don't even try to explain. I'm not a numbers person." Zo scanned the store. "I need to find George. Have you seen him?"

"Not since this morning."

"I'm going to check my yard," said Zo. "I'll be back. Get the candy dishes out of the storage room, will you?"

Harley nodded, and Zo started for the gate. She found George in Cunningham's garden, which was a tangle of dead vines and crunchy leaves. When George saw her, he rolled onto his back, stretching in the dirt. His white stripes of fur turned light brown.

"You know you're not supposed to be in Cunningham's garden," she whispered as she came closer.

George turned on his side and lifted a paw, pausing before giving it a lick. He squinted at her. Maybe he noticed her costume.

"Like my outfit?" She switched the black fabric tail back and forth.

George began his bath. He wasn't impressed.

"I told you that cat gets into my garden," hollered Cunningham from his deck. "I see him there, like a mountain lion."

Mountain lions were a real problem in the area, but Cunningham was exaggerating. George was only as big as a baby mountain lion.

"Sorry, Cunningham," Zo apologized. "No harm done. The garden's long dead."

"That's not the point," said Cunningham. "George needs boundaries. If he thinks he can get away with it in the fall, he'll do the same in the summer."

"Don't worry," said Zo. "He won't do it again. He understands he's in trouble."

"It looks like it."

Enjoying the last drops of sunshine, George was nibbling on a stray weed. Zo picked him up, knowing full well the dust would transfer to her black costume. She'd have to fix it before the parade.

George flopped in her arms, trying to free himself from her grasp.

"Do you need some help?" asked Cunningham.

"No, I got him." But she could have used the help. George was not only heavy but strong. When he didn't want to do something, he made it known. Getting him up the deck steps was a challenge, and she was relieved once they were inside. He leaped out of her arms and onto the kitchen table, shaking the antique piece of furniture with his girth.

"George!" she cried. "Not the table."

He crouched into a ball, then darted off when she reached for him, leaving behind a fluff of fur. She picked up the hair and tossed it in the trash, silently cursing the fall shedding season. It was more of a year-round thing with George. She had to sweep her hardwood floors every other day

to keep up, but he was worth it. He had personality, and she admired his
independence, even when it was a pain in the neck.

Now to find the lint roller and deal with the fur and dust on her costume.
After giving her outfit a quick roll and washing her hands, she finished
the appetizers for tonight's party. She'd already cut the veggies and made
the monster munch snack mix, but she still needed to heat the dip and
assemble the pinwheels. Beth was bringing the desserts, Jules was bringing
the drinks, and Max was bringing chips, a bachelor staple. Hattie agreed to
make her famous apple pumpkin. It was loaded with spiced apples warm
from the oven. They were delicious with ice cream.

Since this was her friend Beth's first Spirit Spooktacular, Zo gave her
a quick call to make sure she knew the schedule of events. She'd moved
to the area this spring and spent most of her time in the canyon, where
her lodge was located.

"Yes, I know the schedule," said Beth. "I'm coming early, before the
parade. What else can I bring?"

"Just your lovely family." Beth was married and had two girls, Meg and
Molly. Her mom, Violet, or Vi for short, also lived with them. She helped
manage the resort. "I can't wait to see the girls."

"I'll warn you that Meg is *under* dressed for the occasion," said Beth.
"I guess rock stars wear very short skirts."

Zo chuckled. "I'm sure she's just trying to be...authentic."

"*Right*," said Beth. "I'm sure it's about authenticity. More likely it's her
new group of friends. They're going as an all-female rock band."

"That's cool," Zo exclaimed. "What's wrong with that?"

"One word: eyeliner. You'll see when I get there."

They said goodbye, Zo still chuckling as she ended the call. Meg was
a levelheaded kid—at least she was this summer. Maybe the new school
had changed her, or her new friends. Zo hoped Beth was overreacting.
She didn't want to see Meg in trouble.

After giving the house a once-over, making sure it was party-ready, Zo
returned to the store. Harley was pouring candy into an oversized orange
bowl. Zo grabbed the other giant-sized sack of candy and poured it into
the Frankenstein stand by the door. Then she turned on the twinkle lights
in the front window. The police were marking off the street, which meant
treat-or-treaters would be there soon. The youngest children would be the
first to arrive.

At least she assumed they would be first to arrive—before Justin Castle
barged through her door. He had a cameraman with him, so she figured
he was on assignment for the local television station. His was the most

recognizable face in Spirit Canyon: tan, young, and haughty. He believed the sun rose and fell on his "special" reports, and Zo knew he had a lot of young followers—mostly of the female variety—but didn't understand why. Sure, he was handsome. With his stylish hair and trendy clothes, he defied the image of the Old West. Still, Spirit Canyon was full of adventurers, hippies, and nature-lovers who'd traded bigger cities for the haven of Spirit Canyon. He wasn't the only young guy who sported J. Crew. But maybe he was the most visible.

"Happy Halloween, Zo," greeted Justin. "Think you have a shot at the pumpkin contest?"

"I think we have a good shot. Look for yourself." She motioned toward the front window.

"I saw it on the way in," Justin dismissed. "Mark, get that for the video."

The cameraman uncapped his camera and zoomed in on the pumpkin.

"We're covering the winners and the parade on the ten o'clock news."." Justin perused one corner of the store, then the other.

Zo wondered what he was looking for. It couldn't possibly be a gift.

"Isn't this where Marianne Morgan died?"

Ah. That was it. The more encounters they had, the less she liked him.

Harley dropped a piece of candy. She wasn't as good with people as she was numbers and hated conflict. When someone argued about a price or return, she became as quiet as a calculator. But Zo wasn't afraid to talk to guys like Justin. She met a lot of them working at the *Black Hills Star.* The only way to deal with them was head on.

"She had her book signing here," Zo corrected.

"But you found her," pressed Justin. "At your store."

He circled the merchandise. Zo knew he was taking mental notes. He had no interest in her or her shop. He only wanted what was useful to him, and that was making a name for himself. The murder of a famous author would help him achieve that—if he covered the story right. And obviously, he'd already done some digging. Someone had told him about her discovery but whom? Brady Merrigan wouldn't have shared the detail.

"I was walking home from Spirits & Spirits," Zo corrected. "Anyone might have found her."

"At *your* store?" questioned Justin. "I don't think so." He picked up a candle, pretending to check the price. "Didn't you say she was dressed like a witch? Hat and all?"

"I didn't say anything," said Zo.

"Hmm. Must have been someone else. But you *did* see her. You found her. What did she look like?"

The ghouls are out early this year. "Marianne was my guest and a good writer. If you think I'm going to describe her death to you, you're wrong." "Just her injury," Justin clarified. "I heard she had a gash on her head." Zo pointed to the door. "Get out."

He took a step toward the door and tripped on a black cat statue. She and Harley shared a puzzled look. What was it doing in the middle of the floor? The thought no more than entered her mind than she thought of Marianne. Zo chuckled. Was she cursing Justin with bad luck?

He yanked his camel hair jacket. "Fine, but your pumpkin is going to be a footnote in my broadcast. The tiniest blurb."

"Not if it wins," Harley piped up. "Then we'll be the top story."

Zo bemoaned the thought. Though she wanted to win the contest, being interviewed by Justin would be like having surgery on live television. She wouldn't put it past him to bring up Marianne's murder again.

"Come on, Mark. Pack up."

Mark was standing next to the door and opened it. Justin breezed through, not bothering to hold it for his cameraman.

Harley put her hands on her hips. "I hate that guy."

"Hate's a four-letter word at Happy Camper," said Zo.

"Fine," Harley said. "I dislike that guy a lot. I dislike him more than any man on the planet."

"Much better," laughed Zo.

Chapter Eleven

Their first trick-or-treater was a toddler dressed like Cinderella. Her blue gown was almost as long as her sullen face. Zo detected a problem in the kingdom, and she needed to fix it. Maybe a couple candy bars would help. "I love your dress." Zo held out a pail of candy. She hoped giving the toddler her choice of chocolate would improve her mood. "Is it new?"

"Yes," she said with a small sigh, sifting through the bowl with a dimpled hand. "But my glass slippers broke."

"Cheap junk," the toddler's mom mumbled.

The girl plopped a Snickers in her pumpkin pail.

"Oh dear," Zo empathized. "If only your fairy godmother were here." She considered the problem for a moment. "You know, I don't have glass slippers but I do have a pretty sweet pair of cowboy boots." She walked over to her kids' corner, where she had several play items, including costume boots.

The girl's face brightened. "Mommy, can I have them?"

"How much?" asked the mom.

Zo waved away the question. "On the house. Consider it my Halloween treat." She winked at the girl. "The next person might get a trick."

Relieved, the mom thanked Zo and switched out the shoes for the boots. The mom and daughter both left with smiles on their faces.

"Another satisfied customer," proclaimed Zo.

"When they don't pay, they're not customers," said Harley, who was a stickler for profits.

"You're starting to sound like Jules." The ten-dollar boots were worth making a genuine connection. There were too few of those these days, in her opinion. She wanted her customers to know she cared, and not just about their purchases. She hoped each and every one of them could find something in the store that spoke to their experiences.

She and Harley took the candy outside, where they would greet the rest of the trick-or-treaters. Some people stopped and asked about her pumpkin. Wherever did she find a pumpkin so large? Others ran by, collecting candy as fast as they could before the parade began. They needed to hurry if they wanted a prime seat.

Zo spotted Jack before she saw Beth. He was carrying a cooler, presumably filled with desserts. His wife had a tendency to overdo. Though Zo had said bring one dessert, Beth probably brought a dozen. She used to be a party planner for the Waldorf Astoria in Chicago. She believed more was always better.

"Hey, Jack." Zo handed Harley her candy bowl so she could show Jack where to put the desserts upstairs.

"They're coming," whispered Jack. "Beware."

"That doesn't sound good," Zo whispered back.

"It's not," agreed Jack. "Beth's still peeved about Meg's skirt."

"It's Halloween," said Zo. "What's the big deal?" Meg came into view, and Zo understood the big deal—or small, as it were. The skirt was a tiny square that barely covered Meg's bum, let alone her midriff, which had a bellybutton piercing.

"It's fake," explained Jack as they approached. "The piercing, I mean."

"What the heck happened?" Zo whispered.

"Puberty," he said out of the corner of his mouth.

"Hi Meg," greeted Zo. "Hey Molly. Beth, it's good to see you. Where's Vi?" Vi was Beth's mom, who lived with them at Spirit Canyon Resort.

"She's watching the lodge. We have a full house." Beth nodded toward the cooler. "I brought apple, pumpkin, and French silk."

Zo took in Beth's beautiful costume, a green-and-white flowered gown and an enormous straw hat with ribbon. Beth was dressed as Scarlett O'Hara. With his slicked hair and fake mustache, Jack had to be Rhett Butler. "I said *one* dessert," joked Zo, showing them upstairs. Her deck was strung with pumpkin party lights for the occasion.

"Spirit Canyon Lodge isn't a downtown business, so I thought I should bake extras." Beth indicated the lights. "How fun are these decorations? It's going to be a great party."

"*Real great,*" Meg muttered.

"I'll take that." Beth grabbed the wine from Meg's armpit and gave it to Zo. "A hostess gift."

Adorable, and so like Beth. The wine was dressed like a scarecrow. As the owner of the premiere resort in Spirit Canyon, Beth was good at details. She pampered guests with little luxuries that made their stays memorable.

"Thank you," said Zo. "I'll put it inside with the pies."

"Can I help?" asked Molly. Molly was three years younger than Meg. Puberty hadn't hit her yet, thank goodness. She wore a Velma costume from the Scooby Doo gang.

"I'd love some help," said Zo. "Could you grab the door?"

Molly held it open as they brought the cooler and wine inside. "Aww," Molly cooed. "Is that your cat? Can I pet him?"

"Go ahead." Zo put the French silk pie in the fridge. "Just don't pick him up. He can be grouchy."

"I don't know if she could pick him up," said Jack. He stashed the cooler around the corner. "He's huge."

"Can I go now?" pleaded Meg. "I'm meeting friends at the parade."

"We're all leaving in a minute," Beth answered, her voice not giving an inch. "Be patient."

Meg let out an audible groan.

"I need to get back to the trick-or-treaters anyway," said Zo. "We can go."

"What's your cat's name?" asked Molly.

"George," answered Zo.

"*Mom*," Meg whined.

Beth's only answer was a stern look.

"George. That's a good strong name," said Molly. "That's what my grandma would say."

"Yes, she would." Zo prodded Molly toward the door. In high-heeled boots, Meg led the way down the stairs. She was anxious to get to her friends and took two at a time. "Honey Buns is giving out chocolate muffins, by the way," added Zo. "They're not to miss."

"Ooh, chocolate." A curl popped out from under Molly's Velma wig as she bounced down the steps. "I'm hitting all the stores."

Harley returned Zo's candy bowl, and Molly selected several treats. Zo offered it to Meg, and Meg snatched up a candy bar, giving Zo a little smile of thanks. Zo remembered what it was like to be a teenager. Any kindness was appreciated at that age.

The street was now full of kids running helter-skelter with candy pails. Some families saved seats on the curb with blankets; others had folding chairs. Walking toward Happy Camper, Tiffany Snow had a chair under each arm and two kids in tow. As they approached, Zo noticed the children weren't wearing costumes, which was strange. The boy and girl looked the same age as Beth's kids, if not a bit younger. Why weren't they dressed up? Tiffany stopped in front of the store. "Beth! I hardly recognized you in that dress. Who are you supposed to be?"

Zo guessed she didn't watch classic movies. Anyone would recognize the iconic flowered dress and straw bonnet as Scarlett O'Hara's.

"Hi Tiffany," said Beth. "Scarlett O'Hara. My husband is Rhett."

"I can never get my husband to come to these things," Tiffany explained. "Too crowded. It's hard to get in and out of them." She gave Zo a once-over. "A black cat. How appropriate."

Zo wasn't sure how to take the comment, so she smiled. "Don't let me step across your path tonight."

"The kids didn't dress up?" Beth glanced at Tiffany's children.

"No," said Tiffany. "I forbade it." The boy and girl, who were talking to Molly, stopped and glanced at her. They looked miserable. "You can't blame me. The day brings out the worst in children. Regular kids dressed like…" She looked at Meg. "Well, you know."

Zo was dying for Beth, who was uncomfortable enough with Meg's attire without this do-gooder pointing out its flaws. And who did Tiffany think she was anyway? The Halloween police? This was Spirit Canyon. People went all out for the parade. Even old men and women dressed as train robbers and saloon girls. If she didn't want to participate, she should've stayed home.

"I don't think there's any harm in dressing up." Beth's cheeks were pink with embarrassment. "It's just for fun."

"Exactly," Zo agreed. "In Spirit Canyon, it's wrong *not* to partake in the festivities."

Tiffany's puffer vest swelled with indignation. "I'm partaking by being here. Come on, kids. I see an open spot by Roberto."

She rolled the *R* in his name as if she were fluent in Spanish. Zo highly doubted it.

Roberto and his son's attendance was interesting. Zo supposed they'd be home, mourning Marianne's death. Or at least Roberto would be. Everyone grieved differently, though, and maybe getting out among friends helped. Tiffany acted *friendly* as she put her arm around him, consoling him on his loss. Too friendly? Zo decided to reserve a spot next to them. She wanted to know just how close they were.

"Help me with these chairs before you go," Zo said to Beth. She handed Jack her goody bowl. Temporarily, he and Molly took over candy duty.

"I want to make sure we have our seats saved before the parade starts. Follow Tiffany."

Beth grabbed a chair and forced another on Meg. "I think I've had enough Tiffany for one day."

"Same, but Marianne wouldn't like Roberto getting chummy with her so soon after her death." Zo tucked the chair under her arm.

"How do you know?" asked Beth. "Are you communicating with the dead now?"

"Maybe," said Zo.

Beth shot her a curious look.

Zo explained. "Some strange things have happened since Marianne's death. I get the feeling that she wants me to solve her murder."

"If that's true, she's haunting the right person. I know that firsthand. If anyone can catch a killer, it's you." Beth set down a chair near the curb. "Does here work?"

They were three seats away from Tiffany and Roberto. "Perfect," said Zo.

"Can I go now?" Meg plopped her chair down with a clang.

"Yes," said Beth. "But keep your phone on. I'll be checking on you."

Meg was gone with a roll of her eyes.

Beth shook her head. "See what I have to put up with?"

Zo unfolded another chair. "Jack said Meg was going through some… changes."

"That's putting it mildly," said Beth. "One minute she's laughing, the next she's crying. I'd need a crystal ball to figure her out her moods these days."

"Jules might have one on sale," joked Zo. "I can check."

Beth laughed. "I'm willing to try anything." She set up the last chair. "So how are you? Tell me about something that doesn't involve teenage hormones."

Zo showed her the necklaces. "A match was found in the theater during the renovation. My full name is Zoelle." It was the first time she'd said it aloud. A little foreign, a little fun, the name was hers alone. She liked saying it, though it would take some time getting used to it.

Beth's gray eyes grew wide as she examined the jewelry. "It's your birth mom's?"

"I think so," said Zo.

"It has to be. It's obviously a woman's necklace, and who else but a mom would wear her daughter's name around her neck?" Beth grasped her own necklace. It had two tiny shoes with Meg's and Molly's birthstones. "It's a mom thing. Trust me."

"You might be right," agreed Zo, starting back for Happy Camper. "It was found in the women's dressing room."

"I can't wait for you to find her." Beth linked her arm with Zo's.

"You're not going to tell me to use caution or be careful or hold back?"

Beth's hoop skirt swung back and forth as they walked. "Absolutely not. First, it wouldn't do any good, and second, it's *your* story. You have every right to know its beginning. I know your mom feels the same way."

Zo mulled over her words. Beth was a mom. If anyone could speak for moms, it was Beth, right? "You don't think she'd be mad?"

"For finding her?" asked Beth. "No, I don't."

Zo wished she were as confident.

Beth tipped her straw hat toward Zo. "Look, I can't speak for the woman, but as a mom, I know she cares about her daughter. It's the reason she left you at the police station—to keep you safe from harm. The necklace was to remember you. Why wouldn't she want to know how you are now?"

The way Beth described it made perfect sense. Zo wanted to believe it. But she knew some stories took unforeseen twists. She just hoped her story wasn't one of them.

Chapter Twelve

Zo returned to her candy post, and Jack and Beth took Meg trick-or-treating. Harley refilled their buckets twice before foot traffic died down and the parade began. The last float would include the mayor, who would announce the winner of the pumpkin-carving contest. She and Harley could hardly wait. Maybe Zo was partial, but she believed they had a real chance at winning. The detail on the leaves was impeccable, and she'd challenge anyone to find a carver as masterful as Harley. Hopefully the townspeople thought so, too.

Leaving the candy buckets on the bench next to the front door, Zo and Harley walked to their saved seats. Glancing back at the lighted pumpkin in the window, Zo decided it didn't matter if they won. The pumpkin was perfect for Happy Camper. No matter the outcome, she'd always remember it as one of her favorites.

Zo took the seat closest to Roberto, and Harley sat next to her. No sense in sticking Beth, who was still trick-or-treating, near Tiffany. Besides, Harley knew Alex. They might be able to talk about college. She glanced between the two. *Or not.* While Harley sported purple hair streaks and a Superwoman cape, Alex wore a football jersey and eye black. They might not have that much in common.

"Hey, Roberto," Zo said. "How are you holding up?"

Tiffany gave Zo a thin smile and turned in the other direction, talking to a mom at her side.

"Hanging in there," said Roberto. "I had to get out of the house for a little while, and Alex wanted to come. It's his last year at home."

"I heard," said Zo. "Harley said he's going to college out East next year. Congratulations."

"Thank you." Roberto's brown eyes brimmed with pride. "But the praise goes to Alex. He did all the work."

Zo nodded. "The studying paid off. Good for him."

Beside her, Harley snorted. Zo remembered her mentioning him not being much of a scholar. She wasn't sure how he planned to get into an Ivy League school in the first place. "Will he be playing football?" The costume was the only guess she had.

"Water polo," Roberto answered.

"*Water polo*?" questioned Harley. "Where'd he learn to play *that*?"

Zo, too, was surprised. They had a lot of activities in the Black Hills, but water polo wasn't one of them. Alex looked athletic; he had a stocky frame and large shoulders. Maybe they were from swimming.

Alex leaned past his father, into the conversation. "You ought to get out more, Harley. There's more to life than working." He stuffed a handful of popcorn from Pop and Shop in his mouth, a smug smile on his face.

"Some of us have to pay our own way," Harley shot back.

It was a sentiment Zo seconded. She understood Roberto's pride; he only wanted the best for his son and could give it to him. But Alex's entitled attitude? She didn't get it at all.

"Oh, I've paid," Roberto explained. "I worked two jobs when he was young for an opportunity like this. Don't think it came easy."

Jules said he was a hard worker, perhaps too hard. He had a sincere face that leaned toward serious. There was a touch of sternness in it. But his brown eyes were warm and kind like the silver streaks that softened his dark hair. Too bad Alex wasn't more like his father.

"Come on, Pop." Alex gave his dad a shove. "Don't get started on *that*."

Like a statue, Roberto didn't budge. His smile was tight-lipped. "You're right. No need to go down memory lane."

"You own Dakota Shipping," asked Zo. "Is that right?"

"That's right," confirmed Roberto. "Built it myself from nothing. It was voted the number one transport company in the area."

Tiffany's friend left, so Tiffany leaned forward to join the conversation. "You're such a good businessman and father."

Alex looked at her as if she were the dumbest person in the world, but Roberto enjoyed the compliment. "Thank you."

Beth, Jack, and Molly were combing for a break in the crowd. Zo waved at them, and Molly choose the easiest route—through the middle of the street. Jack and Beth followed breathlessly behind her.

Molly plopped into the seat next to Harley. "Hi!"

"How was trick-or-treating?" asked Zo.

"A-maz-ing." She pronounced all three syllables, holding up her supersized pumpkin pail. It was full to the brim with candy. "I asked Dad to use his pockets for the last three stores, but he said I had plenty already."

Beth repositioned her dress several times before getting it stuffed into the folding chair. "I'm pretty sure someone's not going to sleep tonight."

Molly took a lick of her giant Ring Pop. "Who?"

Zo and Beth laughed.

"Meg's with her friends?" Zo asked.

"Yep," said Beth. "They're having a sleepover. *Five* girls."

Zo wouldn't want to be that mom. When she and Beth were young, they had lots of sleepovers at Spirit Canyon Lodge that didn't include much sleep. Zo would always cherish those memories as some of her favorites.

"Here comes the parade!" Molly pointed down the street.

The Spirit Spooktacular banner announced the start of the festivities. Behind it, puppeteers flew ghosts high in the air. Each ghost had a different face: happy, sad, angry. They were a nice mix of sweet and scary. The parade had officially begun.

Up first was a Jeep dubbed Hocus Pocus. It was filled with cackling witches surrounding a steaming cauldron. They used dry ice to make a spooky fog. Then "Thriller" music started. Black Mountain College's theater department had collaborated with the music department for a performance. Dancing and playing instruments, students were dressed as ghouls, reenacting the iconic Michael Jackson video. It brought new meaning to the word spectacular, and Zo wasn't sure how the next act would follow it. A huge Monster High float appeared, and she had her answer. Not to be outdone, the high schoolers had created a scene from the popular cartoon.

"You should be up there," Roberto said to Alex.

"Dressed like that?" Alex shook his head. "No way."

A wind came up, sending the leaves scurrying down the street. Zo shivered. When the parade was over, she was going to pour herself a cup of the hot cider she'd been giving out to parents. For now, she enjoyed the preschool's *Wizard of Oz* float, complete with an oversized rainbow and miniature Toto. It received lots of oohs and ahs from the crowd, and for good reason. A preschool-aged Dorothy sang "Somewhere Over the Rainbow," melting Zo's heart—and the rest of the crowd's. Beth clasped her hands and said, "Precious!" Jack added, "She's really good." Molly huffed, "I could do that."

Finally, it was time for the pumpkin float, and Harley gave Zo a nudge. Packed with haystacks and glowing jack-o-lanterns, the float announced the end of the parade. Mayor Murphy, dressed like a scarecrow, would announce the winner of the pumpkin-carving contest. She held a large gold envelope in her hand. The crowd clapped as she approached the microphone.

"Happy Halloween, Spirit Canyon!" The crowd responded with another round of applause. "It's been an amazing evening, hasn't it? What a parade. This is my fourth year as mayor, and it's still my favorite night of the year. But you don't want to hear me talk about the last four years, do you? You want the results of the pumpkin-carving contest."

A cheer went up.

"This is it!" said Harley, grabbing Zo's hand. Zo gave it a squeeze.

"The pumpkins this year were bigger and better than ever," said Mayor Murphy. "Thanks to all of the business owners who participated. I don't know where you get your ideas, but keep them coming. I'm already waiting for next year." The mayor opened the envelope. "And now for the winning pumpkin." She paused for dramatic effect. "This year's winner is…Happy Camper!"

The crowd erupted in cheers, and Zo and Harley hugged. Molly jumped up and down.

"Come up here and receive your prize, five hundred dollars and an ad in *Western Traveler*."

Zo pulled Harley's hand. "You carved the pumpkin. You're coming with me."

"Fine," said Harley, laughing.

When they reached the float and shook hands with the mayor, she asked if Zo would like to say a few words.

Zo took the microphone, overwhelmed with gratitude for her store, small town, and community. "Thank you, Mayor Murphy, and thanks to all of you for voting. What a great night! There were so many terrific pumpkins to choose from, and we're honored you voted for ours." Zo glanced at Harley, who was not just an employee, but a friend. "And finally, thanks to Harley for making this night happen. Without her effort and imagination, it wouldn't have been possible."

Harley accepted the praise with a shy smile, and the crowd gave them one more round of applause as they descended the float. Justin Castle was waiting for them with his microphone, and Harley's smile deflated, like a balloon pricked with a pin. Zo understood her reaction, but she was determined not to let Justin spoil their win. She beamed at the camera, holding up her five-hundred-dollar check.

"Congratulations on your win," said Justin. "What do you plan to do with the money?"

"Thank you." Zo blinked at the bright camera light. "I haven't considered it. I'm sure Harley and I will find a good use for it at the store."

Harley nodded.

"With the recent death of Marianne Morgan, do you think you'll invest in any more book signings?" asked Justin.

Zo was taken aback by the question. She shouldn't have been surprised by the unexpected comment. He'd use any weapon in his arsenal catch someone off guard. "Of course we'll continue to do book signings. Our customers love author talks."

"But this author is dead," said Justin. "Do you think there's any correlation between her talk and unexpected death? They occurred on the same day, at your store."

Zo couldn't believe what she was hearing. Justin was leveling an accusation of murder at her or one of her customers, which was just as bad. She did her best to stay calm in front of the camera, but she was pretty sure she was gritting her teeth. "None whatsoever."

Harley crossed her arms.

With Zo's brief response, Justin had no choice but to close the interview.

Chapter Thirteen

Zo and Harley walked back to Happy Camper, where they were met by a small crowd of friends. A few parade goers were still packing up chairs and blankets, but the street was clearing, and police were removing the barricades. It was time for Zo's Halloween party, and they had something to celebrate: their winning pumpkin. Zo bestowed the blue ribbon on their jack-o-lantern with much fanfare from her friends. Molly said it was the "beautifulest" pumpkin she'd ever seen before leaving with her best friend for a sleepover. Cunningham said it was prize worthy. Duncan said Spirits & Spirits' pumpkin was better.

Jules gave him a jab. "Don't say that…out loud," she added in a whisper.

Zo laughed. "Your pumpkin was great. Where's Max?"

"He's coming," explained Duncan. "He's with the street crew."

"Should I shut off the lights?" Harley asked.

"Yep, let's lock up," said Zo. "I see people outside." Business owners were congregating by the door. They were ready for the Halloween party to begin.

Zo hurried to finish closing, asking Beth and Jules to go ahead and get the food ready. Duncan toted Jules's large cooler up the stairs behind them.

Turning the key, Zo heard a noise. She checked over her shoulder and started when she saw a big bear, Smokey the Bear. Max had taken her suggestion.

"Do you like it?" Max pointed to his costume.

"I love it," said Zo. Max wore Smokey's signature brown floppy hat and jeans. The new whiskers on his jawline added to the handsome look.

"I wanted to bring Smokey's shovel, but I figured it might be a hassle to drag it around all night."

"Good call." Zo smiled. "It would have gotten in the way."

They started up the stairs to her deck, aglow with orange lights. Above, the full moon shone against the night sky. With the ponderosa pines in the distance, it was the perfect backdrop for a Halloween party. So was the "Monster Mash" music, playing from the Bluetooth speaker. Zo had synced it from her phone as they ascended the steps.

"Congrats on your win, by the way," said Max. "I voted for you." He turned around and murmured, "Just don't tell Jules or Duncan."

"Thanks. I won't tell." She made her way over to the outdoor fireplace. The night was growing colder, and its heat would warm the entire deck. "Justin did a short interview afterwards. It was dreadful."

"That bad?"

"He made it sound as if the book signing was connected to Marianne's death." Zo switched on the fireplace. "Like it caused it."

"Forget him," said Max. "There's nothing he won't say for five minutes of fame. I don't know when he'll understand Spirit Canyon isn't the town to make him famous."

"I know," Zo agreed. "But it made me think back to the book signing. During her talk, Marianne said her ex-husband was toxic, and when she left, he was there, waiting in the parking lot for Emily, their daughter."

"You think he did something to her?" asked Max.

She adjusted the flame height. "I don't know. It can't be fun, having the whole world know what a jerk you are. She writes about it in the book."

"And he stands to inherit a lot of money," Max added.

"Which is why I need to talk to him, to figure out just how big a jerk he is."

"This isn't a newspaper article," cautioned Max. "You can't investigate on your own. You need to run your theories through the proper channels."

Max was a good guy. He really was. But he knew one way: the straight and narrow. The problem was the straight and narrow didn't always produce results. Life had obstacles, and Zo knew how to get around them. "I thought you *were* the proper channel."

"You know what I mean," said Max. "If the guy's a murderer, it's dangerous to talk to him alone. Brady would agree."

"I hardly think my safety is Chief Merrigan's ultimate concern."

"Did you just call my brother 'chief?'" said a voice behind her. "No matter how long I live, I'll never get used to him being called that."

Zo spun around. The dark hair, the smiling eyes, the green top hat—it was Patrick Merrigan, dressed as a leprechaun.

"Brady was always the quiet one," continued Patrick. "Being jilted changes a man, I guess." He glanced around the deck. "I like what you've done with this place. Is that gas? You must have had someone wire it."

Zo blinked. It wasn't the night playing tricks on her. The man who'd made her life very difficult last year was there on her deck. Months ago, the mention of his name inspired nefarious revenge plots. With a flower in his buttonhole and green, pointed shoes, revenge seemed a little rash now.

"He means the fireplace," Max said out of the corner of his mouth.

"Yes, it's g-gas," she stuttered.

"I've never seen one like that," said Patrick. "I'd like one at my ranch." He crossed his green shoes. "I hope you don't mind my being here. The invite said all business owners were welcome, and I'd like to make amends."

Life was handing her a choice. She counted to ten before deciding not to mind. She wasn't the type of person to hold a grudge. His past actions stung, but now was as good a time as any to give him another chance. He was a business owner and a legitimate guest. The last thing she was going to do was be rude. "Not at all. Thanks for coming. Can I get you something to drink? We're just setting up."

"A beer would be nice," said Patrick.

"I'll be right back," Zo said. Max followed her into the kitchen, where Duncan was placing the stainless-steel cooler on a rolling stand. Inside were beer, spritzers, and soda. Jules brought the perfect assortment of drinks.

"What are you doing?" questioned Max.

"Getting him a beer," answered Zo.

"Getting who a beer?" asked Jules. She and Beth were putting snacks on trays and in dishes.

"*Patrick Merrigan*," Max said.

Jules put down the monster munch. "Shut the front door."

"He's telling the truth," said Zo. "Patrick's on the deck."

"Your deck?" asked Jules. "The deck right above the store you had to relocate to when he wouldn't renew the lease on the one downtown?"

Zo grabbed a bottle of Spirit Canyon's famous pale ale. "That would be the same guy."

"Why aren't you fuming?" Beth fisted her hands on her hips.

"Happiness is a choice," said Zo. The insulted faces surrounding her weren't convinced. "A really *easy* choice among friends like you. In the wild, it's harder." She popped off the beer top. "It's okay, really. He said he's here to make amends."

"So you're not mad?" Beth asked.

"Of course it bothers me," admitted Zo. "But I love my house, the store's doing well, and I just won the pumpkin contest. When I think about it, what's to be sore about?"

"Months of lost work, the hassle of relocation, moving expenses..." listed Jules. She picked up the snacks. "It's Halloween, and there's a full moon. I say we put a hex on him."

Zo chuckled. "We have enough spooky happenings without adding a hex to the mix."

More business owners and their employees had arrived by the time Zo returned to the deck. The crowd trickled into the backyard, where Max hurried to oversee the firepit. Before he made for the steps, she gave him a tray of campfire cones. Wrapped in aluminum foil and filled with marshmallows, M&Ms, peanuts, and chocolate chips, they were a handy snack for bonfires.

She returned to the task at hand: distributing beverages. Patrick was talking to Cunningham, who was dressed like Sherlock Holmes. It was the perfect costume for someone who loved literature. Two white tufts of hair jutted out from a cap, and an ornate pipe dangled from his lips. As she joined them, she noted his trench coat had a herringbone design. Classic.

"Can I get you anything, Cunningham?" she asked, handing Patrick his beverage.

The professor held up a mug. "I brought hot toddies. The slow cooker's inside."

"I thought I smelled cloves." Zo recognized the recipe: apple, cinnamon, orange peel. Mixed with whiskey, the cocktail was a quintessential fall drink. Its only competition was his hot buttered rum. "Excuse me. I need to help Hattie."

Wearing a blue-and-white dress, Hattie Fines was climbing the stairs with her large pumpkin balanced atop a book. Taking the pumpkin, Zo recognized the costume. She was Belle from *Beauty and the Beast*, identical in every way except her hair, which was short, and her red glasses. They hung on a jeweled chain around her neck.

"The astronomy book you requested came in," said Hattie. "I thought I might as well bring it with me."

"Thank you," said Zo. "Let's put it inside with the food."

Just under five feet tall, Hattie moved fast, like a butterfly weaving through the crowd. Zo followed, which wasn't as easily done carrying a pumpkin. She deposited it on the kitchen table.

Hattie handed her the book. "Be careful. It's brand new."

The pages were stiff and smelled like fresh ink. They were chock-full of colorful images of the planets. "I'll put it in my office. Come with me. I want to ask you something." Tucking the book into her desk, Zo told Hattie about the necklace and her name. Had Hattie ever heard of Zoelle before?

"I don't recognize the name." Hattie studied the necklace. "But it's beautiful. When I go back to work Monday, I'll see what I can find."

Zo tucked the necklaces under her catsuit, and they returned to the deck.

"How old are you?" asked Hattie.

"Thirty-three," answered Zo.

Hattie did the quick math in her head. "Did you ask Nikki Ainsworth? She might know why it was in the theater."

"She's the one who told me to talk to the renovation crew."

"It might be worth delving into the theater's past productions. You might find something in a playbill. Nikki's over there with Beth. Why don't you ask her? I'm going to see what that fool Cunningham is up to."

"Good idea," agreed Zo. Nikki was dressed in a flapper dress and fishnet tights. With a gold wig, she looked like Roxie Hart from the musical *Chicago*. She was telling Beth about a theater camp taking place over the holiday break.

"I'm sure your teen would love it," Nikki said.

"Love is in short order these days." Beth released a disappointed sigh. "But I'll ask. I might go crazy with her at the lodge every day over the holidays."

Zo heard her chance to enter the conversation. "Meg is welcome to work with me at Happy Camper over the break. I'm busiest during the holidays."

"That's brave of you to offer." Beth chuckled.

"It's good for teens to be around people their own age," said Nikki. "Plus, I have an actor from Los Angeles flying in for the week. He's very nice looking, if you catch my drift."

"With any luck, she'll go for it," Beth mused. "She's obsessed with celebrities—of the male species. I'll ask her tomorrow."

They all agreed it was a good idea.

"Hattie and I were talking, and she mentioned going through the old playbills," explained Zo. "To see if I can find any connection to the necklace. Would you mind, Nikki?"

"Not at all," said Nikki. "Everything is a bit of a mess from the renovation, but you're welcome to go through what I have. Most of the records are in the storage room. I'm sorting through them to see what else can be displayed. Drop by next week if you'd like."

"I'll do that. Thank you." Something caught Zo's eye, a shiny object on her deck railing. It looked like a piece of jewelry, an earring or pendant perhaps. One of her guests might have lost it. "Excuse me a second."

Duncan stepped in her path. "Jules is looking for you."

"Tell her I'll be right there," Zo muttered, but she was squinting at the item. The moonlight was reflecting off the surface, like the beam of a flashlight.

"It's about the food," Duncan expanded.

Zo decided to go with Duncan. It must be important. That's when she heard the noise and turned around. The metal object sailed off the railing as if it had wings. She and Duncan shared a look. It was the pendant from George's collar.

"That was weird," said Duncan.

Weird didn't begin to describe the sinking feeling in her stomach.

Chapter Fourteen

George's collar was on the deck, but where was he? Though he didn't like wearing it, Zo worried about him getting lost. After many restless summer nights, she bought the collar and engraved the fish pendant with his name and address. He'd tolerated it well—until now.

As if in a trance, she walked over and picked it up. The sight of his nickname, St. George, brought a lump to her throat. Cunningham christened him with it after George chased away a snake in the yard. The clasp was intact but unfastened. What was the collar doing outside? She'd made sure to put him in for the evening. Had someone let him out?

"What is it?" asked Duncan.

"My cat's collar," said Zo. "Have you seen him?"

"No, I haven't." He shook his head.

They walked back into the house.

"There you are." Jules was rinsing a Tupperware container at the kitchen sink. "We're out of pinwheels. Those little suckers are popular—what's the matter?"

"I found George's collar outside," Zo answered. "I need to find him." Like the deck, her house was decorated for Halloween. Many of the knickknacks she picked up for the store ended up in her house. Witches, ghosts, and jack-o-lanterns gave it a cozy glow, but with George missing, it didn't feel like home at all. "Have you seen him?"

"No," said Jules. "But I'm sure he's here. I'll help you look."

Zo checked his favorite places: the chair in her office, the stack of books in her bedroom, the towels on the top of the dryer. But all were empty. *Stay calm. George is a big boy. He goes outside all the time.* But the thoughts didn't calm her. It was Halloween, and for this reason alone, he should have been in the office or bedroom—with the door shut. How could she have been so irresponsible? She couldn't even take care of a cat.

Groups of happy partygoers munched snacks, drank cocktails, and chatted about the busy weekend, but to Zo, they were obstacles to finding George. She wouldn't be able to enjoy herself until she found him. Trying to appear cheerful, she asked if they'd seen him, but it was always the same answer: no. He must have sneaked outside undetected, which itself was a feat. He had a way of making himself known. On a cool night such as this, he normally would have curled up on the lounger, close to the fireplace. But he wasn't overly fond of people, and the couch was full of guests. It was no wonder he hadn't lingered.

As the minutes wore on, Zo couldn't focus on her guests or the party, and she was glad when the first business owners left. Others followed quickly. Patrick Merrigan gave her a hearty handshake, thanking her for a fun evening. Nikki joined him, saying it was the best adult Halloween party she'd ever been to. Cunningham said they should do it again for Thanksgiving, minus the costumes.

Max was still manning the bonfire, and she hurried down the stairs to help him extinguish the flames. *Not that he needed help*, she smiled to herself. He *was* Smokey the Bear; he knew the perils of forest fires. She brought him a bucket of water.

"The camp cones were a hit." Max doused the fire with water. "I'm going to tell our outreach ranger about them. He's always looking for campfire snacks for kids."

"Yeah…" Zo checked under her pine tree. "I'll get you the recipe."

Max mixed the embers and dirt with a shovel. "Peanuts, M&Ms, and marshmallows. Even I don't need a recipe to remember that. What are you looking for?"

She joined him at the pit. "George."

He poured more water on the fire. "Where has he gone this time?"

"I'm worried, Max. I don't want him outside tonight."

He stopped stirring, and their eyes met. The blue sparkle was like a clear path home, reassuring and bright. "We'll find him. I'll help you."

"It's late," she said. "I know you have to go."

"I'm not Cinderella," said Max. "I'm not going to turn into a pumpkin." He held his hand over the wood.

"What are you doing?"

"You know Smokey's rule: If it's too hot to touch, it's too soon to leave." He stood. "This is okay. Let's find that tomcat."

His confidence brought her a breath of relief. Never had it felt so good to have help. He was an expert when it came to animals and had their best interests at heart. He didn't shrug her off or utter some platitude, like, *he'll be back.* She was grateful he was taking George's disappearance as seriously as she was.

"Where did you find his collar?" asked Max, opening her gate. George wasn't in the backyard. They would need to expand their search.

"On the deck," said Zo. "It was so weird. Like it leaped off the ledge to get my attention."

"Like a wind gust?"

"Like a ghost," Zo answered.

Max stopped. They were in front of Happy Camper, and a grin touched his lips.

"I'm sure you don't believe in ghosts," said Zo. They continued past the store and up the hill. "I'm not sure *I* did until Marianne died. But since then, I've experienced feelings I can't explain. Tonight, I felt as if Marianne—or someone—was warning me of George's absence. Ask Duncan. He saw it."

"I'm not sure he's a reliable witness," said Max with a laugh.

"Laugh all you want, but I trust my intuition."

He stopped chuckling.

"Let me guess. You don't believe in intuition, right?"

They stood at the edge of a row of dark ponderosa pines, and Max squinted into the inky night. "I believe in things I can see and touch. Intuition is a little fuzzy for me. Maybe I just don't have any."

"Intuition *is* fuzzy—it's a feeling. You can't touch it, but it's there, like a song. It leads you in the right direction." A breeze came up at their backs, underscoring her words and pushing them toward the forest. She quirked a brow at him. "See?"

"That's called October," Max explained.

The man didn't have an ounce of intuition in his body. Rules had taken him everywhere. She knew other paths. "What about animals? Animal instinct? You believe in that, don't you?"

"It's not the same thing."

"Why not?" she asked. "It's what keeps animals alive. It's how they mate."

He turned to face her. "You're thinking of pheromones. Those are chemical signals."

"Whatever." Zo had never been as good with science as English.

"Pheromones are so small, like tiny particles. They've evaded scientists for years. But you're right about one thing. They draw the male to the female, by the wind." A fresh breeze stirred her hair, and he brushed it back from her face. Electricity charged the space between them. "But you can't see them, pheromones, I mean. It just happens… I'm not explaining it right."

Zo didn't need an explanation. She knew what she felt and trusted her feelings. "That's what I've been saying. Some things are beyond our explanation." A twig snapped in the distance, and she turned in its direction. "George!"

"Let's go." He took her hand and led her into the forest.

Dry pine needles crunched beneath their feet, and an owl hooted somewhere in the forest. Away from the last drops of streetlight, the night grew darker, murkier. Despite George being an expert on the area, Zo was afraid for him. What if he was lost on a night such as tonight? A night when even nice children played tricks. She couldn't bear to think of it. He'd become family to her—maybe a cantankerous relative—but family all the same. She had to find him. She wouldn't stop until she did.

The moon broke free from a cloud, lighting the footpath, but then succumbed to another cloud moments later. Max turned on his oversized flashlight, checking the trees, while Zo called George's name. A half hour later, there was still no sign of him.

"Maybe he's gone back to your house," said Max.

Zo shook her head. "I told Jules to call me if he showed up."

"You might be out of range."

Zo checked her phone. Not surprisingly, she didn't have service. Even in town, it could be sketchy. In the canyon, it was worse. You could go for hours—or days—without a signal. "You're right. Maybe we should head back."

"Just a sec," said Max, craning his neck. "Do you see that?"

At first, she didn't. But as she took a few steps forward, she noticed a reddish orange glow in the clearing. Flames stretched into the night sky, and the smell was unmistakable. Someone hadn't put out their campfire, or if they had, they hadn't done a good job of it. Max broke into a run, and she followed.

Twigs popped and snapped as Max stomped out the fire. It took a couple minutes for him to bury the flames, the bright red blaze turning dull amber. As flames changed to smoke, Zo noticed something unusual in the ashes. In the pile of wood was the remains of a book, a book whose cover she recognized immediately.

"Wait," Zo said. "I know that book. It's Marianne's."

Max kicked the singed book to the side with his foot, and Zo bent down to examine it. It was one from the signing. It had a Signed by the Author sticker on it.

"Careful," Max warned. "It's still hot."

That much was clear from the smoke plumes. She poked it with a stick, opening to the title page. She and Max exchanged a look. It was signed to Roberto, with love.

Out of all the people at the book signing, Roberto was the last person Zo suspected of throwing Marianne's book in the flames. By all accounts, they were a happy couple. At the store, they shared easy conversation, and Roberto was good to Emily. Plus he owned a successful transport company. He had no need for Marianne's money. Even if he did, he wasn't included in her will. So what was his book doing in the flames? Zo would ask him when she brought it back to him.

"I can't believe Roberto would be so irresponsible," spat Max. "I'm going to have a chat with him about fires and the proper way to extinguish one."

Perfect. Zo could tag along. "I'll come with. I want to ask him why he destroyed his autographed copy of Marianne's book. It had to be one of the last things she gave him. It doesn't make sense."

"Unless he killed her," said Max. "Then it's a reminder of her love for him. He'd want to get rid of it."

She gave him a second glance. She wasn't used to him making unsupported claims. Flushed with passion for the forest, he was mad as heck and his jaw clenched. She decided she liked the side of Max she was seeing tonight. "True. We'll ask him tomorrow."

"I'd ask him tonight if it weren't so late," he ground out, walking toward the tree line. "Plus, we still need to find George."

Zo took the book in her hands. It was warm to the touch but no longer smoking. Out of nowhere, a strange gust of wind flipped the pages to the middle of the book. Page 100, to be exact. She dropped it, and Max spun around, seeing the book at her feet.

"Are you okay? I knew that was still hot."

She wasn't about to tell him what happened. He would explain it away as the wind. But they were still deep in the forest, sheltered by towering trees. The wind rarely came in this far. She picked up the book. "I'm fine. Let's head back. Maybe George's home by now."

When they returned, the only people left were Duncan and Jules. Surprisingly, they were sharing a glass of wine by the fireplace. What was next, a truce? Seeing Duncan with his arm across the back of the couch made it seem possible. Zo cast a backward glance at Max.

"That's a good sign, right?" Max whispered as he followed her up the stairs. "Maybe she won't fire him."

Jules heard their footsteps—or whispering. "There you are. Did you find George?"

Zo shook her head. "I guess this means he hasn't come home. Did Beth and Jack leave?"

"Right after you," said Jules. "There was a problem with one of the guest's plumbing. They had to get back to the lodge."

"She left the pies, though." Duncan held up a plate of pie crumbs.

Zo and Max joined them at the fireplace. Spotting the bottle of wine on the table, Zo went to find two more glasses.

"What's in your hand?" asked Jules. Her brown eyes flickered amber in the firelight, and Zo had no problem envisioning her as a witch, at least on Halloween, with the full moon high in the sky.

"It's Marianne's book." Zo placed it on the table. "We found it in the middle of a campfire. Max will fill you in on the details."

She returned with the glasses and poured the wine. Max was finishing the story.

"Roberto's book." Jules tapped her wine glass with her long black nails. "Makes sense. They say nine times out of ten the boyfriend's the murderer."

"They say that about husbands, not boyfriends," Duncan countered. "Roberto's a nice guy. I gave his son guitar lessons two years ago. The kid was a brat, but Roberto was nice. A really hard worker."

"I know that," said Jules. "I dated him."

"Is there anyone in this town you *haven't* dated?" Duncan feigned puzzlement. "I'm starting to feel left out."

Jules set her wine down with a plunk. "You are skating on *such* thin ice. Paper thin."

Zo covered her mouth to keep from smiling.

"There goes the truce," whispered Max.

Unfazed by Jules's warning, Duncan continued. "Anyway, Roberto bought his son a Fender guitar, and the kid complained because it was used. Like I said, an entitled brat."

"I don't get it." Jules shook her head. "How can a kid with a dad like that grow up to be such a slacker?"

"Roberto's trying to save Alex the trouble he went through," said Max. "The problem with that is it creates more headaches than it solves."

Zo sympathized with Roberto. If she had kids, she'd try to protect them. But maybe he'd sheltered Alex too much. There was something to be said for old-fashioned hard work.

Jules stood. "It's getting late." She gave Zo a small hug. "I hope you find George."

"Thanks," said Zo. "I'm sure he'll show up any minute."

"I'll walk you back," said Duncan.

"Not necessary." Jules patted her false sidearm. "I'm packing iron tonight."

"It kind of is," said Duncan. "I forgot my key at the store."

Jules let out a groan and marched down the stairs, Duncan in tow like a reprimanded child.

Chapter Fifteen

If Zo slept poorly when George was in the bed, it was nothing compared to when he wasn't there. Every hour or so, she imagined she heard him and would jump out of bed to check the deck door. A few times, she even went down the stairs and looked into bushes. When morning finally dawned and he hadn't returned, she was beside herself. She spilled the coffee grounds, and then, when the coffee was brewed, dropped her cup. She told herself she was being silly. George was an outdoor cat. He could be gone for days at a time. But this fall had been different. He stayed closer to home, and they, too, were closer. At least she thought they were, until he took off last night.

After a muddled start to Sunday morning, she enjoyed a full mug of coffee on the deck. The sky was cool pink, a new day and month dawning. The trees in the canyon cut a jagged line across the horizon, sharp and saw-toothed against the smooth sky. November meant snow would top the trees soon, softening the sharp edges with powdered white fluff. Winter was like that, insulating the town of Spirit Canyon like thick wool. Zo could hardly wait for the holidays—and holiday shoppers. She had so much planned for the store.

Which reminded her, today was the Harvest Hike at Happy Camper. She and Max would need to talk to Roberto about the burned book before the hike. The idea of seeing Max again gave her pause. Last night felt different, but she couldn't pinpoint how. If something had changed, she couldn't articulate what.

She finished her coffee and went inside. Probably nothing. The moon, the stars, the forest—it was a peculiar evening. Her eyes fell to Marianne's book on the kitchen table. She thumbed through the charred pages. Ashes crumbled onto the antique wood as she flipped to page 100. It was the chapter on poisonous relationships, like the one Marianne had with her ex-husband, Jake. Had he spotted himself among these pages? Zo didn't know him well, but from what she saw at the book signing, he seemed uninterested in Marianne and the event. She could still picture him, leaning against the car with a cigarette in his mouth. If anyone was angry, it was Roberto. Which gave Zo another reason to seek him out.

After breakfast and a shower—and another look around for George—she rode her motorcycle over to Max's house. She needed wind power to clear her head after the foggy night and took her time cruising the quiet streets. Plus, she might spot George.

When she pulled up to Max's bungalow, Duncan was strumming his six string on the porch. She killed the engine. Max was right: country wasn't his forte. But with jeans and bare feet, who cared? She would have paid for that concert any day. She had a feeling the rest of the women in town would, too.

She took off her helmet. "Hi Duncan. Is Max inside?"

Duncan put down the guitar and came over to the bike. "He's in the shower. I like your bike. How about a ride?"

"Now?"

"I'm sorry," he said. "Do I need to make an appointment?"

Zo laughed. "I guess not, but I do rent it out at Happy Camper, if you're interested."

"I had a Harley Davidson, a Road King Classic." He bent down to check out the equipment. "I had to sell it when money got tight. I miss riding."

Zo understood. The canyon byway was the most beautiful drive in Black Hills Forest. Seeing it by motorcycle was like nothing else. "It's not a Harley, but get your shoes. We'll go for a ride while Max finishes showering."

Duncan rejoined her a few minutes later in black boots and a black helmet. They didn't have time for a ride through the canyon, but she could get to the scenic pass within minutes.

He hopped on, and when he put his hands on her waist, she jumped a little. She heard him chuckle through his helmet. He could laugh all he wanted. She doubted there was a woman in town who wouldn't startle at the notion of Duncan's hands on her hips.

Soon she forgot about his hands and everything else. Racing up one hill and down another was thrilling. Hugging the curves of Black Mountain Pass, she enjoyed the view of the exposed rock, the forest, and the lake down below. It felt good to go fast, to clear her mind of the oppressive worry about George. Nature centered her, and she was relieved to let go of the weight if even for a few minutes.

"You're a good driver, Zo Jones," he hollered. "Scary, but good."

She laughed, taking odd pleasure in the ability to frighten him. He held on tighter as she descended the last hill, cruising into town a tick above the speed limit. She slowed down as she approached the first green stoplight and way down as she approached Max's house. He was standing outside. In his green uniform and shiny boots, he looked very official, too official.

"Uh-oh," said Duncan as they approached the driveway. "It looks like you're getting a ticket."

"Can he do that?"

Duncan didn't have time to answer. Max was walking toward the bike.

"You were speeding," accused Max.

"I wasn't," Zo answered automatically.

"Oh yeah?" Max gestured to Duncan's hands, still wrapped tightly around her waist. "Why the vice grip then?"

Duncan hopped off the bike and removed his helmet, smoothing his black hair. Unlike Max's crew cut, his was long and fell over his brow. "For safety purposes, I assure you." He gave Zo a wink. "That ride made me want to get my bike out of hock. Thank you for the motivation. I'm going to write another song."

"Any time," she said.

Duncan handed the helmet to Max. "You're going to want this."

After Duncan left, Max said, "You texted you were on your way."

"I was. I'm here, aren't I?"

"After a detour with Duncan."

"You were in the shower, and he wanted a ride." She flipped open her visor. "I was five miles over the speed limit, tops."

"It's not that."

"Then what?" He couldn't be jealous, could he? Duncan was a playboy, a good-looking playboy, but a playboy all the same. He might send a thrill down her spine, but Zo would never get involved with him. She took one last look at his backside as he shut the door of the bungalow. At least she didn't think she would.

"Forget it," he said. "Do you have the book?"

She pointed to her bag.

He fastened the helmet and jumped on the bike. Unlike Duncan, he kept his hands on the seat handle. *So much for last night.* She plugged Roberto's address into her phone and placed it on the cellphone mount.

Nothing had changed between them. He was still the man who followed every rule, and she was still the woman who did not.

The directions took her to the posh neighborhood of Seven Acres, though Zo was pretty sure each property had only an acre of land. The large houses were surrounded by lush hills. Roberto's drive was lined with fading yellow, red, and orange rose bushes, which was appropriate considering the name of the street was Rose Lane. Zo parked the bike in front of the fourth stall of the towering two story, shook out her hair, and hung the helmet on the back of the bike.

"I didn't have a chance to ask, did George come home?" Max rang the doorbell.

"No," answered Zo. "I searched again before I left."

"Don't worry." Max gave her a sympathetic look. "He will."

Alex opened the door. He was dressed in lounge pants and no shirt, and his hair hadn't been combed. Zo wondered if it had been a late night. Halloween usually was in Spirit Canyon, especially for young people.

"Hi Alex," Zo greeted. "Is your dad here?"

Alex didn't bother with a response. He hollered from the doorway. "Dad!"

Roberto came to the door a moment later, inviting them inside. "Your phone call sounded important, Max. I hope nothing's wrong."

"It is important," said Max. "Thanks for letting us drop by."

"No problem." Roberto motioned to his left. "Let's sit in the living room."

They followed him into the living room, where everything matched, from the curtains to the furniture to the floor rug. It was collage of grays, giving off an air of clean coolness. Zo bet the look was achieved with the help of an interior decorator. Her eyes fell to a silver picture frame of a young family on the console table behind the couch. It had to be Alex's mother, for they shared the same features, including a high forehead. Next to it was an envelope from a university on top of a small stack of mail. It was only the first of November. Why was he getting mail for next year already?

"Can I get you something to drink?" asked Roberto. He took the chair across from the sofa, where Max and Zo sat. "Coffee?"

"No thanks," said Max.

"Congratulations on your winning pumpkin, by the way." Roberto crossed a soft leather shoe over his knee. Despite that it was Sunday, he wore khakis, a polo, and dress loafers. It appeared he always dressed for work. Zo understood the commitment it took to run a business. She, herself, was rarely away from her small shop.

"Thank you," she said. "It was a nice surprise."

An awkward silence fell over the room, and Roberto turned to Max, whose hair was sticking up more than usual because of the helmet. Combined with his perturbed glare, it gave him a devil-may-care look. Zo had the feeling, however, that Roberto would find out in a moment just how much Max cared about the forest. The look from last night was back. His eyes changed from sky blue to stormy gray.

"So how can I help you?" Roberto asked.

"Last night, after the Halloween parade, did you go into the park?" Max's question was tinged with accusation.

"The park?" The question surprised Roberto. Whatever he was expecting, it wasn't that. "No, I came right home. Why?"

"We found something of yours." Max nodded at Zo, and she pulled out the book. A few papery flakes fell on the light-colored rug.

"That's Marianne's book," said Roberto. "It's…burned. Where did you find it?"

"In a bonfire—a bonfire on the verge of rekindling." Max leaned in. "If I hadn't got there when I did, Spirit Canyon might look very different this morning."

"You've got it wrong," Roberto shot back. "I wasn't in the park, and I know how dangerous fires are this time of year. I would never leave one burning. That's not my book."

Zo opened to the title page. "The inscription says otherwise."

"It can't be…" Roberto's brown eyes softened as he reached for the book across the coffee table. His hands were proof of a lifetime of hard work. He studied the print, passing his thumb over the smudged words.

"I could arrest you for attempted arson." Max focused on his reaction. "The judges around here aren't forgiving to people who start forest fires."

Roberto looked up from the book. Max's tone had put him on the defensive, and the two were locked in a silent standoff. As an ex-journalist, Zo knew nothing shut down a productive discussion faster than flinging accusations.

She changed the direction of the conversation. "We don't mean to upset you, Roberto. We know how much you cared for Marianne. Let's start over. If you weren't in the park, did you leave your book somewhere? Is it possible somebody took it?"

"Why would someone steal his book?" Max asked her. "Its value is purely sentimental."

Zo ignored Max. "Maybe your son? Could we ask him?"

He lay the book on the coffee table and stood. "I'll get him."

"Why are you giving him a way out of this?" whispered Max. "We know it's his book. It has his name on it."

"Didn't you see how shocked he was?" she said. "It might be his book, but I don't think he threw it into the fire."

Max rolled his eyes. "Intuition again, right?"

"Right." Zo twisted for the envelope on the console table behind the couch. "Besides, I saw something interesting when we came in."

"What are you doing?" he asked. "You can't open someone's mail. It's a federal offense."

"It's already open." She took out a letter and scanned it quickly. "It's from a coach on the water polo team. He thanks Roberto for his support and says he looks forward to having Alex on the team." She glanced up at Max. "It doesn't make sense. How does he know Alex will be on the team? I doubt the college has sent out formal acceptance letters yet."

"Maybe the Ivy Leagues do things differently."

"Maybe," agreed Zo. "Or maybe Roberto pulled some strings." She turned over the letter. "This isn't on university stationery, just stuck in a university envelope."

Hearing footsteps, she shoved the letter in the envelope and tossed it back on the pile. Alex was pulling on a tank top as he entered the living room. Roberto motioned for him to sit in the chair next to his. Alex landed with a grunt.

"Tell them you weren't in the park last night," said Roberto. "You didn't burn the book."

Alex's young skin had one wrinkle—a smirk. "I wasn't in the park last night. I didn't burn the book."

"This isn't a joke," fumed Max. "So wipe that smug smile off your face."

Roberto's eyebrows knitted together in an angry glare at Max. Zo knew the look of protective father, and that was it. She intervened before Max could say anything else. "Maybe you know someone who had a bonfire last night? Not far from town?"

Alex crossed his arms.

"Alex, answer Zo's question," Roberto demanded. He was protective but also authoritative. He *would* make his son talk.

"Some people from the high school were having a bonfire after the parade," Alex informed them. "They were going to play Midnight Man. I didn't go."

"He was home all night with me," claimed Roberto.

That you know of. "Is it possible one of the kids got ahold of your dad's book? Took it from your house?"

"I doubt it," said Alex, bored. His eyes wandered to his phone, where he checked his social media.

"Then how do you think it got there?" asked Max.

"Marianne was a witch." Alex shrugged. "Maybe she flew it there."

"Alex," warned Roberto.

He looked up from his phone. "What? It's not as if she hid it. She *embraced* it. You were at the talk, Dad."

And so were you. You were being a jerk then, too.

"This book was in perfect condition," said Roberto. "It was prominently displayed on the bookshelf until yesterday. It's obvious to me that someone burned it on Halloween as some sort of cruel joke."

It was obvious to Zo that person was Alex, but Roberto was blinded by love for his son. He couldn't believe he'd do anything so callous. Zo could. He'd acted the same way at the book signing: spoiled, bratty, and rude. Did he think Marianne was trying to take his mother's place? Was that why he was hostile toward her? "I couldn't help but notice the family picture." She nodded toward the console table. "That's Alex?"

Roberto smiled, the warm kind smile for which he was known. The gray flecks in his hair flickered as he turned toward the frame. He looked more like himself. "Yes, when he was a year old. His mother died shortly afterwards, bless her soul. She was killed in a car accident."

"I'm sorry," said Zo.

"Me, too," Max added.

"She was a professor at Black Mountain. Very smart." He gave his son an affectionate swat on the knee. "Like Alex. He inherited her smarts, luckily for us."

"Can I go now?" asked Alex.

"As long as you promise to ask your friends about the book," Roberto insisted.

"Sure."

Roberto watched his son walk out of the room. "I know how he seems, but kids today are different. They don't know how to communicate. It's the technology, the smartphones."

"If you talk to any of his friends, let us know." Max stood. "I'd like a few words with them about fire safety."

And a few words about Marianne Morgan, Zo added silently. She stood also.

"Do you mind if I keep the book?" asked Roberto. "It's mine, and I'd like to see about having it repaired."

"I need it for evidence," said Max. "In regards to the fire."

Roberto reluctantly handed him the book. A second later, Max dropped it, and it landed on the coffee table with a plunk. Zo reached for it.

"Leave it," said Max. "I...I don't think it will hurt if Roberto keeps it."

Zo wondered about his change of mind but said nothing. She thanked Roberto for his time before they left.

Putting on her helmet, Zo said, "Are you going to tell me what that was about? Back there with the book?"

"No, I'm not." Max got onto the back of the bike. "You're just going to have to use your intuition."

Chapter Sixteen

After dropping Max off, Zo made lunch at home. Then she changed clothes for the Harvest Hike. The hike was a one-and-a-half-mile trail to Spirit Canyon Falls, the popular waterfall pictured on postcards. She tossed on her Take A Hike long-sleeved shirt with a plaid vest and orange hiking boots. In her backpack, she tucked in staples including a map, compass, and first-aid kit. The writing paper, for journaling, was downstairs in the store. The group would pause near the lower observation deck to write. They would add the sheets to their scrapbooks when they returned to Happy Camper. She couldn't wait to see Max's entry.

If he didn't like the journaling exercise, it would be his own fault, she mused as she hitched her backpack over her shoulder and locked the door. He was the one who signed up. His reasoning still evaded her. Did he think she was unqualified to lead the hike? She would disabuse him of that notion today. She knew her limits and would never put a group of tourists in danger. Strenuous hikes and trails, the ones deeper in the woods, she left to professionals. Her hikes were recreational and usually involved a theme or holiday. This one was based on gratitude and perfect for November.

"Where do you want the Gratitude Tree?" Harley asked when Zo came through the door. Always on task, she was busy switching out Halloween décor.

"Near the front window," Zo answered. "Where people can easily get to it." The Gratitude Tree was a big hit with her customers last year. They wrote what they were thankful for on gold, brown, and orange pieces of paper. By the end of November, the bare branches would be covered with "leaves" of gratitude.

"I set up the scrapbook table in the back corner." Harley wore a gray cotton jumpsuit and army boots that matched her long-sleeved shirt. "I couldn't find the glue guns."

"I'll get them," said Zo. "They're in the back." She'd just finished laying out the supplies when Max arrived.

"You're early," she said.

"I wanted to remind you about the Trip Plan," said Max. "Did you complete it?"

Dang it. With everything going on, she'd completely forgotten. She rummaged for it in the paper stack beneath the counter.

"You didn't lose it, did you?"

She glanced up. The green vest he was wearing made his eyes look the same color as the forest pine trees. For a moment, she forgot what she was doing. Then his brow furrowed, and she remembered. The Trip Plan. She found it under a flyer for this year's Holidazzle, which reminded her. She needed to get moving on her "Spirit of the Season" column. "Here it is."

"It's incomplete."

She pulled out a folder. "I know, but I have all the signups right here."

"In an emergency, it's nice to have quick access to the information." Max grabbed a pen out of the holder. The daisy on top looked hysterical in his large hand. "I'll finish it before we leave. That way you'll have an example to follow."

"Thank you." She wasn't sure she meant it. She didn't like him meddling in her business, or giving her more work to do. Hers was a one-woman operation, two-person on nights and weekends. If she could embed the form online, it might work. Right now it was just another piece of paperwork she didn't want to complete. But she believed in trying everything at least once.

When all ten hikers had arrived, she informed them of the plan. The group started off toward the woods, in the direction of the trailhead. The curvy path was cool and covered in pine needles. Towering evergreens surrounded them, shading the trail. As they walked, Zo told them a little bit about wildlife in the area, including bison, mountain goats, bighorn sheep, turkeys, and woodchucks. Max was quick to jump in and add mountain lions to the list of animals. Zo noticed the group huddled a little closer after the mention.

They came to a creek, and Zo allowed everyone a few moments to rest or take pictures. What had they observed so far? Could they capture it with a photo? It was a perfect opportunity to fill their scrapbooks later. She also encouraged them to hydrate during the break. If anyone felt hungry, she had energy bars in her backpack.

Max sat down next to her on a bench. "I admit, the hike's a lot different than I thought."

"How?" Surrounded by women in their thirties, forties, and fifties, she could see one major difference. He was the only guy on the trip.

He shrugged. "I've hiked this trail a million times, but it's not the same. The pace, the little tidbits. I'm enjoying it more this time."

"Thanks," said Zo, smiling. "That means a lot."

For the rest of the journey, she pondered Max's compliment. She was relieved he was enjoying himself. He didn't mention any other dangerous animals, and when they reached the lower observation deck of the waterfall, he didn't caution them about the slippery rocks. Zo did that. She'd seen overzealous tourists fall into the water while taking selfies. Instead, she encouraged them to find a quiet spot on the bridge or a rock, listen to the sounds of the spray, and think about what they were most thankful for right now. As she journaled, one idea monopolized her pages: Spirit Canyon. Houses changed, tourists came and went, but Spirit Canyon remained the same. Ruggedly beautiful, life-giving, and inspirational, it signified home to a girl who didn't have a permanent address. It filled her cup with daily gratitude.

A hiker asked a question about a bird, and Zo followed her to the bridge. She listened to the description, then took the hiker's binoculars to see for herself. Perched near the top of the waterfall was a majestic bird of prey native to the area.

"It's a red-tailed hawk," said Zo, peering through the lenses. "See its dark head, white throat, and red tail? The curved beak—" She stopped talking. On a lower shelf, something orange caught her eye. Too large to be a rodent and too furry to be a land animal, it was out of place. Her heart fell to her stomach. George! As if feeling her eyes on him, he turned his head and meowed. "Go get the ranger," Zo said to the hiker. "Please, hurry."

Max was there in an instant. "What is it?"

Only then did she pull her eyes away from the binoculars. She gave them to Max. "It's George." She heard his breath catch in his throat. It was the scariest sound in the world. It confirmed George was in danger.

"Don't worry," he said with certainty. "I can get to him."

"He's my cat. I'll go."

He gave her a sideways glance, the binoculars never leaving his face. "This is what I do, Zo. For once in your life, trust me."

He was a trained professional, an expert on the national park. But deep in her heart, she didn't know if she could do what he asked. George meant everything to her. If something happened to him, she'd never forgive herself. And the truth was, people had a history of letting her down.

"Please." He touched her arm with his free hand. "We don't have time."

Max had a better chance of rescuing George, and George liked him. He wouldn't resist. Zo nodded her assent before she could take it back, and he was off.

While Max scaled the stony cliff, Justin Castle arrived with his camera crew. One of the participants had posted a picture of the scene on social media, and spotting it, he came running. Any trouble in town got him excited—and kept him in business. He looked on the scene giddily, like a child in a store window. In a quiet town of ten thousand people, he was thrilled to have something to report for the six o'clock news.

Zo kept her distance, instead gathering with the women in the group. Never had she been so grateful to be surrounded by positive energy. They put away their plans for the afternoon and their journal exercises. They watched and prayed as Max closed in on the waterfall. No one mentioned getting back.

The terrain was rocky and slick from the water, but Max was experienced and knew where to step. He was sure-footed and careful. Through the binoculars, Zo could see the flex of his muscles as he climbed. If only he could climb faster. She was worried George would dart away before he could get to him.

Max's movement drew attention from the red-tailed hawk, its head turning sharply. The bird zeroed in on George. Though George was a large cat, hawks were strong. They were carnivores and could carry up to sixty pounds in their talons. Small animals, including cats, dogs, and foxes, weren't safe from their hooks. But from this angle, Zo didn't think the hawk could get to George. He could attack him, though, and hawks were very territorial. Even with Max approaching, the bird might make a move.

"That bird isn't going to—" started one woman. She covered her mouth before she finished.

"Why doesn't the ranger scare it away?" said another group member.

"He can't." Zo understood the predicament. "The noise might startle George. He doesn't want him to run."

"How will he get him down from there?"

Zo shook her head. "I don't know. I've been asking myself that same question." The climb was tricky without George. With a furry, frightened, sharp-clawed cat? She couldn't even imagine what to do. What if George was hurt? What if he wouldn't let Max carry him? What if—God forbid—Max dropped him?

Zo's mouth began to water and her armpits sweat. Then the shaking started. One of the women took the binoculars from her.

"Don't worry," the woman said. "He's got this. I know he does. He's almost there."

Zo nodded. Even through the panic, she could see he was getting close. The problem was the hawk was closer, too. It swooped to the ridge near George. She covered her eyes.

After a long moment, the hiker said, "He's there!"

Zo took back the binoculars. Max hovered near George, checking him over carefully. The seconds ticked past like hours. Max gave a thumb's up sign, and the group cheered. Zo released a breath. George was safe.

Max removed gloves and a folded canvas sack out of his backpack. It took Zo a moment to realize his next move. He would have to put George in the sack to transport him. *George wasn't going to like that.* Zo worried he'd resist. But he must have been too frightened to fight, because Max had him in the sack within a few seconds. Max climbed to the top of the waterfall, where he was soon met by a ranger in a four-wheeler.

Zo's phone rang. It was Max.

"I'm taking him to the animal hospital to be checked out," said Max. "You get the group back to Happy Camper. Call me when you get there."

"He's okay though?" Zo asked.

"Let's make sure." A pause on the line. "He's fine as far as I can see."

Zo heard a meow.

"He doesn't like being in this bag," said Max, "but he hasn't lost any strength."

George might not like being confined, but they were only minutes from town. He would make it. With her hands still shaking, Zo hoped *she* would. "I don't know how to thank you." The words caught in her throat.

"It was no problem," said Max. "Really. I'm just glad he's all right. You're okay to get back to the store?"

Zo swallowed. "Of course. I'll have Harley do the scrapbook session and meet you at the vet's."

"Darn it," said Max. "I won't be able to show off my glue gun skills. I've been practicing."

"That's okay," said Zo. "I have a feeling you'll get another chance."

Chapter Seventeen

Justin Castle stopped Zo on her way back to the trail. Like a boulder on the path, he was an obstacle to overcome. Dressed in a snappy sweater vest and jacket, he was better looking than a boulder, but a boulder all the same. With his cameraman recording, he asked what her cat was doing so far from home and if she planned on reimbursing the town for the use of governmental resources. He blinked, waiting for an answer.

"If by governmental resources you mean Max, I'm happy to pay him for his time," said Zo. "But he was participating in the Harvest Hike. He wasn't on the clock."

"Servants of the law are always on the clock, Ms. Jones." He took a short bow. "As am I."

"How sad for you," said a group member.

"And me," muttered Zo. She wanted Max's heroic action covered on the news, but Justin always had to spin his stories, to make them more controversial than they were. Max had rescued her cat, plain and simple. By the time the rescue aired on the evening news, the story would be entirely different.

They started back for Happy Camper, leaving Justin to glare at their backs. Zo assured the group they didn't need to hurry, but concern must have still been written on her face. They wouldn't hear of stopping and zipped through the woods at a breakneck pace without so much as a water break.

Luckily Sunday afternoons were slow, and Harley said she could take over the scrapbook project without any trouble. Zo gave each of the hikers a free Happy Camper water bottle for their kindness. Then she grabbed her cat carrier and hurried off to meet Max at the pet hospital.

He and George were in Exam Room 1 with the veterinarian. When Zo opened the door and spotted George sitting on the counter, her emotions broke again.

"George! Are you okay?" She tossed the cat carrier on the floor.

"Other than a little overweight, he's just fine," said Dr. Iron Cloud with a chuckle. He took a step back from the counter, sliding his glasses to his forehead.

Zo picked up George and hugged him to her chest. He didn't bite or scratch her. Maybe he was too surprised at her reaction, or maybe he was relieved she was there. "How did you get so far from home?" The only answer was a muffled meow. Very un-George-like. She put him back on the counter.

"A big cat like this?" said Dr. Iron Cloud. "The wanderlust doesn't surprise me. He's not the kind to stay indoors. Max told me he was near the waterfall."

Too worried about George, Zo hadn't noticed him there. Max was sitting calmly in the corner chair. Her eyes flew to his with appreciation. "Max saved him. Did he tell you that?"

"He didn't have to." The doctor petted George's head. "It's not the first animal he's rescued, and I'm sure it won't be the last. He's a regular hero in my book."

"Mine, too."

Standing, Max waved away the compliments. "Thanks, you guys, but I was just doing my job."

Dr. Iron Cloud turned to Zo. "Everything looks good, so you're free to take him. If anything changes, though, bring him back."

"Thank you." After the doctor shut the door, she gave Max a hug. "And thank *you*. I don't know what I would have done without you today."

"You would have climbed up the cliff and rescued him yourself," said Max with a laugh.

"That was my plan, but I don't know." She shook her head. "I froze. I think I had a panic attack." Recalling the moment made her shiver.

Still holding her, he rubbed the sides of her arms. "It's okay. It happens. I'm just glad I was there to help." He pulled back, a smile on his face. "Makes you wonder if having a guide along for every hike would be a good idea…"

A chuckle bubbled to her lips. "Let's not get carried away. Help me get George into the carrier."

"*That* carrier?" he said.

"It was the biggest one they had." Zo opened the door. She could handle the carrier if Max could handle George.

In one fluid motion, Max had him into the crate. Orange fur stuck out of the holes, but it couldn't be helped. He was big and hairy. George's meow was back to normal as she hauled him to the front desk, where she paid the bill.

"Do you want to come to my house for a cup of tea?" she asked, tucking away her wallet. "I could use one after the day I've had."

"Unless you need help with George, I promised Duncan I'd stop by Buffalo Bill's. He's playing with a Rascal Flatts cover band." He raised his sandy brown eyebrows. "You're welcome to join me."

She bit back a smile. "A tempting offer, but I don't want to leave George alone."

"I understand." He walked her to her car. "I would rather get a tooth pulled than listen to Duncan play another song. But I feel bad for the guy. I couldn't say no."

"You're too nice, Max." She slid the cat carrier into the seat beside her.

"You know, I get that a lot."

"I don't doubt it." She buckled her seatbelt. "See you tomorrow."

Harley was locking up for the evening when Zo pulled into Happy Camper a few minutes later. Zo heard the telltale click after she shut off the engine. She couldn't believe how late it was.

"How did the scrapbooking go?" Zo called out. She grabbed George's crate from the passenger seat.

"They loved it." Harley approached Zo's Subaru Outback. "They asked what you had planned for Christmas."

"I need to figure that out—soon. My column is due Friday. That's my official deadline."

Harley stuck a finger in George's crate. "So here's the big guy causing all the problems."

George growled.

"He needs to rest," explained Zo. It surprised her how quickly she'd make excuses for her cat. She wondered if mothers felt the same inclination.

"He needs *something*," mumbled Harley, who was not a cat person. "I'll see you tomorrow."

"You don't have class?" asked Zo. She was usually alone on Mondays.

"It's fall break, remember?" Harley slipped on the army jacket tied at her waist. "I don't go back until Wednesday."

That's right. There was no school on Monday or Tuesday. She'd be at the store both days. Which reminded her of a question that had been nagging her all day. "I just remembered a question I wanted to ask you. When did you get your acceptance letter from Black Mountain College?"

"March," Harley answered. "Why? You're not thinking about changing careers on me, are you?"

"Not at all." After living next to Cunningham for a year, school was the last place she wanted to be right now. "It's about Alex. He already received a letter from the water polo coach. I thought it was strange."

Harley shrugged. "I don't know anything about sports—unless scrapbooking counts."

"It does in my book," said Zo with a laugh. "See you tomorrow."

Harley waved goodbye, and Zo walked up her deck stairs. George made the climb as hard as possible by shoving himself into the rear of the carrier, upsetting the balance. Once inside, she opened the crate, and he bolted, low-walking across the kitchen floor and into the living room. From under a chair, he peered at her as she poured food into his dish. The stare down lasted no longer than a minute. Then he was busy munching his dinner while she made tea.

Nothing said fall like apple cinnamon, and after the day she had, she needed a comfort tea—and teapot. As the water heated, she took down her single-serve apple teapot. It had its own infuser, which she filled with loose-leaf tea. She warmed her hands on the apple-shaped pot while she waited for it to steep, the smell of cinnamon wafting up from the spout.

As the tea took effect, she breathed a sigh of relief. George was safe, the Harvest Hike was over, and the scrapbook event was a success. She could turn to other things now—like her Happy Camper column. It needed to include businesses that were giving back to the community for the holidays. Her laptop on the kitchen table was a reminder of the work that needed to be done for the article. She flipped it open.

She'd talked to Nikki about the theater. They were doing a holiday food drive. One sack of groceries would purchase a ticket to this year's production of *A Christmas Carol*. Next, she needed to talk to Hattie, who always planned something special for the library. But right now her screen was pulling her in another direction. Her Internet application was open to a page about water polo. She'd been searching for teams in the area and found nothing.

Zo tapped the screen. "Zero," she said aloud. Like Harley, she wasn't familiar with the sport, but something was amiss. If Harley didn't receive her acceptance letter until March, why was Alex receiving letters from the water polo coach in November? Was it possible he'd already been accepted by the college?

She typed in the name of Alex's Ivy League school and, after scrolling through various menus, found an application timeline. It was just as she thought. Even if Alex did the early action option, the soonest he would get his acceptance letter was mid-December. Other applicants would receive theirs by late March. College coaches recruited early, even before students applied, but did they also send letters, thanking parents for their support? Zo had a feeling something else was at play besides the game of water polo.

George jumped on her lap, interrupting her musing. His purr was a welcome intrusion. She leaned back from the computer and scratched his ears. She would look into it later. Right now she needed to spend some much-needed time welcoming home her cat.

Chapter Eighteen

The next morning, Zo stood back to admire her work on the chalkboard tent outside Happy Camper. It announced her November promotion, Marshmallow Mondays. Above a swirling cup of hot chocolate, she'd written, MARSHMALLOW MONDAYS START TODAY! in colorful bubble letters. Customers could enjoy a free cup of hot chocolate on Mondays from now until the end of December. Last year, customers loved it. The hot chocolate carafe became the metaphorical town water cooler, with people popping in to sip, gossip, and shop. A jar of colorful marshmallows sat next to the pot. In December, she would put out candy canes.

December, she repeated to herself as she opened the door. The nip in the air told her it was right around the corner. She poured hot cocoa into her Happy Camper mug, a taste test to make sure she got it right. Rich, chocolatey, and steamy, it was perfect—more than perfect. It put her in the mood for holiday music, and she decided to grab the Christmas albums out of storage, to give them a shine before the start of the season, and the holiday gift cards. She brought them to the register, where George lay on the counter taking his bath. When Harley arrived, she'd take the gift cards to the construction workers at the theater. It was still amazing to her that complete strangers had discovered something so personal about her. They'd gone out of their way to be helpful. She wanted to repay the kindness.

For now, she drank her hot chocolate and read the paper—as much of it as she could anyway with George's tail in the way. Interestingly, he hadn't begged to go outside today. Maybe he'd had enough of the great outdoors after seeing it up close. He seemed perfectly content to hang close to her.

"*Marshmallow Mondays*!" Harley called out as she breezed through the door. "The most wonderful time of the year."

"I'll get you a cup," said Zo.

Harley unwrapped her purple scarf and hung it with her coat in the backroom. "Is it too early to frost the windows?" she hollered.

"A bit." Zo handed her the hot chocolate as she approached the register. "Let's wait until after Thanksgiving."

Just as they began to share their morning mugs, Justin Castle came through the door like a cold burst of air. Harley shot Zo a glance, her hot chocolate still raised to her lips.

"What fresh hell is this?" muttered Zo, quoting Dorothy Parker.

Justin pointed to the table of seasonal books, which held copies of Marianne's book. He barked orders at his cameraman. "Zoom in on this. Film the 'happy' stuff. It'll be an ironic twist for the piece."

Reluctantly, Zo set down her mug. It was too early for Justin—and on a Monday to boot. "What are you doing?"

"Good morning." Justin motioned to a mug that read Gratitude Is an Attitude. "Get this, too, Mark. I'm doing an exposé on Marianne's death."

The cameraman hovered over the merchandise.

"I got word this morning that her death wasn't an accident—blunt force trauma to the head. It looks as if we have another murderer in town." He arched a slim eyebrow. Zo was pretty sure he waxed them. "You're not going to scoop me this time, Zo."

She grabbed the cup out of the cameraman's hand. "What do you mean 'scoop you'? I'm not in the newspaper business anymore, obviously." She flashed him the cup. "I own a business, a business you keep trying to disrupt."

He gave her a smile. His cool blue suit jacket made his teeth look even whiter—if that was possible. A sparkle could show up at the corner of his mouth like in a toothpaste commercial, and she wouldn't be surprised. "Don't pretend you don't know what I'm talking about," he said. "That little incident over Memorial Day? You were the town hero for unmasking the murderer."

"That's an overstatement," said Zo. Harriet Hobbs, her newspaper editor, had noted more interest in her Happy Camper column after the event, however.

"Really?" he said. "Why would my boss suggest talking to you then?"

"Maybe he thinks you need to find inner peace."

From the counter, Harley sputtered a laugh.

Justin glared. "Laugh all you want, but you're tangled up in this. The entire store is. So is your friend, Julia Parker. I know Roberto is her ex-boyfriend. Don't think I'm not checking up on *that* lead next."

Zo wondered where he was getting his information. *She* didn't even know Jules dated Roberto until last Thursday. How did Justin?

"When can we sit down for an interview?" he asked.

The nerve of this guy. "Let me tell you something my first editor told me. Honey attracts more flies than vinegar. If you want an interview, you should try being nice."

"My broadcast is number one in the area," boasted Justin. "I don't need advice from you."

"Suit yourself."

"No comment, then?" Justin looked pleased with himself.

"No comment." After they left, Zo turned to Harley. "I always feel like I need a shower after talking to him."

"I don't know why he's so popular." Harley was still glaring at the door.

"Two words: great hair." Zo grabbed her vest from the hook in the back room. "I'm going to drop off a few gift cards at the theater. I'll bring us back lunch. What would you like?"

"Ooh, a salad from Green Market," Harley requested. "And you'd better warn Jules about Justin. I have a feeling she's next on his hit list."

"Agreed," said Zo. "I'll see you at lunch."

Zo started toward the theater. The streets were calm and quiet, a nice change from the busy weekend. The hum from the corner café was the only sound Zo heard as she crossed the street. A crumbly brick building, it didn't have a sign except Café, and locals called it *The Café*. This morning, like every morning, folks were filling up on eggs and bacon, pancakes and sausages, and jelly-filled donuts. Crowded with people, it wasn't a restaurant mentioned on the tour guides. And luckily, too. Its obscurity kept prices low.

The theater was also noisy, but, unlike the happy humming café, the sound was disruptive. Nikki was arguing with Marianne's ex-husband. Neither noticed as Zo entered the lobby; the disagreement was that intense. Zo scanned the posters on the wall, not wanting to pass out her gift cards until Jake left.

"It's rightfully mine, you blood-sucking thief," shouted Jake. "The will says so. It's all there in black and white. Everything belongs to me now."

"Marianne was a season subscriber," said Nikki. "You don't *need* a ticket."

Jake jutted out his chest, which also expanded the size of his belly. His flannel shirt stretched tightly across his midsection. "You think I'm not smart enough for your shows? Let me tell you something, I'm smarter than you think."

When Nikki didn't respond, the lobby fell silent. Coolheaded, she wasn't about to let a man like Jake Morgan intimidate her or goad her into a screaming match. After a few minutes, she calmly gestured toward the door. "I'd like you to leave."

"You would, would you?" He took another step toward Nikki. "Well I'm not going to."

Zo decided it was time to intervene and walked over. She wasn't going to let Nikki face the bully alone. "Is something wrong?"

Nikki's cool eyes never left Jake's. "Jake was just leaving, before I call the police."

"The police don't scare me." Jake rocked on his heels. "I got nothing to say to them."

Zo pulled out her phone. "They might have something to say to you."

"Man, you women are testy," said Jake. "Forget it. I'll come back when you're ready to talk."

"Don't bother," said Nikki. "Our conversation is over."

"That's what you think," Jake proclaimed.

Zo's eyes followed him out the door. "So that's Marianne's ex."

"A piece of work, isn't he?" Nikki smoothed her blond hair, which was tucked into a French twist. "As if I don't have other things to worry about besides this weekend's seats. If you ask me, it's a little premature for him to be taking in a show. His wife of twenty years died four days ago. How can her box seat matter to him right now?"

Zo agreed. He seemed too excited about his new wealth.

"Anyway, I'm sure you didn't come here to hear my problems—or Jake's," said Nikki. "How can I help?"

Zo handed her a gift card to Happy Camper. "My way of saying thanks for giving me the necklace. I also brought a couple for the crew. They told me they found the necklace in the dressing room."

"That's so kind of you." Nikki's shoulders relaxed in her well-tailored blazer. Apparently, Jake had made her more tense than she let on. "Have you found out anything else about your birth mom?"

"Not yet," said Zo. "At the Halloween party, Hattie mentioned going through old playbills. I think that's a good idea."

"Absolutely," answered Nikki. "I have a box of them in the basement storage room. I just haven't gotten that far yet. Later, it might be fun to hang some on the walls or in a display case. Would you like to take a look?"

"That would be wonderful," said Zo. "Unfortunately, I don't have time today. Another day?"

"Stop by any time," said Nikki. "Just make sure to wear your old clothes. The place is a mess." The phone in the will-call booth rang. "I need to grab that. The crew is in there." She pointed to the theater.

Zo walked in. The smell of paint told her the group was still working in the balcony, so she took the side stairwell up to the second floor. Sean was fastening new chair cushions. Deep crimson, they matched the theater curtain on the stage below. Like the main floor, the balcony would soon be ready for use.

"You're back," said Sean.

"I wanted to say thanks for finding my necklace and for your work on renovating the theater." Zo handed him an envelope. "It looks amazing."

He wiped his hands on his jeans before taking the card. "What's this?"

"I own Happy Camper," Zo informed them. "It's a gift card to the store, just a small token of appreciation. Without work like yours, Spirit Canyon's history would vanish. Thanks to you and your group, the theater will be here for years to come."

"You didn't have to do that," said Sean. "We feel the same way. That's why we volunteered."

"You're not getting paid?"

He shook his head.

Zo was impressed. "Wow, even more reason for the gift cards." She scanned the balcony. "Are the others around?"

"I sent them for more supplies," said Sean. "I'll make sure they get them if you leave them with me."

Zo gave him the rest of the envelopes. "Tell them thank you, will you?"

"Sure thing," he said.

Zo went down the steps, out the door, and toward Spirits & Spirits with a new zip in her step. It wasn't the cold air that had her moving quickly. It was the sense of community spirit. *This* is what she wanted to get into her column, the feeling this time of year brought with it. She needed to do something extra special at Happy Camper. The theater was doing a food drive. Hattie was probably doing a book drive. Zo had done a toy drive last year. What could she do this year? She was still racking her brain when Duncan came up behind her in the Spirits & Spirits parking lot.

"Come with me, and don't say a word," Duncan whispered.

"Is this a stick-up?" said Zo.

"No, but I like the way you think," murmured Duncan. "Follow me." They ducked into the alley behind the store.

"So what's this about?" asked Zo.

"You're writing a column about giving back for the holidays, right?"

Maybe Jules had been giving him mind-reading lessons. Zo had considered the article all the way here. "Right. Why?"

"I've been thinking about doing something at Spirits & Spirits," said Duncan.

Zo shot him a look. "At *Jules's* store."

"I came to you first because I knew how Jules would react," said Duncan. "Just this way."

"And I'm supposed to...?"

"Be more open." Duncan gave her shoulders a shimmy. "You're adventurous. Spontaneous." He quirked a brow. "A risk-taker."

Far less handsome men had turned her head with talk of adventure. She needed to move this along. "Okay, tell me your idea."

His eyes flickered. They lighted up the drab sky, which had turned steel gray. "A little concert, Sips and Swings. I'll play the guitar, and Jules will serve the wine. All proceeds for the concert will go to charity."

It was a solid notion. But Jules might wonder if it was just another way to promote himself or his guitar lessons. She told him.

"That's where you come in," Duncan answered. "If you say you came up with the idea, she'll take it more seriously. It won't sound self-serving."

"*Is* it self-serving?" She noted the scales of justice tattoo on his arm. Maybe he was being honest.

"No," said Duncan. "It's about giving back, to the community."

"I have to give you props for not smiling," said Zo. "You almost had me."

"What would it take to convince you?"

Not much, Zo thought, but she kept that to herself. "How about a reason? Besides the community."

"I live here, too, you know." His face softened. "It'd be nice to be a part of something."

At a core level, she understood the need to belong. It wasn't until she opened Happy Camper that she felt connected to the community. It sounded as if Duncan was searching for a way in, and if she could help him, she would. "All right. I'll put in a good word for you, but I'm not going to lie. You have to tell her it's your idea—and no country music."

He stuck out his hand. "Agreed." He frowned. "Your hand is cold as ice. Take my coat."

"I'm okay," said Zo.

He wrapped an arm around her shoulder as they walked around the corner and into the parking lot of Spirits & Spirits. "Is that better?"

Was hot chocolate better with peppermint schnapps? Heck yes it was better. Up until the moment Justin Castle's lackey shoved a camera in their direction, she'd felt like she was wrapped in a warm blanket.

She kicked herself for not calling Jules right away. She had no idea Justin would show up so soon.

"Hello again, Zo." Justin looked between her and Duncan. "I hope we're not interrupting."

Zo shrugged off Duncan's arm. "Your purpose in life is to interrupt. What do you want?"

"We're here to talk to Julia," said Justin.

"About what?" Duncan's eyes had a new hardness to them.

"That's none of your business," argued Justin.

Duncan didn't move from the front door of Spirits & Spirits. His arms across his chest, he stood sentinel, blocking the door.

Until Jules jerked it open. She was dressed in black leather pants that showed off her stunning full figure. "Does someone want to tell me what's going on? I've got a tarot-card reading in ten minutes, and you all are blocking the path." She looked at Duncan. "You're late."

"Justin is here about Marianne's death." Zo sputtered out the words as quickly as possible. "He wants to talk to you."

Justin tilted his head. Not a hair moved. "Marianne died under suspicious circumstances. We need to talk."

"Let the man through." Jules held open the door. "If I know anything, it's suspicious circumstances."

Justin paraded past Zo with a smug look on his face. His cameraman followed.

"What are you doing, inviting him in?" whispered Zo.

Jules held up a hand, her white shirt sleeve billowing in the breeze. "You have to handle guys like Castle head on. Trust me. I know what I'm doing."

Zo hoped so. In her opinion, Jules had a little too much confidence in her otherworldly abilities. Sometimes Zo wondered if she'd convinced herself she was invincible.

But there was nothing she could do when Jules shut her out. Leaving her and Duncan in the proverbial dust, Jules ducked in the other room, far beyond Zo's reach or influence. The only thing left to do was bring Harley lunch.

Chapter Nineteen

Zo was grateful for the crunchy carrots in her salad. She could chomp on them without saying a word to Harley about the ordeal at Spirits & Spirits. Here she was, trying to save a friend from a headache, and the friend embraced said headache. What was Jules thinking? Zo had no idea, except one—sales. She wouldn't have been surprised if Justin left with a growler of local brew before the conversation was over. What's more, Duncan looked miserable watching the two of them disappear behind her consultation curtain. He didn't have a chance to tell Jules about Sips and Swings, and Zo didn't have the opportunity to back him up. She stabbed a cucumber.

"Just so you know, cucumbers aren't dangerous," said Harley, pulling her eyes away from the computer. "A broken plastic fork is another matter, however. My friend had to have five stiches because of one." She returned to the computer screen, eating her salad. "Went clear through the roof of her mouth."

Zo scrunched up her face. Harley was a treasure trove of youthful facts. "Ew."

Boot heels alerted her to a customer, and Zo put down her fork to greet the newcomer. It was Brady Merrigan. "Officer Merrigan. I'm starting to wonder if I should sign you up for a frequent shopper punch card. The holidays are right around the corner."

"It's the first week of November," said Brady. "Don't talk to me about the holidays."

"Understood," said Zo, "but we'll have to talk about them soon. My column is due Friday, and I need to know what the station is planning for charity."

He let out a whistle. "Dag nabbit, I forgot all about it. Let me get back to you."

"Before Friday," reminded Zo. "Thursday at the latest."

"Yes, ma'am." He flipped open his notepad. The writing on the page was meticulous, bulleted, and numbered. He obviously cared about his work as much as the town. "But first, I'm here about a restraining order. For one Nicole S. Ainsworth against Mr. Jake Morgan. She said you overheard him harassing her this morning and could corroborate her story?"

Zo applauded Nikki's move. It was smart to keep Jake from pestering her at the theater, and he was sure to return another day. He'd said as much before he left. "Yes, I was there. He was very pushy. Belligerent."

"Why don't you tell me about it?" said Brady.

She reiterated the story. "If you ask me, despite being obnoxious, it's a little premature. The last thing on his mind should be his ex-wife's box seat."

"Technically it's his, at least until the end of the year," said Brady. "Nikki says Marianne renewed it every year for the last five years. She thought of the box as hers."

"Don't you think it's strange, though, considering everything he'll acquire?" questioned Zo. "Why bother Nikki about the seat?"

"She says they never got along when he and Marianne were married. She encouraged Marianne to leave him." Brady tapped his notebook, perhaps mentally underscoring his decision. "Which makes the visit sound like harassment. He's rubbing her face in the fact that everything belongs to him now."

It made sense. Jake seemed like the kind of person who needed to have the last word. And if he murdered Marianne, it was her last word—and breath. "Does he have an alibi?"

He shut his notebook with a smile. "Does he have an alibi? You know I can't discuss the case with you, Zo. But nice try. I admire your determination. It's served you well over the years."

She shrugged. Determination and a little luck went a long way.

Brady stopped short of opening the door. He turned around with his hand on the knob. "By the way, my brother Patrick told me about the costume party. It was a neighborly thing of you to do."

"Don't mention it," said Zo. This was as close to a thank you as she would get, but she appreciated it all the same.

With the touch of his hat, he was gone, like a cowboy in an old western. She went back to her salad, but it had lost its appeal. Tossing it in the trash, she trolled Sunday's old newspaper, looking for antiques. With the aftermath of Spirit Spooktacular, she hadn't had the chance to check upcoming auctions. She noticed a collection of first edition Louis L'Amour books. She circled it with her aqua-colored pen. Hattie Fines would want to know about that. Closing the paper, she told Harley she was going to the library.

Zo considered the library "Hattie's library." The little brick building at Main and Juniper was her domain. Hattie managed four book groups, three hobby groups, and children's story time. If something was going on at the library, chances were she'd had a hand in putting it together.

This afternoon, however, she wasn't organizing events. She was arguing with an employee when Zo arrived. Zo hadn't seen the woman before, and Hattie was really peeved. Zo thumbed through a copy of *Time* magazine at Hattie's desk while she waited for them to finish, but it was hard not to overhear bits of their conversation. The newbie was not following directions.

Hattie stomped over to her desk wearing a shirt that read, THE PAST, THE PRESENT, AND THE FUTURE WALKED INTO A BAR. IT WAS TENSE. She stowed her red glasses on top of her spiky hair. "Zo. What a relief to see you."

"Trouble in book paradise?"

"New employee," said Hattie. "I assumed by her age she'd know a few things. Boy was I wrong."

Zo gave the woman a glance. Like Hattie, she had gray hair, but hers was pulled into a severe bun. Also like Hattie, she wore glasses, but hers were round and sat primly on the end of her nose. She wore an A-line skirt and pink cardigan.

"Hired by the city," continued Hattie. "Her name is Agnes. I think she's about a hundred and three."

"*Hattie.*" Zo stifled a laugh. "That's terrible of you."

"Why? I have my senior discount card." She tossed her hands in the air. "I can say stuff like that. Anyway, you didn't come here to read *Time*. What's up?"

Zo pulled out the auction clipping from her vest pocket. "First editions. I thought you might want to come with me."

"Yes, I do." Taking a seat at her desk, Hattie found a black Sharpie and wrote the time on her desk calendar.

"There's one other thing."

She put the cap on the marker. "You have my full attention."

"My name, Zoelle." She scratched her head. "Do you think it means anything? Anything that might give me a clue about my birth parents?"

Hattie slid her glasses to her eyes and started typing. "It means *something.*" She clicked a few times, then rotated her screen. "Every name does. Let's look. It's not popular, according to this chart, and was even less so in the eighties."

Zo squinted at the screen. The chart showed an uptick in its use in the last few years.

Hattie clicked another link. "Elle is the French word for she, and you *are* a girl."

"Thank you for clarifying that," said Zo with a smirk. "I've always wondered."

Hattie ignored the joke, clicking more links. "And Zoë is a very French name."

"Uh-huh," said Zo. Put them together, and they didn't mean a thing.

Hattie leaned back in her chair, plopping her glasses on her forehead. Her eyes twinkled with an idea. "You know what I think?"

"I've seen that look before," said Zo. "I have a feeling you're about to tell me."

"I think your mom might be French."

Zo liked the idea. After living in South Dakota all this time, she'd laugh if she found out she was French. Not that South Dakota's history books weren't filled with French explorers. The state capital is Pierre, named after Pierre Chouteau Jr., but instead of pronouncing it like the French, South Dakotans pronounce it like *pier*. A shrugging off, of sorts, of the fancy name. "I suppose she could be French. If it's true, it might help me track her down."

"Is that what you want?" asked Hattie, with the knowledge of a friend who'd shared many experiences. "To track her down?"

"I have to follow this new lead," said Zo. "I can't ignore it."

"Sometimes you get caught up chasing a story, even when it's your own—"

"—and the chase can be more exciting than the catch," Zo finished. "You don't have to remind me. Believe me, nobody gets that better than I do." Hattie had her best interest at heart; she knew that. But part of Zo was missing, like a page ripped out of a book. She could flip to other pages, but those pages couldn't replace the missing words.

"I'm not trying to discourage you," Hattie assured her. "It's just that you went through a phase like this a few years ago. It let you down."

"I'm older now. I don't have the same expectations as I did then." Zo straightened the magazines on Hattie's desk. "I don't want a relationship. It'd just be nice to know."

She pushed back her chair. "If there's anything I can do to help, I will. You know that."

"I do," said Zo. "And I appreciate it."

Hattie helped out a patron with a renewal. When she was finished, Zo asked her about the library's seasonal charity drive. "Do you know what you're doing? My column is due Friday."

"Diapers for dues," said Hattie, sticking a returned book on a cart. "For every diaper donated, the library will forgive a dollar's worth of library fees. According to my calculations, you owe me sixteen diapers. I think they come in packs of twenty-four."

Zo caught her drift and loved the extra push. "I'll bring the entire package."

"That's the spirit," said Hattie.

The new hire joined them at the reference desk. She had a magazine clutched to her pink cardigan sweater.

"What is it, Agnes?" Hattie asked.

Agnes gave her a quick peek of the woman's magazine. An article about sexual health was on the front cover. "Do you have a slip for this? I don't believe it should be displayed in public, for everyone to see."

"It's a public library." Hattie said, her hands on her hips. "The point is for everyone to see it."

Agnes stiffened, her bony shoulders like two pebbles under her thin cardigan. "To think my tax dollars fund such vulgarity." She turned on her square heel and marched away.

Hattie shook her head. "See what I mean?"

Yes, Zo could see. First Jules and now Hattie had employee troubles. She was going to walk—no, run—back to Happy Camper and give Harley a raise.

Chapter Twenty

Later that night, Zo and George were in the back room of the store, sorting through the holiday décor, when the six o'clock news came on the television. Harley had a date, and Zo was using the TV for background noise. Mostly, she and George were playing with the silver garland in the Christmas box. Until Justin appeared on the screen. Then she put down the tinsel and turned up the volume. He had an update about a special report, airing Friday night.

"We know her as Zo Jones, the Happy Camper," said Justin, in a voice-over. Several items of Zo's merchandise came into view.

She smiled. Her stuff was so dang cute. Just look at those Daydreamer coasters.

"She's the shop owner who wants to make sure you have a good day." A shot of Zo and Duncan, arm and arm, splashed on the screen. They were smiling.

Zo's hands flew to her mouth. What the heck? Justin must have taken the picture at Spirits & Spirits.

"But when asked about the death of Marianne Morgan, Ms. Jones wasn't so happy." Zo appeared on the screen, hands on her hips. "No comment." Justin's voice returned. "What happened that fateful day after Marianne's book signing at Happy Camper? And was Zo's friend Julia Parker involved?" The screen panned Spirits & Spirits, where Jules disappeared behind a curtain. Her voice, however, was loud and clear. "Did I love Roberto Salvo?" A chuckle. "Do vampires love garlic? I despised the man." Justin's powdered face appeared on the screen. "Tune in Friday night, for my special broadcast: Murder in Spirit Canyon."

The weather came on, but Zo was too stunned to watch. Justin Castle was a cad, but this was lower than low. He hadn't said she and Jules were involved with Marianne's death, directly, but he might as well have. The insinuation had gone too far. If she weren't at the store all alone, she'd march down to the station right now and tell him what she thought of his "special" report.

Her phone rang. It was Jules.

"Did you just see that?"

"Do vampires drink blood?" said Zo. "Of course I saw it. Why did you tell Justin you despised Roberto?"

"He kept saying I was in love with him, that I wanted to steal him back from Marianne." Jules huffed a breath. "It was driving me crazy. You didn't fare much better."

"A little better." Zo tucked away a stray ornament. George had batted it from the box to the middle of the floor. "No comment is better than saying I despised someone."

"The insinuation is the same," argued Jules. "What are we going to do?"

Zo shut the holiday box. "I'm going to go to the station and tell them what I think of Justin's special report. It's slanderous."

"You can't hire a lawyer. They cost too much."

It was true. She didn't have the money or the time to fight a legal battle right now. But they had to do something. Jules was brainstorming as they spoke. Zo could hear a pencil tapping on the other end of the line.

The tapping stopped. "I got it," said Jules. "I'll summon Marianne's ghost at a séance. She'll help us solve her murder before the show airs on Friday. And if that doesn't work, I'll employ a curse."

Okay maybe it wasn't a pencil. Maybe it was a wand.

"We'll do it tomorrow night, at the Zodiac Club," Jules continued. "We're meeting at Happy Camper. It's perfect."

Holding a séance in the middle of a gift shop? It didn't sound like an ideal setting to Zo. "Really?"

"Marianne spent time there the night she died," Jules said. "We'll have better luck communicating with her."

That might be true. Zo had experienced a few strange incidents at the store, and Marianne was murdered nearby. Still, the idea was a stretch, and Zo wasn't sure summoning a ghost, even if possible, would help. With her store's reputation on the line, however, she was willing to try anything. "Fine," Zo agreed. The bell signaled a customer's arrival. "You send the email to the group. I have to go."

When she got to the front of the store, she realized it was Max. Dressed in forest ranger green, he looked as if he'd had a day. Several speckles of mud covered his pants, and his boots revealed similar distress.

"Are you okay?" asked Zo. "It looks like you were attacked by a mud puddle."

"A ranger's four-wheeler was stuck," Max explained. "We had a time getting it out." He gestured toward Main Street. "I was at Buffalo Bill's having a beer when the news came on. I decided to stop by."

Zo was glad he'd seen it. He would understand how frustrated she was right now. "Can you believe it? If we don't get this thing figured out before Friday, I don't know what I'll do. Who knows how far Justin will go to get a scoop."

"You seemed okay to me."

Okay? She was pretty much the opposite of okay.

"With Duncan."

She recalled the flash of them on the news. "Oh that. He wants to do a charity concert at Spirits & Spirits. He wants me to convince Jules it will work."

"Ah," said Max. "That explains why he had his arm around you."

"What is that supposed to mean?"

"It means I'm not an idiot," said Max. "The only person Duncan's trying to convince is you. He knows your type."

She laughed. "Do tell. What's my type?"

"The leather-jacket-wearing type."

"You have a good memory," said Zo. Her ex-boyfriend Hunter wore a leather jacket. Max hadn't forgotten. "But Duncan's serious about the charity concert. He wants my help."

"That's not all he wants," he muttered, bending down to pet George, who had come out of the backroom to greet him. "Hey big guy. How's he doing?"

"Good." Zo was glad for the break in conversation. For once in his life, George had done something charitable. "He's been inside all day."

"What are you going to do about Justin Castle?" Max scratched George's chin.

"Jules is putting a curse on him," said Zo. "I'm not sure I'll need to do much after that."

"Tell me you're joking." Max looked up, his eyes shaded by his thick lashes.

"I'm *kind of* joking" said Zo. "She's going to perform a séance at Happy Camper tomorrow night. She thinks Marianne will reveal the killer, and we will be cleared from suspicion."

"Great," Max said. "If Brady hears, he'll be more convinced than ever that Jules had something to do with Marianne's death. He thinks she's a witch."

"She *is* a witch."

"I wish you guys would stop throwing around that word." Max stood. "I don't like it."

"I know," said Zo, smiling.

Max wasn't smiling. He was crossing his arms.

Zo quit teasing him. She cleared her throat. "Don't worry about Brady. He was in the store today, and he was all right. He needed confirmation about something. Jake was yelling at Nikki at the theater, and I saw it. It was pretty intense. She filed for a restraining order against him."

"Smart move on her part," said Max. "It sounds as if Jake is dangerous. Do you know anything about him or his relationship with Nikki?"

"No, but there seems to be some long-standing animosity between them." George meowed from the counter, complaining loudly about the time. It was past his dinner hour. She took out a can of tuna fish. "Nikki resented the way he treated Marianne."

"He stood to gain the most by Marianne's death, and we know he's violent."

"Brady wouldn't tell me if he had an alibi," said Zo. "Will you?"

Max shrugged. "If I could. I'm on a need-to-know basis with Chief Merrigan. There are a lot of things I don't need to know, it would seem. I'll talk to Jake and see what I can find out."

"Let me come with," said Zo. "I won't get in the way, I promise."

"You know I can't do that." Max watched George eat his food, avoiding her pleading gaze. "You have no reason for being there."

Zo had an idea. "I do have a reason, though. I'll be right back." She scurried to the storage room and opened the back door. Jake's hubcap was still sitting next to the garbage bin. Grabbing it, she hustled into the store. She held up the dented automobile part. "See? His hubcap. It fell off the day of the book signing. I need to bring it back to him."

Max examined the part.

"I think it's vintage."

"It's something," Max muttered. "What about the store?"

"Harley's working tomorrow," said Zo. "After I open, I'm free all day."

"Fine," Max agreed. "I'll see you in the morning."

Zo smiled a goodbye.

After he was gone, she put on *The Perry Como Christmas Album*. Sure, it was early, but she had more holiday boxes to sort. And she needed inspiration for her charity drive. Sorting through last year's merchandise, she considered her options. Her customers were generous and always willing to give back to the community, but Zo wanted to give them something for their thoughtfulness.

Unhappy with his dinner, George peered into the box, his long orange paws dangling over the side. She scratched his ears. "What do you think? Do you see anything good in here?"

His answer was yes, a holiday pillow. He tried to make a bed of it before she grabbed him and placed him on her lap. Under the pillow was a box of red-and-white mugs that had been incredibly popular last year. In curly font it read, "A hug in every mug." That gave her an idea.

"Mugs for hugs!" she said aloud.

George meowed and jumped off her lap.

Zo donated to an organization that helped foster children with supplies such as skateboards and duffel bags. They were small items but made a big difference to kids who were used to dragging their clothes from place to place in garbage bags. For every twenty dollars customers donated to the organization, Zo would give them a holiday hug mug. If she ordered them in bulk, she would receive a discount on the price.

She darted upstairs to grab her laptop, returning seconds later. With an hour before the store closed and no customers, she had plenty of time to start her "Spirit of the Season" column. In an inspired burst, she wrote quickly, sketching out the idea for the holiday drive. She moved on to the theater and library, not stopping until she hit the police station, a blank in her Word doc. She would need to talk to Brady before finishing. With nothing more to do tonight, she shut her laptop, locked the door, and turned the sign to CLOSED.

Chapter Twenty-One

Tuesday morning, when Zo came down to open Happy Camper, Melissa Morris was waiting for her. Wearing a long-sleeved shirt, puffy vest, and curly ponytail, she looked like the busy but efficient mom she was. The Visitor Center across the street was lucky to count her as an employee, for she knew everything about Spirit Canyon. If a visitor needed information, Melissa was the gal to give it—and receive it. She was always fun to talk to, if a little bit of a gossip.

"The girls and I saw Justin's broadcast last night," Melissa sympathized. "We couldn't believe what he said about Happy Camper."

Zo unlocked the door, and Melissa followed. The "girls" were Melissa's three daughters. Zo always thought of them as a singular unit because that's how Melissa talked about them. "I know. I can't imagine what he'll say during Friday's special report."

"Can't you do something to prevent it from airing?" Melissa asked.

Zo switched on the lights. "I don't know what I could do. Besides, what can he say? Marianne had her book signing here, yes, and her body *was* found near the store. But what do those two things really have to do with her death? There's no connection."

Melissa's eyebrows disappeared under her bangs. "Still, it doesn't sound good."

Zo flipped on her computer and sighed. "I know."

"Is there anything I can do to help?"

"You could tie him up in the basement of the Visitor Center," Zo said with a smile. "Just until Friday night."

"As fun as that sounds, I don't think my husband would go for that—or my eldest daughter. She watches the news every night and has a terrible crush on him." Melissa shook her head. "Unbelievable, right?"

"Not really," said Zo. "He's good-looking guy and popular with the girls."

A knock came from outside, and Melissa checked at the window. "Oh man. It's Tiffany Snow. She's at the Visitor Center. I'm sure she's there to sell me one of those dang wreaths. Doesn't she get that I have kids? I buy enough of that crap from them. Most of my paychecks go to overpriced candles and tasteless cookie dough."

"The woman's relentless." Zo told Melissa about the Halloween parade and her kids not wearing costumes. They looked miserable.

"It doesn't surprise me," said Melissa. "She and I sparred off once about the Easter Bunny. I told her to keep her ideas to herself. I don't care what the occasion is. Any time is the right time for a crème-filled chocolate egg."

"I agree one hundred percent."

The knocking became more insistent. Tiffany hollered out Melissa's name.

"If I were you, I'd check into *her* whereabouts the night of Marianne's death." Melissa adjusted the purse on her shoulder. "If she knew Marianne was a witch, there's no telling what she might have done to stop her from poisoning her children's precious brains."

"You think so?"

"I *know* so," said Melissa. "When it come to her kids, she's the worst kind of zealot. The overprotective kind." She grabbed the door handle.

"Thanks for stopping by," said Zo. "We'll talk later—after she leaves."

With a smile, Melissa was gone, and Zo finished opening the store, but all the while, her mind was on Tiffany and Melissa's remarks about her. It was hard to imagine any person being that overprotective of their kids. Did Tiffany really believe Marianne was a danger to her family? Even if she did, the world was full of threats. Tiffany couldn't protect her kids from every one of them.

Yet, the night of Marianne's death, Tiffany was at Spirits & Spirits—alone. She was selling holiday wreaths. Maybe she and Marianne had a confrontation about the book or even the wreaths. Tiffany wasn't at the store long before she left in a huff. She could have met up with Marianne on the way home. If they had a fight, she might have knocked her unconscious, leaving her for dead. Plus Tiffany was the type of person who would add the witch hat, making Marianne look like an evil person.

The door opened, and Harley and Max walked in. They must have arrived at the same time, for they were in mid-conversation.

Harley changed topics when she spotted Zo. "One, yes I saw the broadcast. Everyone I know has asked me about it. And two, where did you get that scarf?"

Zo touched the gold and blue scarf in her hair, tied into a short ponytail. She loved how the material looked with her gold hoop earrings. "At the Cut Hut. They just unpacked a new box of them. I saw a bright purple one with your name on it."

"I'm so stopping after work." Harley took off her jacket.

"Sorry, no forest green, though," Zo said to Max with a smile.

"That's okay," said Max. "Are you ready?"

"Yes." Zo told Harley her plans to return the hubcap. "I'll be back this afternoon. Do you want me to pick up lunch?"

"I brought my own." Harley held up a tiny cooler.

"Your car or mine?" Zo asked Max.

"Let's take your bike," suggested Max. "Do you mind?"

Zo tried to conceal her surprise. Her attempts must have failed because Max followed up with a laugh.

"What?" he said. "It's a gorgeous morning, and Jake lives in the canyon."

She grabbed her helmet from underneath the counter as well as the dented hubcap. "I have no problem taking the bike. I want to get it out as much as I can before the snow flies. Do you need a helmet?"

"No, I borrowed Duncan's. It's in the truck."

A drive through the canyon could be chilly, so she picked up her leather jacket from the backroom before heading outside. She shrugged it on, glad she'd worn her jeans and knee-high boots.

"Sorry to say, I just have my forest ranger-approved green with me." Max grabbed the helmet.

"I like it." He looked adorable in the insulated forest ranger coat. It made him look softer, less serious. "How do you know Jake lives in the canyon?" said Zo, fastening the hubcap to the back of the bike. She slid on her helmet.

He showed her his phone. On it was a picture of the temporary protection order.

"Brady served it yesterday," said Max. "Not without fanfare either. Jake made a big stink at the station. I told Brady I would swing by Jake's house this morning to remind him of the stipulations."

"I suppose you didn't tell him I was going with you."

"I might have left that part out," said Max with a smile, flashing a set of straight, white teeth. They were a nice contrast to his new beard.

"I'm proud of you." Zo flipped down her helmet visor and hopped on the bike. "Rule bending, bike rides—what's next? A tattoo?"

He sat behind her. "Let's not get ahead of ourselves. Besides, I'm scared of needles."

"You're kidding." She started the engine. "A big strong forest ranger like yourself, scared of needles? I don't believe it."

"It's true. They hurt."

Her laughter trailed behind them as they headed out of town toward the canyon. Passing under the rocky arc was like entering a different world, one without consistent phone, internet, or satellite service. When tourists wanted to get away from it all, they came here. This time of year, with the fall colors fading from yellow to brown, it was worth disconnecting. Just five minutes in the fresh mountain air lifted her spirits, and despite her worries about Justin and the store, the longer she drove, the more she started feeling like herself again.

Being in the canyon fortified her spirits. It always did. From the time she was a young girl, zooming to Spirit Canyon Lodge on her ten-speed bike, she felt as if she could do anything after a ride through the canyon. It was the strength of the place. It transformed everything it touched. Even visitors.

She wondered if Max felt something as well. Maybe that's why he mentioned taking the bike. He was determined to be professional, but out here in the canyon, she wanted him to let go a little. To forget he was a responsible forest ranger. She made a quick decision, not slowing down when she went around a familiar pass. That's all it took for him to grab on to her waist as the motorcycle hugged the curvy road. Close together, they flew around the pass, Zo not thinking about anything except the beautiful fall day and the feel of his hands around her.

She kept up the speed all the way to Jake's house, a ranch surrounded by a circle of half-dead trees. Two old cars in different states of repair were parked near the house, and Jake himself was under the hood of the Chevy. He wore jeans and a flannel shirt and put his hand up to his brow to shield his eyes from the sun when he heard them drive up. Clouds were coming in from the west, but for now, the sun was still bright, high in the sky.

"What can I help you with?" Jake hollered.

They removed their helmets and dismounted the bike. Zo grabbed the hubcap. "This fell off your car the other day at Happy Camper. I wanted to return it."

Jake walked over, wiping his hands on his jeans. "Thanks. Things are always falling off that car." He spied a glance at Max. "Who are you?"

"I'm Max Harrington, a Law Enforcement Officer for Black Hills National Forest. I rode along to remind you of Nikki Ainsworth's protection order."

Jake let out a guffaw. "You don't need to remind me. I hate that woman. I was only collecting what is rightfully mine. After all the money my ex-wife squandered on the theater, the least Nikki could do is give me the seat."

"You'll have a chance to tell your side of the story in thirty days, at trial," Max explained. "Until then, please keep your distance from Ms. Ainsworth."

Jake pointed at Zo. "You were there. Tell him I didn't do anything wrong."

"I didn't hear the entire conversation," said Zo. "But you seemed upset."

"Look at that fancy theater." Jake wiped his brow with a handkerchief he retrieved from his back pocket. "She's like a queen on her throne, giving orders. I won't stand for it."

Max crossed his arms. "You will stand for it, or you'll face up to a year in jail or a two thousand dollar fine or both."

Jake pressed his lips together into a belligerent pout. "Is that all, Officer?"

"One question, then I'll let you get back to your work," said Max. "Where were you the night Marianne died?"

"I already answered that." Jake squinted at Max's uniform. "Are you sure you're a cop?"

"Just answer the question," pressed Max.

Zo was upset for Max. It was bad enough when Brady challenged his authority but this guy? He had no right to question Max.

"I was with my daughter, Emily."

"All night?" asked Zo.

He pointed a stubby finger in her direction. "I might have to answer his questions, but I don't have to answer yours, girly. Justin Castle says it's no coincidence Marianne was found at your store, and I believe him. He's got a report coming on Friday, and you'd better believe I'll be watching. The whole town will, so careful what you say about me."

Zo felt a surge of anger rush to her head. She took a step closer to him. "Is that a threat?"

Max stepped between her and Jake. "Thank you for your time, and remember what I said about Ms. Ainsworth."

A smug smile crept up on Jake's lips as Max linked his arm in Zo's and led her to the motorcycle.

"You're just going to let him get away with threatening me?" said Zo.

"He knows who you are, and you're not supposed to be asking questions. I am."

She handed him his helmet. "I didn't realize I rated so low on your scale of protection."

"I'm pretty sure you can protect yourself. You've told me so a million times." He leaned in closer. "The reason I didn't react is because of Happy Camper. With one call to Justin, he could make the special report even more *special*."

Max was right. Jake was eager to mention Justin's special report on Happy Camper. What if the whole town felt the way he did? What if they were convinced she was involved after the show aired? "What am I going to do?" she asked with a groan. She hopped on the bike.

Max took a seat behind her. "You're going to drive back to Spirit Canyon, at the speed limit, and we're going to talk this through. If that doesn't work, you're going to summon help from the other side at tonight's Zodiac meeting."

When she didn't respond, he poked her waist. "Hey, that was a joke."

"It needs work," said Zo, but she relaxed her shoulders. It felt good to have him near.

Chapter Twenty-Two

After closing the store, Zo and Harley set up the table Zo used for special events. Jules wanted to use it for the séance because Marianne signed books at the same table. As it turned out, the night was too cloudy for stargazing, and most of the Zodiac Club wouldn't be attending the meeting. Gatherings would be hit-and-miss from now until spring. Tonight, Jules encouraged people who believed in the hereafter to join. Nonbelievers, according to Jules, would disrupt her psychic energy and should stay home.

Zo decided she was a believer. Too many odd occurrences had happened to be coincidences. First the planner, then the black cat statue, George's collar, and finally Roberto's book. Marianne was trying to tell her something; she just had to figure out what that was.

"Tell me why I can't stay again?" Harley pulled her cross-body purse over her head.

"Because Jules says nonbelievers break the circle of communication," said Zo, placing candles on the table. "Marianne won't be comfortable with your presence."

"Jules can say anything she wants." Harley swiped her heavy bangs to the side. "Marianne liked me. You know she did."

"I know." Zo smiled. "Who wouldn't like you?"

Max knocked on the door.

Harley pointed at him. "If I can't come, he can't."

"He's not." She opened the door. Max was wearing a black thermal shirt and black jeans. Except for his light hair, he blended into the hazy night. "Hey Max. What are you doing here?"

"The better question is why does Duncan get to come to your séance and not me?"

"Seriously?" said Harley, still looking at Zo. "It would be my one-and-only chance to hold hands with the guy."

"First of all, it's not my séance," Zo explained. "It's Jules's thing. She makes the rules. Second, Duncan is a musician. He's more...open to suggestion than you are."

"*I'm* open to suggestion," Max insisted. "One hundred percent open." He emphasized each word separately.

Jules walked in as he was declaring his openness. She was wearing a purple dress and black headscarf that hung to her waist. "You're as closed as a clam, Max Harrington. Both of you need to leave before you sully the energy."

Zo loved how certain she was of everything, including the uncertain.

Duncan breezed in behind Jules wearing a leather jacket. He gave Zo a wink. "Hey Zo."

Max threw up his hands. "It's the coat, isn't it?"

Zo took Max's arm and walked him to the parking lot. Harley followed. "I would love to have you guys here. You know I would. Come back in an hour. I'll give you all the details."

Harley's brow puckered.

"I promise," said Zo.

"Fine," Max agreed. "One hour."

"I have a test to study for," said Harley, "but I want all the details when I come in to work tomorrow."

"You got it." Zo turned to go inside. During her side conversation with Max and Harley, the rest of the participants had arrived. Hattie and Zo's ex-boyfriend Hunter were there, as well as a man Jules described as her *doorkeeper*. He would keep evil spirits from entering the conversation.

Jules gathered up people's phones, temporarily, and placed them under the counter. Then she shut off the lights. A small side lamp illuminated the area.

"Friends, you know why we're here," Jules announced as she lit the candles on the table. She tucked the lighter in her dress pocket. "To gather information from our dear friend Marianne about the night of her death. It's important for Marianne to feel welcome and to join us at her leisure. Don't overwhelm her with side questions. I will lead the conversation. Does anyone have questions before we begin?"

Hattie pointed to Jules's water glass. "What's that for?"

"Communication," said Jules. "Sometimes it's easier for the dead to communicate through an object. Any other questions?" When all was silent, Jules asked them to join hands to create a circle. After a moment, she said, "Marianne Morgan, we are gathered here tonight in hopes that you'll join us. Please feel welcome to enter our circle whenever you're ready."

Zo waited for a rush of energy. She was disappointed to feel nothing. She glanced at Jules, who had her eyes closed. Zo took a breath, shut her eyes, and cleared her mind. She wanted this to work. She *needed* this to work to exonerate herself and her store. So many odd occurrences had happened; Marianne had to be giving her signs. If she could just give her a few more, possibly in the direction of her killer, Zo would be forever grateful.

The water splashed, and Zo opened her eyes. Everyone was staring at the glass of water in front of Jules.

"If you are present, Marianne, let it be known by moving the water once more."

A splash landed on the tablecloth, and Zo's heart knocked in her chest. She wasn't afraid of ghosts. Heck, she'd grown up with the idea in Spirit Canyon. But to know that one was in her presence? That was a little different.

"Thank you for joining us, Marianne," said Jules. "We're glad you are with us. When you're ready, we'd like to ask you a few questions about your death." The candles flickered wildly. "Take your time," said Jules. "We understand it's difficult."

Sitting next to her, Duncan squeezed her hand. Until then, Zo didn't realize how strongly she'd been gripping his.

The flickering subsided, and Jules continued with her questions. "Dear sister witch and friend, were you murdered? Move the water if the answer is yes."

The water splashed. Zo pressed her lips together to keep from gasping. She knew Marianne was murdered; the police knew Marianne was murdered. But to have her confirm it was unreal.

"Who did this terrible thing to you?" asked Jules.

A flurry of activity ensued. One candle went out, and a nearby Halloween decoration fell off the clearance table. Sitting on the other side of Zo, Hattie arched a gray eyebrow.

"I'm sorry," said Jules. "That was a poorly worded question. Was the murderer someone you know? If the answer is yes, indicate with water."

The water sloshed in the glass.

"Good," said Jules. "Was it someone you argued with?"

The water moved again.

"Was it someone you disliked?"

Nothing happened, so Jules continued. "Was it someone you liked?"

"I don't think that's a fair question," Hunter interrupted. "How could she like someone after they killed her?"

Jules's eyes narrowed on Hunter. "I'm asking the questions. Don't break the energy with skepticism."

"It's not skepticism," argued Hunter. "It's input—informed input. I've done quite a bit of research on dreams, apparitions, and myths."

"Then you know to keep your mouth shut," Jules ground out.

The room cooled. Zo glanced down at her arms, where she could see goosebumps. It wasn't her imagination.

Jules took a breath and continued. "Let's try another question. How did you die?"

The water swirled in the glass, and the glass tumbled over. As the water streamed toward him, Duncan jerked back, breaking the circle. "Sorry about that," Duncan apologized. "I was just a little surprised, that's all."

Everyone joined hands again, but the energy was gone. It was as if the last fifteen minutes hadn't happened. Jules thanked Marianne for coming, but Zo knew she was gone already. Nothing moved or flickered or indicated that she was still with them.

They released hands but stayed at the table.

"Well, Marianne was definitely murdered," said Hattie.

"By someone she knew," Zo added. "Which doesn't exactly narrow it down…"

"It does," surmised Duncan. "We know she wasn't murdered by a random serial killer."

"We knew that already," said Hunter.

"Maybe if you wouldn't have opened up your big trap, we'd know even more," Duncan argued.

Zo bit back a smile. Hunter did have a big trap. It was one of the reasons they'd broken up. He loved talking about himself and not much else.

"Maybe if you had worn less cologne, she would have stayed longer," retorted Hunter. "Zo has to be ready to pass out."

Actually, she was enjoying Duncan's cologne, albeit a little strong for her taste. The musky scent was nice.

"Boys, please act like adults," Hattie instructed. "I'm just glad she showed up at all. Truth be known, I was a little skeptical when we first started. I've never been to one of these things." She slid her red glasses to the top of her head. Her hair stood up like gray spikes. "I've read about them, though."

Zo stood to grab a towel. She needed to wipe up the water before it stained her tablecloth. What she saw in the store window froze her in place. It was Justin Castle and his cameraman, Mark. Justin pointed to the camera and smiled. They had recorded the entire session.

If Zo could have disappeared into the netherworld with Marianne, she would have, for she knew exactly what this meant for her and the store. Part of her, a very small part, believed Justin wouldn't air it, that it was against his ethics. The other part of her, the ninety-nine percent, knew he didn't have a moral fiber in his being. He *made* news; he didn't just report it. If there was a way to get tonight's séance into his broadcast, he would make it happen.

"We have company," Zo muttered.

"You should have let Max stay," said Duncan. "He could have arrested him or something."

"That's exactly what I was thinking." Zo's eyes didn't leave the window. She marched up to the door and flung it open. "What do you want?"

"Well, well," said Justin. "The most *interesting* things happen at this store."

"What are you doing here?" Zo asked.

"A friend told me the Zodiac Club was meeting here tonight," explained Justin. "I'm thinking about joining."

Zo checked her camper wall clock. "It's over, and you weren't invited."

He gave her a fake frown. "I'm crushed." He crossed his arms and leaned closer. "Tell me. Did Marianne *say* anything?"

"I'm not telling you a thing," said Zo. "You'll have to make something up for the ten o'clock newscast."

He tilted his head. "If you insist. Come on, Mark. Pack it up."

She slammed the door in his face.

"You shouldn't have done that," said Jules, blowing out the remaining candle. "It's going to come back to haunt you."

"He'll have to get in line," said Zo. "I have enough spirits chasing me."

Duncan laughed.

"Don't encourage her," said Jules. "It's bad business to make enemies. That's what got *you* into trouble this year."

Duncan's look soured.

Hattie stood. "Jules is right. Justin knows he can get to you, Zo. That's why he does it. He's been gunning for you since Memorial Day. Everybody loved that story."

Hunter took Zo's hand and kissed it. "Patience has never been one of your attributes, love."

"And humility has never been one of yours." Zo yanked her hand back and wiped the water off the tablecloth, folding it into a square for laundering.

She tucked it under her arm. "When I was a journalist and someone said 'no comment,' I took it to mean 'no comment.' It was the safest response. With Justin, it's just the opposite."

"Spirit Canyon is a small town." Hattie helped Zo put back the chairs. "Ninety-nine percent of the time nothing happens here. Reporting the news is an uphill climb." Seeing Zo's glare, she added, "I'm not defending him. I think his actions are unconscionable. But you have it easier with your Happy Camper column."

Zo didn't disagree. It was probably why her column was so popular. People came to Spirit Canyon to get away from the news. It was a vacation destination, but it didn't give Justin the right to slander someone's good name or store. She glanced around. Happy Camper was her home, and while that might not mean a lot to Justin Castle, it meant a heck of a lot to her. Houses were just buildings. A home was somewhere you felt safe, secure, and loved. Happy Camper had become that for her. And no one would take it away.

After Hunter folded the table and returned it to the storage room, Hattie left. So did Hunter and the doorkeeper. When Zo realized she was alone with Jules and Duncan, she knew it was the perfect time to pitch Duncan's musical concert. She nonchalantly picked up the fallen Halloween mask. "My column is due this Friday. Duncan had a neat idea for your store. Has he told you?"

Duncan mouthed the words, "thank you."

Jules scanned Zo with tawny eyes. It felt as if she were reading Zo's mind. "What idea?"

Zo gestured to Duncan to continue.

"I'd like to do a holiday concert," said Duncan. "The money raised could go toward charity."

"How does it fit with the theme of the store?" asked Jules.

Jules was doing calculations in her head. Did the event jibe with her business? Would it raise lots of money for charity? Would it be smart for her bottom line?

"People like to sip drinks and listen to music," said Duncan. "You serve the wine. I'll play guitar. We could call it Sips and Swings."

"I like it," said Zo. "It's catchy."

"What do you think?" Duncan asked Jules.

She looked between Zo and Duncan. "I think you two could be a very dangerous combination." She tossed her handbag over her shoulder. "But I like the idea. You can add it to the column, Zo."

"Thanks, Jules," said Duncan. "You won't regret it."

She threw a glance over her shoulder. "I'd better not."

Duncan flashed her one of his megawatt smiles. "Wait up."

Jules flittered a hand in the air. "I'm not walking you home." She let the door close behind her.

Duncan grabbed his leather jacket. "That went so much better than I thought it would. Thank you."

"Don't mention it," Zo said. "It's going to be a great event."

"So is it true what Max says?" Duncan zipped his coat. "Do you really dig guys in leather jackets?"

She wished she had somewhere to look besides his playful eyes, but she wasn't going to give him the satisfaction of looking away. "I can't deny it. They seem to be my type."

"What about Max? Is he your type?"

Zo evaded the question. The last person she was going to discuss her love life with was Duncan Hall. "I don't think he owns a leather jacket."

He touched her chin. "Your eyes betray you, Zo. I can see how much you care."

They stood like that for a moment, eyes locked. Zo decided Jules was right. They were a dangerous combination. Zo was attracted to Duncan like a child to a cookie jar. It was instinctual and bad for her health.

A noise at the window broke the spell. They turned to look. It was Max, tapping on the glass.

"Speak of the devil," said Duncan.

Max walked in. "I hope I'm not interrupting."

"I was just leaving." Duncan patted Max's shoulder. "We're getting you a leather coat, buddy."

"What was that about?" said Max when Duncan left.

"Rawhide," said Zo. "Plain and simple." That's what she was telling herself anyway.

"What happened at the séance?" asked Max.

"Can I tell you upstairs, over a glass of wine?" asked Zo. "It's been a long night." A glass of wine with Max was just what she needed to relax.

He agreed, and she shut off the lights and locked the door, happy to put the spirits to rest for the evening.

Chapter Twenty-Three

Wednesday morning Officer Brady came to Happy Camper—again. This time his visit wasn't about Nikki. It was about her and last night's séance. Justin Castle aired it on the six a.m. news. Zo was thankful she'd missed it until Brady told her the details of the account: the black store, the burning candles, the circle of hands. It sounded like something out of a horror film. The truth was it was a request for information from the other side, nothing like what Brady described. She could imagine how Justin had twisted the scene to make it as provoking as possible.

"At least not many people are up that early," said Zo, trying to look on the bright side. She plated George's tuna fish, placing it on the floor behind the register. George stared at it from the pile of books on the counter. If she thought he would stoop to eating on the floor, she was dead wrong. Zo took the plate and set it on the counter.

"Oh, he said it would run again at noon and ten." Brady checked his Timex. "It'll be on again in about an hour."

"It figures," muttered Zo. She'd have to tune in this time.

"So I have to ask you, did Marianne…say anything?"

Zo could feel her jaw slacken with surprise.

Brady coughed. "For my report, of course, I have to ask."

He didn't *have* to ask. He was just as suspicious as the rest of the town. Superstition cloaked the city like a thin fog, settling into cracks and crevices too small to see. For some reason, Zo thought being a cop made him immune to it. But anyone in the canyon was susceptible. "She said she knew the person who killed her."

He frowned, putting an elbow on the counter. "Any mention of a purse?"

"Whose purse?" Zo asked. "Marianne's? Is it missing?"

"I guess she didn't," said Brady. "Never mind."

"You brought it up."

The curiosity left his face, and he stood taller. "Yes I did, and now I'm changing the subject."

He'd drawn an imaginary line in their conversation, but she wasn't afraid to cross it. Their history wasn't all sunshine and rainbows, but it was genuine. In Spirit Canyon, that meant something. "Come on, Officer Merrigan. This store means everything to me. If you know something about Marianne that could clear the store, you should tell me."

His face didn't change, but his shoulders lowered. "Yes, her purse is missing. Her death appears to be a robbery gone wrong."

It was an interesting idea, but it didn't make sense. Marianne said she knew her killer. Thefts were random, at least the ones she'd followed at the newspaper. "How could that be?"

"A lot of tourists were in town for Spirit Spooktacular," Brady continued. "It's possible that a purse snatcher came up behind her on her way home. They struggled. It got violent. He knocked her in the head, stole the purse, and left her on the street."

Zo understood money was involved, but a purse snatcher? She didn't think so. The reason was more personal. "There could be another reason her purse is missing."

"I'm all ears."

"I don't know." Zo shrugged. "It's just that we don't have a lot of robberies in Spirit Canyon. Plus, why would the robber disguise Marianne as a witch?"

"To give himself more time to get away," explained Brady. "It obviously worked. She'd been dead awhile when you found her."

The decorations, the fog, the clock striking midnight. Recalling the evening made Zo shiver. She wouldn't easily forget the sight.

George strode across the counter, breaking the silence that had fallen between them. Brady leaned over to give him a scratch. "I saw this little guy was stranded near the waterfall. It's surprising what makes the news in this town."

Little guy? Did he mean the giant impasse near his face? "He was. Thank goodness for Max Harrington."

Brady blinked. "Saving animals is part of Max's job."

"Not domestic animals," said Zo, petting George. "He went out of his way to help us."

"Out of the way describes it, all right," grumbled Brady. "I'd rather he stayed in the forest and out of my investigations."

Brady didn't appreciate Max's fifteen minutes of fame. Cops in small towns could be undervalued and rarely made the news. When they did make the news, it was because they did something wrong or didn't do enough or didn't do it fast enough. In Marianne's case, for instance, Justin was doing his own investigative reporting since the case was at a standstill.

"You know what they say, 'two heads are better than one.'" Zo gave Brady a smile.

"You have enough cute sayings in here, Ms. Jones. I don't think you need to recite them out loud." He touched his cowboy hat. "I'll be in touch."

After he left, she noticed the tuna was still on George's food dish. It was the second time he hadn't finished his meal in as many days. Maybe he didn't like the new brand. For a tramp, he was incredibly finicky. "What's the matter with you? Are you on a diet?"

His only response was a nip on her hand. He was not only done with his food but also her petting.

Zo switched on the old Magnavox in the backroom, waiting for Justin's noonday report. Until then, she restocked her Happy Camper line, which had been depleted during Spirit Spooktacular. She was putting out fall notepads when she heard Justin's report from the backroom. Leaving the stock, she rushed to see if it was as bad as Brady claimed. Twenty seconds later, she decided it was. It was hard to make out the participants, because the room was cloaked in darkness, but her face was as clear as a mountain morning. With her eyes closed, holding the others' hands, Zo imagined anyone seeing the broadcast would assume she was a witch or into black magic of some kind. Never mind it was Jules's modus operandi.

The screen changed, and Justin's face appeared. "Did Zo Jones make contact with Marianne on the other side? Did she explain what happened that fateful day of her book signing? Find out on Friday's special report."

She switched off the TV. Someone had entered the store—Cunningham. He must have come directly from school because he was wearing a brown corduroy jacket with suede elbow patches. Plus he had a dusting of chalk on his sleeve.

"This is an unexpected surprise," said Zo. "What are you doing here?" She had an idea. If there was any time a teacher needed a friend, it was November.

"I'm quitting my job," he proclaimed. "This spring, it's goodbye cruel words."

She picked up her box of notepads. "I think you mean *world*."

"No, I mean words." Cunningham gave George a bow. "Good afternoon, St. George. How would you feel about performing another miracle? I need you to make something disappear."

George squinted at him. He was looking curiously at Cunningham's messy stack of hair. Maybe Cunningham had resorted to pulling it out.

"The papers?" asked Zo.

"Of course it's the papers," said Cunningham. "When isn't it the papers? I can't keep up. I'm only one man."

A man with an aversion to grading. "You said the same thing last year. Hang in there. You only have a month to go before winter break."

"I'll be dead in a month," claimed Cunningham. "Buried in run-on sentences."

"Who cares as long as they're writing." She refilled the pencil box next to the notepads. "You're a literature teacher, not the grammar police. Don't take the errors so seriously."

"How can you say that?" asked Cunningham. "You were a journalist."

She gave him a sideways glance. "One whose job was cut because of the decline of the written word. Keep teaching, Cunningham. We need you. *They* need you." She handed him a journal. On the cover was printed YOU ARE THE AUTHOR OF YOUR LIFE STORY. MAKE IT A GOOD ONE. "This is on the house."

"Thank you, Zo. I know why I came in here now." He took a breath. "I feel better already."

"It's the pumpkin spice," she said with a smile. It wafted through the store in the fall. "I'm glad you stopped by anyway. I wanted to ask you about college admissions."

He tilted his head to one side. "You've decided to enroll in my class this spring, haven't you?"

She laughed. "No. I'm wondering how a student would know he's been accepted to college before the acceptance letters have gone out. He's already talking to a coach about next summer."

Cunningham let out a huff. "Athletic departments. A student should be allowed in on academic merit only. Period."

"That's the thing. I don't think this student has merit or talent." She leaned in. "The coach is from a water polo team, and we don't have any leagues in the area."

"Money is driving the deal, plain and simple."

"How?" asked Zo.

"The parents probably donated a good deal of money, on or off the books. Are they wealthy?"

By the looks of the Salvo house they were. She nodded.

"I thought so," said Cunningham. "It's a sad fact of college life. It's getting more attention than it used to, but still not enough in my opinion."

Money, again. It kept cropping up. Marianne had a ripped check in her hand. Could it have been Roberto's check to the university? Marianne might have confronted Roberto about his donations to the college, attempting to destroy the latest payment. In his attempts to retrieve it, he could have hit her.

Zo shook her head. Roberto seemed to care for Marianne. Could he really hurt her? Maybe not, but his son Alex could. Alex had words with Marianne at the book signing, he laughed at her. He wasn't afraid to confront her—or burn her book.

Furthermore, Brady said Marianne's purse was missing. Could her death really be a robbery gone awry? Zo doubted it but needed to pursue any idea that might clear the store before Friday's broadcast. If she could entertain the notion of a séance, surely she could entertain the notion of a robbery.

"Hold the door, Harley," said Cunningham. "I'm headed in that direction."

Zo bid Cunningham goodbye. She was glad to see Harley, even if she was dressed in all black. "How was the test?"

"Terrible," said Harley. "I hate geography. How was the séance?"

"Terrible," Zo repeated. "You can see a recap of it on Justin Castle's evening broadcast."

Harley unwrapped her scarf. It was black like her outfit. "You're kidding."

"I wish."

"What are you going to do?" asked Harley.

"Now that you're here, I'm leaving for *Canyon Views*." She shrugged on her leather jacket. "Harriet might be able to help."

Harley wished her luck, and Zo headed toward the small 1970s building two blocks from Main Street. Harriet Hobbs was Zo's newspaper editor and friend. They'd met several years ago when Zo was working at the *Black Hills Star*. She was the one who'd suggested the Happy Camper column when Zo opened the store. She knew it would be a perfect fit. "It'll keep you sane" were her exact words. Going cold turkey would be too much for a ten-year veteran in the business. A column that supported her interests was just what Zo needed, and Harriet gave it to her.

That was her last and only favor. Zo grinned as she opened the door to the newspaper office. Even though Zo's column was for entertainment purposes, Harriet still had exacting standards. *Canyon Views* was her baby. It relayed the flavor of the Black Hills and was everybody's favorite local read. If something was happening in the area, Harriet knew about it—or wanted to know about it. Hers was a revolving door of information.

Harriet sat at her oversized desk, chewing Big Red gum. Zo knew the brand because it's what Harriet chewed since she quit smoking several years ago. Zo thought of her every time she smelled cinnamon.

Harriet spotted Zo the moment she entered the office. Little went unnoticed by her hawk-like eyes. "I hear you're in the witchcraft business now," she said as Zo approached her desk. The creases from her smile were the only wrinkles on her smooth brown skin. Despite being fifty, she didn't have a deep line on her face. "I've been thinking of changing your column to the Creepy Camper—just for Halloween."

Zo fell into the chair across from her. "It was bad, wasn't it?" She desperately wanted to hear that it wasn't.

"Yes, but not as bad as Friday's report will be."

Zo moaned. Harriet wasn't the person to go to for warm fuzzies. "I need to figure out what happened before my reputation goes up in a puff of spiritual smoke."

"Any ideas?"

"Brady Merrigan thinks Marianne might have been killed during a robbery," said Zo. "Her purse is missing. Were any other robberies reported that night?"

Harriet turned her oversized computer monitor toward Zo. "It's easy enough for your number one editor to find out." Her red nails clicked on the keys. A page of police calls populated the screen. "A few domestic disputes, neighbor complaints, pumpkin smashers. I don't see any thefts." She scrolled through a few more pages. "What else do you have?"

"Even if it wasn't a robbery, money was somehow involved." Zo told her about finding a ripped check in Marianne's hand.

"Who was she paying in the middle of the night? And for what?" Harriet rotated her monitor, ready to do some more searching.

"Possibly her ex-husband, Jake," said Zo. "Nikki says Marianne supported him during their marriage, and he doesn't have a job."

"If anyone had dirt on her, it would be her ex." Harriet tapped her fingertips. "It's possible she didn't want it surfacing before her national book tour."

It was an interesting notion, one Zo hadn't considered. It made her think of another. "The other possibility is Tiffany Snow."

Harriet stopped snapping her gum. "The PTA mom who sells those wreaths for Christmas?"

Zo put her elbows on the desk. "Hear me out. Tiffany had a fistful of checks at the book signing, and she claimed Marianne's book was demonic, a bad influence on children. She said her daughter mistakenly picked it up because of its cute cover."

Harriet leveled a look at her.

"Plus she was very chummy with Marianne's boyfriend, Roberto, at the Halloween parade. Her husband was nowhere to be seen." Zo paused for emphasis. "He doesn't like social events, despite being married to the queen of community service."

"Now we're getting somewhere." Harriet returned to her computer. "Why was Roberto at the parade in the first place? His girlfriend just died."

"His son graduates in the spring," explained Zo. "It's his last Spirit Spooktacular before he goes off to college."

Harriet acknowledged the statement with a mumble. She was too busy reading to respond properly. Whatever she found must have been interesting because she kept nodding at the screen as if having a conversation with it. Zo wished Harriet would have kept the monitor pointed in her direction. Finally, Harriet turned the monitor. A young girl wearing a sleeveless shirt, ripped jeans, and heavy black lipstick populated the screen. Several teens stood behind her. The blog caption read, "The Sisters of the Undead."

"Interesting, Harriet, but hardly the time for a look back at Goth subculture."

Harriet pointed to the girl in the center. "That's Tiffany Turner, or as we know her, Tiffany Snow. Turner was her maiden name, according to the blog."

"Get out of here." Zo moved closer to the screen. She didn't recognize the peppy mom from the book signing, probably because a black veil covered most of her face. With a second look, however, Zo could make out Tiffany's features, but just barely. Tiffany was not only young but thin, too thin. All of the girls looked pale, gaunt, and unhealthy. "What is this?"

"It's a mommy blog." Harriet scrolled down. Other pictures of teens appeared. "It has a history of dangerous 'cult cultures.' It looks as if Tiffany was part of one when she was a teen in Arizona. It made the news when one of the girls took her own life."

"That's terrible," said Zo. Maybe Tiffany was passionate for a good reason. It made sense why she attacked Marianne's book, at least partially. Zo still believed she should have read it first, but maybe it reminded her of her own time in the "Sisters of the Undead." She wouldn't want to read what was inside if the cult had scarred her. Losing a friend to suicide would be unbearable.

"It is terrible, but this mom's doing her best to help other moms recognize the warning signs. Her own daughter is in recovery." Harriet clicked a tab devoted to healing. "Pretty comprehensive, really."

Zo digested the new information, running the scenario out loud. "If Tiffany saw Marianne as a threat, she might have struck her in a moment of passion or defense."

"It might have also been preemptive." A journalist slid a piece of paper in Harriet's bin, and Harriet said, "Wait." She scanned the paragraph and handed it back to the writer. "John belonged to the Elks Club, not the *Elk* Club. The man is dead. Get it right." The journalist slunk back to his desk with his obituary.

Zo reminded herself to reread her Happy Camper column twice before printing it. "What do you mean by preemptive?"

"It's like we were saying earlier." Harriet crossed a leg over a knee. "Only different. Maybe Marianne wasn't paying anyone. Maybe someone was paying *her* for her silence. I can't imagine Tiffany wanting this information spread around Spirit Canyon, especially with her hoity-toity reputation."

Zo could count on Harriet for a different perspective of a story. She had at least two ways of looking at things, and sometimes five or six. "Marianne wouldn't take a bribe, would she?"

Harriet shrugged. "How would we know? We weren't her best friend."

"True." Yet Zo had read her book and been inspired by it. Maybe it was the reader in her, but it was hard to see the author as anyone but a decent human being. She brought other women up, not tore them down. Passing judgment wasn't her style, let alone taking bribes. "Maybe Tiffany tried a bribe, and Marianne wouldn't take it. Maybe that's the reason the check was torn."

"I wouldn't rule anything out," said Harriet. "It's another possibility. That's all I'm saying."

Another possibility was the last thing Zo needed. She needed answers, like two days ago. "Thanks, Harriet. It always helps to talk to you. I'll be in Friday with my column."

"Or earlier," Harriet called after her.

Chapter Twenty-Four

It was two o'clock, and school was in session. Zo could take a trip to the elementary school to find out more about Tiffany. If anyone could get the insider scoop on Tiffany, it was Beth, who was picking up Molly. She sent her a quick text. Could they meet at the school? Her response was short and sweet: "Yes. Bring chocolate."

Thirty minutes later, Zo was meandering through a line of cars with two chocolate eclairs from Honey Buns. Though school wasn't out for another thirty minutes, parents waited in cars, reading magazines or updates on their cell phones.

Zo opened the door of Beth's SUV. "It's like the paparazzi out here." She hopped inside. The warmth of the car was welcome, for the wind had picked up. It had an extra snap to it that said November.

"You do *not* want to be at the end of that line when the kids come out," proclaimed Beth. "You'll be stuck for twenty minutes." She took the bag Zo handed her. "Tell me about Ms. Perfect. You mentioned her in your text."

Zo relayed Tiffany's involvement with the "Sisters of the Undead" while Beth munched on her éclair. "It was a cult, then?" Beth took a tissue from a floral package in her middle console and wiped her hands.

Zo had just taken her first bite, so she nodded.

"I'm shocked," said Beth. "I wouldn't have guessed she was involved in anything like that."

"It can happen to anyone," Zo explained. "That's what this blogger wants other parents to know. She made it her mission to warn them."

"You can't just go up and ask Tiffany about it, though." Beth waved to a parent walking by. "What are you going to say?"

"I'm going to buy a Christmas wreath."

Beth lifted her eyebrows.

"And I want you to come with me." Zo dusted off her hands. "I need a look inside that big manila envelope she always carries. A ripped check might tell me if she was with Marianne the night she was killed. Is she here?"

"Of course she's here." Beth handed her a tissue. "She volunteers every afternoon."

Zo wiped her hands and threw the tissue in the empty sack. "Perfect. Let's go."

Beth gave her a look that said she didn't understand what she was asking. "I'll have to park—in the lot. It will take me a half hour to get out of here."

"Sorry. I'll make it up to you."

"I want one of those Happy Camper mugs, the ones with the fall leaves. Two, actually." Beth smiled. "I need one for Jack."

"Done," agreed Zo.

Beth flipped on her blinker and swung her SUV into the lot. Heads turned as she and Zo walked up the path to the elementary school. The other parents must have been wondering what forced Beth to leave a perfectly good spot in the line. Beth pushed a button, and the school buzzed them in. The secretary waved, forgoing visitor passes. She recognized Beth, and only a few minutes remained of the day. Molly and the rest of the kids would be out soon.

"Molly's in the same class as Tiffany's daughter," explained Beth, leading her down the first hallway. "That's how I know her."

The younger kids already had on their coats. Molly's class was shoving folders into backpacks and zipping them up. When Molly saw them, she came running. She gave Zo a big hug. "What are you doing here Zo?"

"Hello to you, too," muttered Beth. "I'm your mother, remember?"

"Hi, Mom," Molly added.

"I need to buy one of those wreaths from Tiffany." Zo checked the hallway, crowded with kids. "Have you seen her?"

"Mrs. Snow?" Molly pointed to her classroom. "She's inside."

The bell rang, and a wave of kids flooded the hallway. Beth grabbed Molly's backpack and coat from her hook, stopping to say hello to the teacher at the door. Tiffany was inside the classroom, just as Molly had said. She was cleaning off a table with a sanitizing wipe, her daughter waiting next to her—impatiently. It looked as if the kids had done a craft that required a lot of glue.

"Hi Tiffany," greeted Zo. "I never got a chance to order my wreaths. Beth needed to stop in the school, so I figured I'd tag along and see if you were busy."

Tiffany quit wiping the table. "I'm never too busy to sell wreaths."

Molly and Tiffany's daughter chatted while Tiffany grabbed her designer purse from under the teacher's desk. She pulled out the glossy order form. "There are several different options this year: holly, no holly, ribbon, or pinecone."

Zo unfolded the brochure. The options as well as the prices had gone up. She swallowed her reservations. It was for a good cause. "I'll take two with pinecones."

"A classic," said Tiffany. "You can't go wrong with that one. Would you write your name on the back? There's a form." She handed Zo a pen.

Zo was thrilled to find a list of names and addresses of all the people who'd ordered wreaths. All seventy-five lines were nearly filled, so Zo took her time writing out her information. Discreetly, she was scanning the names for Marianne's. Her pen stopped when she found it near the middle of the list. Marianne had ordered a wreath with ribbons. The purchase was listed along with her name and address.

Finished with the teacher, Beth joined them in the classroom, greeting Tiffany with an overly sweet hello. Beth was laying it on thick. Their talk gave Zo a little more time to study the information.

Marianne purchased a wreath the day of the book signing. That had to be important. If Zo could take a peek inside the envelope, it would confirm what she needed to know. The problem was Zo didn't see the envelope. "Do you take checks?"

Tiffany paused her conversation with Beth. "Yes."

Zo took her checkbook out of her backpack, waiting for Tiffany to grab the envelope. Instead she kept talking to Beth. Tiffany needed help with the class holiday party next month and wondered if Beth would be around to help.

"Of course," said Beth. "I'd love to."

Beth's December was scheduled to the hilt. It would be one of Spirit Canyon Lodge's busiest months. Lots of tourists came to the Black Hills to ski, snowmobile, and snowshoe. The last thing Beth needed was to plan a classroom party. Zo gave her a look that conveyed her gratitude as she tore the check from the book. "Do you need me to put it in something, an envelope?"

Tiffany took the check, folded it, and put it into the back pocket of her super skinny jeans. "I have it at home."

Shoot. Zo wouldn't be able to get a look in the envelope after all. Still, she had found Marianne's name, which was something. If only she could get her eyes on the other checks. "My neighbor Cunningham—Russell

Cunningham—might want a wreath if you're looking for more donations. Do you mind stopping by the store some time? He's right next door."

"No problem," agreed Tiffany. "What about you, Beth? How many wreaths do you need for the lodge? I don't think you've ordered." She blinked her curled lashes.

"I don't believe I have." Beth took the form from Zo, not bothering to conceal a glare.

A classroom party and wreaths? Oh, boy. This was going to cost Zo more than mugs.

They were on their way to the middle school to pick up Meg when Zo offered to repay the favor. She promised to contribute prizes to the classroom shindig: miniature writing sets. They contained candy cane pencils and red-and-white paper. With a handful of candy, they would make the perfect party favors.

"Wrapped in cellophane bags." Beth turned down a side street near the middle school. It, too, was busy and lined with cars.

"Done."

"With curly ribbon."

"Of course," said Zo. "What's Christmas without curly ribbon?"

Beth let out a breath, pulling up closer to the school. "I can do this. It's one little party, and I'm great at parties."

That was an understatement. With her years of experience organizing parties at the Waldorf, Beth could throw together a child's party with the wave of her magic hand. The lodge must be really busy for her to second-guess it.

"Uh-oh," said Molly's little voice from the backseat.

"What is it?" Beth asked.

"Meg is in a car—with a boy."

"Where?"

Molly's finger punched the window. "There."

Zo followed the direction of her finger. Molly was right. Meg was sitting next to a boy in a four-door sedan that had seen better days. It didn't look as if anyone else was in the car.

"Megan Elizabeth!" Beth exclaimed. "What are you doing?"

"I don't think she can hear you." Molly's voice was mature and practical.

Zo bit her lip to keep from laughing. Beth was mad as heck. She didn't want to make it worse by laughing at Molly's obvious—but funny—statement.

"That boy has to be in high school." Beth leaned over the middle console. Her chestnut ponytail dipped over one shoulder. "What's he doing over here?"

"I think he's giving her a ride home," explained Molly.

"Oh no he's not." Beth laid on the horn. Several drivers glanced in her direction. One threw up his hands. Beth mouthed the word *sorry.* "Roll down your window, Zo."

It would be better to walk up to the car, but Zo didn't dare refuse the maniac's request. Zo had never seen her like this. In their youth, she was always the calm, sensible one. Now she was a mom on a mission. Zo obeyed and rolled down the window.

"Megan! Get over here this instant."

Molly slunk down in the backseat. Even for a second-grader, her mom's actions were embarrassing. Zo couldn't imagine what Meg was feeling.

When Beth didn't get a response, she put the car in drive, still calling Meg's name out the window. Zo could have sworn Meg saw them, but the car took off in the opposite direction.

"If she thinks she's going for a joy ride with that *dude*, she has another think coming." Beth stepped on the gas. "Are you buckled, Molly sweetie?"

"Yes," Molly answered.

"I wonder if you should call her on her phone?" asked Zo. "It might be safer than a car chase."

"Don't worry," said Beth, taking a corner a little too quickly. The SUV hit the curb, and her long brown ponytail jumped off her shoulders. "I'm in complete control."

The sedan was several blocks ahead of them, so Beth had some catching up to do before she would reach them. She zigzagged through traffic until the car was within sight. The problem was Main Street. It narrowed to one lane in each direction and was notoriously clogged with tourists. The stoplights put them several car lengths behind. It wasn't until after driving through downtown that the road widened and they finally caught up.

At a stoplight, Beth pulled up alongside the sedan and hollered at Meg to roll down her window. Meg stared straight ahead, her brown ponytail looking very much like her mother's. But she could ignore her mother's protests for only so long. Everyone within a one-block radius could hear Beth's demands. Eventually Meg rolled down her window.

"Oh hey, Mom." Meg was nonchalant. "What are you doing here?"

"What am *I* doing here?" repeated Beth. "What are *you* doing here? Tell that boy to pull over."

"We're meeting some friends for pizza," explained Meg. "I'll be home afterwards."

"No you're not," Beth insisted. "You're going to pull over and get in this car right now."

Meg had no intentions of getting in the car with her mother. She was playing it cool for the young guy in the car. He did a nice job of acting, too. He pretended not to see the concerned mom with her head hanging out the window. He and Meg shared a look that conveyed the hilarity of the situation. Beth didn't find it quite so funny.

"You, pull over—now!" exclaimed Beth.

The light turned green at that moment, and the sedan pulled away.

Beth gave Zo a look of astonishment. "Can you believe it? I would have never disobeyed my mother like that."

Molly piped up from the backseat. "That's not what Gran says. Gran says you were a 'handful.'"

"That's not true." Beth stepped on the gas. "Tell her, Zo."

Zo lurched forward in her seat. "Your mom was a good kid." It was Zo who got them into mischief. Rules changed from house to house. It made getting into trouble easy. Bringing your best friend along for the ride was even easier. But those days were far from Beth's mind. Her only concern was Meg and how to stop her.

"See?" Beth gripped the wheel. "I was a pillar of good behavior."

That was taking it a bit far, but far be it for Zo to disagree with a mom on a mission. A siren blared, cutting off further conversation. Zo checked the mirror. A police car was behind them with its lights on.

"Are those for me?" asked Beth.

"I think so," said Zo. "I'd pull over."

"What about Meg and that thug?" Beth pulled over to the side of the road. "They'll get away."

Thug? He looked like a perfectly normal teenager to Zo. But she supposed that's what mothers called boys who took their daughters away in speeding cars. "We can search the pizza places. There are only four in town, and they drove by one of them. That leaves three."

Beth didn't respond. She was watching her rearview mirror as the police officer approached, citation device in hand. A large shadow shaded her side of the car.

"Mom's getting arrested!" Molly couldn't conceal her excitement. A car chase and a chat with a police officer? They were much more interesting than her usual sandwich and glass of milk after school.

A black Stetson hat filled Beth's window, and Zo groaned. Two visits with Officer Merrigan in one day? It was enough to recollect further childhood truancies. He'd been present for more than one of them.

"Well, well, well," said Brady. "If it isn't Thelma and Louise. Is it just me, or do you two still get into a lot of trouble?"

"My mom's a pillar of good behavior," chimed Molly from the backseat.

"Hello, there." Brady tipped his hat to Molly.

"Look, Officer, could we hurry this up?" asked Beth. "My daughter's in a strange car with a boy. I need to go find her."

Brady was taken aback by her words. This was not the same woman from Memorial Day. This was the mother of a teenager in peril. "What strange car? When was she taken?"

"After school," said Beth. "Around three o'clock."

"Could you describe the car or driver?" asked Brady, lowering his electronic device. He obviously thought Meg had been kidnapped from the way Beth was relaying the story. Zo decided she better set the record straight.

"She got into the car *voluntarily*," explained Zo. Brady bobbed his head lower to meet her gaze. She cleared her throat. "They're going for pizza."

"It doesn't make it right!" said Beth. "Plus they were speeding. I know they were because I was following them. You need to follow that young man and give him a ticket. That'll teach him!"

"Like it did you or Zo?" muttered Brady. "I'm sorry about your daughter going out with a boy, but it doesn't give you an excuse to speed. You were going six miles over the limit. Downtown, that's a lot. Someone might have been injured."

"We're a mile from downtown," Beth informed him. "I would never harm anyone."

Zo would bet Beth was thinking about the murder at the lodge now. Brady had accused her of killing one of her guests over Memorial Day weekend, and Beth hadn't forgotten. Zo interceded before Beth said something that would cost her—in fines. "Beth's just concerned for her daughter. Surely as a…human being you understand."

"I understand." He held out a ticket. "I understand you and your friend still think you're above the law. Someday you'll learn."

Beth snatched the ticket out of his hand. "Today isn't that day, Officer. I'm too busy raising a teenager. They're a whole other species." She rolled up her window, leaving a gaping Brady Merrigan to stare after her as she merged into traffic.

Ten minutes later, they pulled into Mile High Pie, the new pizza place in town favored by teens and young adults. It not only had decent pizza but WiFi and charging stations. Patrons didn't have to worry about running low on batteries while filling up on pizza. The entrance was marked by a pizza with toppings balancing precariously and reaching into the sky. It wasn't a mile long, but customers got the idea. The boy's car was parked sideways in the lot.

Beth turned off the ignition, and Zo touched her arm. "Let me go in and get Meg."

"I want to come, too!" pleaded Molly from the backseat.

"Just me," said Zo. "It'll be less embarrassing for her."

"I *want* her to be embarrassed." Beth narrowed her eyes. They were steel gray. "She should be embarrassed about the little stunt she pulled."

"You don't mean that," said Zo. "You're upset. It's hard being a teenager, especially in a new town. You can hold off on the lecture until you get home."

Beth relaxed her shoulders. The tiniest smile played on her lips. "Since when did you learn so much about irresponsible teens?"

Zo gave her a grin. "Since I *was* one for years."

"Fine," agreed Beth. "Go. But tell that boy you've got your eye on him!" she hollered as Zo shut the car door.

Zo had no plans to tell him anything. She was going to give Meg an indication and hope she followed it. Zo assumed she would. Meg was a good kid. Besides, she wouldn't want to draw more attention to the situation than necessary.

The pizzas sold by the slice smelled heavenly and so did the breadsticks. Zo wondered about something to-go. She usually grabbed pizza at Lotsa Pasta downtown but decided to place an order. It would give her a reason for being here, besides retrieving Meg.

She texted Beth, asking if she'd like veggie or barbequed chicken. Beth responded with veggie—and the eye-roll emoji. They'd already indulged in a chocolate éclair. Zo placed her order and stepped to the carryout queue, where she noticed Roberto's son waiting. He was passing the time scrolling on his phone.

"Hey Alex."

His brown eyes were his father's but lacked the same warmth and generosity. They dismissed her with a glance. "Hey."

"Have you had their pizza?" asked Zo. "I heard it's pretty good."

"Yeah," said Alex. "It's good."

"How's your dad?" Since he'd gone back to his phone, Zo was left to look at his dark hair, pulled back from his forehead with the help of a styling product, probably something expensive. From the creases in his Oxford shirt to his hip jeans, he appeared ready for the Ivy Leagues.

"He's fine." He squinted, seeming to remember something. "He saw you on the news. Did you really have a séance at your store?"

An idea dropped into her head. Instead of changing the subject, she would use it to her advantage. "I did. We were able to reach out to Marianne."

He squirmed, looking more like a teen than an adult. "She never liked me, you know. She'd say anything just to be with my dad."

"Why didn't she like you?" asked Zo.

"The lady was a witch. What can I say?"

"Is that why you burned her book?"

His eyes widened. "Is that what she told you?"

Zo kept her gaze steady. Marianne didn't tell her, but she let Alex believe it. Zo knew he was the only one with access to the book. Unless Roberto burned it, which was highly unlikely.

"She wanted my dad's money," explained Alex. His eyes flashed black. "That's why she was mad about college. She could say whatever she wanted about values and work ethic, but I knew the truth. She just didn't want my dad spending his money on me."

"Is that why you burned her book?" Zo repeated.

"Dad needed to get her out of his head," said Alex. "Having that stupid book lying around wasn't helping. He'd been staring at it for days. Since you brought it back, it's even worse. He has it in a plastic bag like it's some kind of antique. So thanks for that. Really appreciate it."

The self-centered teen had turned it around, placing the blame on her. If his dad was suffering, it was because he loved Marianne, but Alex obviously didn't see it that way. He'd gotten rid of the book. Had he gotten rid of Marianne, too?

Marianne opposed his fancy college. Alex said it was because of the money, but Zo didn't believe it. Marianne had plenty of her own money from her book advance. Plus she was a believer in working one's way up, so it wasn't college itself she objected to. Zo needed to figure out what was—and if it was worth killing for.

A number popped up on the monitor, and Alex shifted from one foot to the other. Order 454 was being taken out of the oven. It must be his.

"If you talk to her again, tell her to buzz off, would you?" He put his phone in his pocket. "My dad and I don't need any visits from the other side. We're doing just fine without her."

From the kitchen, a pizza box slid under the warmer, and Alex approached the counter. An employee handed him the order, and he was gone.

Zo went to Meg and her friends at the corner table. Except for a few choice words Zo overheard as she neared, the kids were perfectly behaved. Three girls and three guys were huddled together, looking at something funny on a phone. A girl jerked it away when she noticed Zo.

"You ready, Meg?" Zo nodded toward the pickup counter. "Pizza's about done."

Meg pushed back her chair. "See you guys."

"You have to go already?" The boy from the car tugged Meg's hand, and Zo ignored the irritation growing inside her. She understood how Beth lost her cool now. Something instinctual took over when it came to loved ones. It was hard to explain, and Zo might not have even believed it if she hadn't experienced it for herself. She felt a strong desire to protect Meg from harm, and right now, that meant the young man.

"I'll call you later," said Meg.

Zo and Meg silently collected the veggie pizza, and Zo was pleasantly surprised by its weight. They really did pile on the toppings here.

Meg held open the door for Zo. "Thanks."

"What for?" said Zo.

"For not letting my mom come in here like a crazy person," Meg answered.

"I know you'll disagree, but I kind of like seeing your mom act like a crazy person." Zo shrugged. "It makes her seem more normal in a weird way."

"Normal is the last word I'd use to describe her lately," mumbled Meg.

Seeing Beth's makeshift sign language from the SUV, Zo had to agree.

Chapter Twenty-Five

Zo, Beth, and the kids enjoyed the pizza at Happy Camper. Harley was closing, and Zo wanted to share. With the five of them huddled around her table in the backroom, Zo experienced a warm fuzzy feeling of family, a family that didn't include a husband or children but a family all the same. It's what she cherished about the store. Happy Camper had become a front porch of sorts for the people who mattered to her. It welcomed new friends from all over the country who came to visit the Black Hills. Zo hoped they would return again and again, and the store would be here to welcome them. From the gains made in the summer, she felt positive about the future. For the first time since she'd opened, she contemplated adding another employee. With the holiday season approaching and college in session, the idea was plausible, but she knew Harley needed the hours and didn't want to reduce them. If her walking tours became more frequent, however, she would need another person.

Max popped into her head the way he always did when she thought of anything related to hiking, biking, canoeing, or camping. Picking up the pizza plates and tossing them into the garbage, she could hear his voice warning her about the dangers of the forest. A chuckle crept up on her. He'd probably want to screen a new employee himself. Unless he was looking for part-time work. In that case, she could just hire him. She could picture him in his forest-green uniform, marching people up the hill and to the path that led to the waterfall. The scene didn't exactly scream *happy camper*, but it did make her smile.

The bell on the door interrupted the imaginary scenario, and Zo motioned for Harley, who was still eating, to stay seated. Tiffany was there with her two kids in tow. No longer did Zo see her as an overzealous mother with perfect hair and clothes to match. She was a woman with a past, one she didn't want repeated. Like most people, Tiffany was much more complicated than she looked. It had been a mistake to dismiss her as a town do-gooder.

"My last stop of the day." Tiffany held up her bulging manila envelope.

"I didn't think I'd see you so soon," said Zo. Tiffany had more sales than the last time Zo had seen the envelope. It would take her awhile to rifle through the checks. Thank goodness Beth and the kids were still here. Hopefully they would provide enough of a distraction to give Zo time to take a peek.

"Orders are due tomorrow," explained Tiffany. "It was now or never."

"Molly!" Tiffany's daughter squealed. The two girls joined in a hug. Molly dragged her to the Gratitude Tree, where they scribbled on leaves. Tiffany's son stood next to her, looking around for something else to do.

Tiffany nodded toward the tree. "I see you've switched out your Halloween décor. It's cute."

"I like keeping up with the seasons," said Zo. Another customer entered, and Harley appeared from the backroom with Beth. Meg was left alone to finish her pizza in peace. After the talking-to Beth had given her on the way to the shop, it was probably a welcome relief.

"So your neighbor…" started Tiffany.

"Let me give him a buzz." Zo wished she'd called Cunningham earlier. She should have known Tiffany would be right over when it came to wreath sales. If Cunningham was still in his grading funk, though, he would be happy for the interruption. She pulled her phone from her back pocket and pressed his number.

Cunningham answered on the fifth ring, and Zo explained her reason for calling while Beth chatted with Tiffany. Under her breath, Zo told Cunningham she needed him to come and bring his checkbook. He didn't need much encouragement to flee his papers. She heard him open his door as he said goodbye.

Zo clicked off the phone. "He's on his way."

Tiffany nodded. She and Beth were already making class party arrangements. A few minutes later, Cunningham entered Happy Camper, looking bleary-eyed. A sleep wrinkle crossed one cheek.

"Sorry, Cunningham," Zo apologized. "Were you sleeping?"

"No, no." He cleared his throat. "I was grading papers."

"Must have been interesting reading." Tiffany and Beth were still chatting, so Zo gestured toward the envelope. "I'll show him the options."

Unfortunately, Tiffany handed her the order form, not the envelope. Zo cursed her bad luck. She should have just grabbed the envelope in the first place. Tiffany was so busy planning the party, she wouldn't have thought anything of it. Zo showed Cunningham the pictures of the different wreaths.

He was considering his options carefully. "This one's a little too rustic, don't you think?"

"We live in the middle of a forest," said Zo. "Rustic is kind of our thing."

"But I like a little color..."

Zo rolled her eyes. "Then get this one."

"Hmm," mumbled Cunningham. "I just wish the bow was maroon instead of red."

Zo had no idea he was so fastidious about home décor. "It's nice. It will look great with your tree." Under her breath, she added, "Did you bring your checkbook?"

"Of course I did." Cunningham pulled it from his jacket pocket. Unlike Zo's, the leather cover looked worn and well used.

"Write your name and information on the back of the form," Zo instructed. "I'll get you a pen." She grabbed a daisy pen from the cash register, and Cunningham wrote out his information painfully slow. He had beautiful penmanship, though.

"Do I make the check out to the school?" Cunningham asked when he was finished with the order form.

Tiffany's ears perked up at the word *check*. She paused her conversation with Beth, pointing to the words on the bottom of the form. "You can make it out to Great American Wreaths. Our school gets proceeds from the orders. If we get enough of them, the kids might win a Kindle!"

"That's wonderful." Zo reached for the envelope. It was now or never, and she needed to get a look at those checks.

"I got it, thanks." Tiffany gave her a smile. "Next year I'm going to have to recruit you for sales. You've made four today."

Zo smiled back through gritted teeth. Nothing ever went as planned, and she was running out of time—and people to buy wreaths. She wracked her brain for ideas, but came up empty. Tiffany was about to leave.

Just then, the door blew open, and a gust of wind took the envelope, scattering checks everywhere. It was raining money. Tiffany shrieked in dismay, but Zo couldn't have been happier. She had a feeling Marianne had something to do with the turn of events. Maybe a customer left the door open, but the day was calm. A force of nature was to thank for Zo's good luck.

"No worries." Zo grabbed the envelope. "I'll get these picked up in no time. Harley, give me a hand." Everyone got busy gathering the spilled contents.

Having the envelope gave Zo the advantage of glancing at the checks as she tucked them inside. It was easy to look for rips as she sorted them carefully. Halfway through a stack, she noticed Marianne's check. It was in perfect condition. It also matched the one in Marianne's hand the night of her murder, which meant the check belonged to her.

Marianne paid someone in the middle of the night. But who and for what? Did she change her mind? Is that why a piece of the check was still in her hand? Was it the reason she was killed? Zo sat back on her heels. It was another dead end, yes, but also another possibility crossed off the list. Tiffany hadn't killed Marianne. Who had?

It was the question she was still pondering later that night while writing her Happy Camper column. For Zo, writing had always been relaxing. She wasn't easily distracted from the clicking of the keys. But tonight was different. She was restless and had a hard time focusing on the words.

George let out a troubled meow, and Zo gave him a glance. Maybe he was having a hard time relaxing, too. He stopped bathing, a lengthy ritual that involved a lot of licking. Since he was a Maine Coon, it was a process. But a low moan told her something was wrong. He kept reaching for a spot behind his neck. Falling short, he lay back down, squinting at her with two distressed eyes. Something was very wrong.

Zo went to him, glancing through his fur, starting with the spot on his back that was causing him trouble. He opened his mouth to bite her. She dodged the attempt. The area was obviously tender. Had he hurt himself during his overnight escapade? She slowly ran her fingers through his fur. She stopped, noticing a small white bump. George growled, but she didn't let his deep rumble deter her. Upon closer inspection, she realized it was a tick. At least that's what she thought it was. She couldn't see the bug itself because it was burrowed into George's fur, quite deep into the skin.

George decided he'd had enough of her examination. He squirmed on his side, out of her reach. Zo checked the clock on the wall. It was after eight, and the vet wasn't open. She'd never get the tick removed by herself, and leaving it there was dangerous. It might be the reason he hadn't been eating or gone outside. She'd chalked up his behaviors to missing home but realized now it was probably the tick. A knot tightened in her stomach. The tick needed to go ASAP.

She pressed Max's number on her cell. When he answered, she explained the situation. "I don't know how it happened. I use once-a-month flea and tick prevention. I should have seen it sooner. He hasn't been eating well."

"It's okay." Max's voice was calm. "I'll be right over."

By the time Max arrived, she was fighting back fear and not doing a very good job. She was kicking herself for not seeing the warning signs earlier.

"Hey, are you all right?" he asked.

She nodded. She was now. "He's in my office."

Max followed her into the room, kneeling beside George. He moved with calmness and concern. George didn't flinch from his touch. He trusted him.

Zo realized she did, too. That's what the feeling was: trust. A lightening of the heart. A single tear slid down her cheek. It felt good to let it go.

Max looked at her quizzically. "I'm pretty sure I can save the cat, but I don't know about the cat mom."

She waved away the comment. "I'm sorry. I'm just so worried." But it was more than that. Max had opened a door in her heart that had been closed a very long time. A floodgate better described it.

"Don't worry." Max took gloves and tweezers out of his red first-aid kit. He looked like a doctor getting ready for surgery. "I can remove a tick. Would you grab a container with alcohol? I'd like to save it for the vet's office. If George does have an infection, it'll help identify it."

A new fear twisted her stomach as she hurried to grab the supplies. She hoped George didn't have an infection. He looked healthy. Until tonight, she hadn't noticed anything bothering him. That had to be a good sign. Focusing on the task at hand, she found a small Tupperware container in the kitchen. Next she grabbed the alcohol from the bathroom cabinet. She set them down next to Max.

"Shut the door, will you?" Max said. "I don't want George going anywhere."

Slowly, she closed the door. Basking in Max's attention, George didn't notice. She inched toward the pair, kneeling beside Max. One hurdle had been traversed. She hoped she could make it two.

George sat up. He must have been able to detect her anxiety. She was sweating buckets of it. Luckily Max was as cool as the hardwood floor. He poured the alcohol in the container and grabbed the tweezers without arousing suspicion.

"Do you think you could hold him?" asked Max.

"I can try." His fur was already parted where Max had examined the tick. All she had to do was keep it there for the next minute. It would be no easy task.

"Here we go," said Max. "Keep him steady."

George was not only a furry cat, he was also a strong cat. She could feel the muscles beneath his coat as she put her hands on him. Max moved in with the tweezers, and she turned her head. She couldn't watch what was about to happen.

Seconds later, Max said, "You can let him go."

She blinked, relaxing her grip. "You're finished?"

George bounded off the chair.

Max snapped the container lid shut. "Yep. All done." He took off his gloves.

"Where did you learn to do that?"

"All forest rangers have to take Ticks 101." Seeing her gullible reaction, he grinned. The whiskers on his face were darker, handsomely outlining his jawline. "I'm kidding. The first time I did this, I nearly threw up. I was so nervous. You wouldn't believe how many dogs get ticks in the forest. I got better with practice."

She released the breath she'd been holding. The tick was gone, and George seemed fine. The pounding of her heart was growing quieter. "Do you think he'll be okay?"

"I think so. Take him to the vet, just to make sure. Don't forget this." He pointed toward the container with the bug in it.

They stood.

"I don't know how to thank you." Zo returned his smile. "I seem to be saying that a lot lately."

Max tilted his head, the lamplight catching the playfulness in his eyes. "It does have a familiar ring."

"It means a lot to me," said Zo. "More than you know."

He took a step closer, his hands brushing her upper arms. "I'm happy to help, seriously. No thanks necessary."

"It's not just the cat," Zo continued. "I mean, it *is* the cat, but it's more than the cat." She was at a loss for words or perhaps didn't want to say them out loud. She couldn't bring herself to admit her new feelings. She feared he wouldn't understand.

"I know." Something flickered across his face, and she recognized it as desire and felt it, too. Her lips parted, and it was all the indication he needed to kiss her, softly at first, then more deeply. His passion surprised her, and she reached for his broad shoulders. He slipped his hands around her waist, pulling her closer, and the world fell away.

She wasn't inexperienced; she'd felt passion before. But this was something else. He was telling her he understood without saying a word. The way he held her said everything. In his arms, she felt safe and warm. She told herself to hold back, not to give herself away, but dismissed the warning. The lightness in her heart was addicting, and her cares disappeared. She wanted to feel this way forever.

George, not so much. The swerve of his heavy body between them forced her to pull back. She glanced down to make sure nothing was wrong, but one look into his tiger eyes told her he was jealous of the attention she was receiving. Now that he had their notice, he jumped on her desk, half his rump covering her laptop keyboard. She rolled her eyes at Max. George was doing just fine.

"That was a heck of a thank you," said Max. "I wonder if I should check for more ticks."

Zo smiled. "It's been a long night." She nodded toward her computer. "I should finish my column. I have a feeling fur face just deleted half of it."

He squeezed her hand. "I understand."

She believed he really did.

Chapter Twenty-Six

That night, Zo didn't sleep, and it wasn't just the kiss with Max that kept her up. Okay, a lot of it was the kiss, but it was also George. With the tick gone and his energy back, he wanted outside. He meowed at the deck door, then jumped on her bed to underscore the complaint. At one point, she heard another noise, and went to see what the commotion was. She found George sitting on her oversized kitchen windowsill, fluffed to twice his size. Something had him spooked. She peered over his shoulder to see what was the matter.

The night was jet black, the pine trees imperceptible from the dark sky. She craned her neck, a single street light visible in the corner of her window. A large man with a baseball cap shuffled down the street. Was he what had George blown up like a balloon? That must have been it. Although it was hard to see, Zo didn't see any forest animals. A deer or stray raccoon hadn't wandered onto her deck. She grabbed George and walked him to his cat bed in her room. He immediately jumped out.

"Fine, but you need to be quiet," Zo insisted. "No more meowing."

He sauntered out of the room, and Zo listened. No protests at the deck door. The man in the cap must have been the problem. She closed her eyes, and her mind wandered back to the kiss with Max. How had they been close enough to kiss? Had she made the first move, or had he? They were usually on the opposite sides of everything. Not tonight. Tonight they were closer than they'd ever been, and it felt nice. Better than nice.

She shook off the memory, trying not to place too much emphasis on it. She'd been distressed, worried about George. She'd feel differently in the morning. But right now, it felt good to recall the safe feeling of his arms wrapped around her. She gravitated toward guys who were the opposite of Max: reckless, feckless, hopeless—any of the *less* words. Dating them was thrilling but not much else. The feeling Max gave her was exciting in a different way. Maybe it was dangerous also, because it meant more. The last thing she remembered before dozing off was his warm skin and solid heart drumming against hers. At least, that was the fantasy until she awoke to real pounding—at her door.

She squinted at the clock. It was four in the morning. What was going on? She stumbled out of bed, grabbing her robe. "I'm coming," she hollered. "Just a minute." It felt as if she'd just gone to sleep, but she knew she must have been sleeping a couple hours or more.

Red and blue lights illuminated her living room curtain. What the heck? Were the police outside? A deep voice confirmed her suspicions.

"It's Officer Merrigan, Ms. Jones."

She opened the door. "What's happened? Is something wrong?"

Brady looked over her shoulder. "We got a call about suspicious activity near Happy Camper. Are you okay?"

Zo blinked. "I'm fine…I think." The deck door was locked. She flipped on a light. Nobody had been inside. It was the same kitchen she saw before going to bed.

"What about the store?" said Brady.

She groaned. "Oh no. I'll meet you downstairs."

He took a step forward. "Let me come with you. Someone might have broken in."

She walked to the indoor staircase that led to the store, happy the door was still locked. Even if someone was inside Happy Camper, they hadn't been in her upstairs living space.

"I'll take it from here," said Brady, pulling out a weapon. "Stay behind me."

"Is that a gun?" Zo didn't know how she felt about a firearm in her house, burglar or not. Happy Camper was a peaceful place, and she wanted to keep it that way.

He didn't answer. He crept down the stairs in stealthy silence, Zo a few steps behind him. Seeing him in action gave her a new appreciation for his work. He had no idea what he would find downstairs yet met it with determination and courage. It was a different side to him she didn't often see.

"Wait."

Pausing in the stairwell, she obeyed his order. She listened for evidence of a break-in—footsteps, voices, glass—but heard only the click of Brady's boots on the floor. The silence was paralyzing and went on forever. She imagined someone lurking in the darkness, lunging at Brady when he least expected it. She wished he'd turn on the lights or call "all clear" over his radio. He did neither. He crept through the store for what seemed like hours. When he finally switched on the lights, she sucked in a surprised breath.

He returned to the stairwell. "Didn't mean to startle you. You can come out now."

"Did you see anything?" Zo rubbed her eyes.

"No."

She tied her fuzzy robe tighter, feeling a little silly to be standing there watching while Brady checked out the store. She should be helping or offering him coffee or something. Truth be told, she was in a daze. It was as if she were watching a scary movie, and she was a woman in distress, frozen and unable to move. She shook off the drowsy feeling. She hated that cliché and wanted to help. She walked to the windows. "The locks are intact."

"The door is secure also." Brady glanced her way. "It may have been a false alarm."

"Who called it in?"

"It came in over the anonymous tip line," said Brady. "A woman. She didn't leave a name."

Zo checked the cash register. It hadn't been tampered with. She closed the drawer. "Earlier, a man was outside my house. I noticed him when I got up with my cat. Could that be him?"

"What did he look like?" asked Brady.

"He was large, heavy. He had on a red baseball cap."

"Was he near the store?"

Zo nodded. "He might have been. He was passing under a streetlight."

Brady's radio buzzed. A voice came over the line. "I got something out here, Chief. You'd better come see."

Zo and Brady shared a look.

Brady told the officer he'd be right there and unlocked the front door. Zo followed. An officer was holding something silver in his gloved hand. A tire iron? A crowbar? Some sort of tool for a car. It was also a tool that could be used to break into a store. Had Brady scared away the crook just in time?

"I found this near the garbage bins, behind the store," the officer informed them.

That didn't make sense. A criminal wouldn't bother to throw away his tool, especially if he was in a hurry. But why else would the officer be putting it in a plastic bag marked Evidence? Zo scratched her head, willing away the fog that enveloped her mind.

Brady examined the tool. After inspection, he and the officer locked eyes.

"What is it?" asked Zo. Something had been communicated between the two men, but she didn't know what was said.

"We won't know for sure until it's been tested," Brady explained. "But it looks like blood."

"Blood?" repeated Zo. "No one's been hurt."

The hum of their radios was the only response.

She felt as if she were on another planet, observing a new life form for the first time. Why weren't they speaking? Then it struck her. They weren't thinking about a possible break-in anymore. They were thinking about Marianne. It was her blood on the tool. At least that's what they assumed, and Zo did, too. Marianne was struck in the head. This could be the murder weapon.

"Wait," said Zo. "Do you think this was the weapon used to kill Marianne?"

"We'll know for sure once we test it for DNA," said Brady.

"I don't understand." Zo shook her head. "What's it doing here?"

"I think you'd better come down to the station with me."

"Why?"

"To give your statement," Brady answered.

"I didn't do this," pleaded Zo. "You searched my place the night Marianne was found. Remember? Why wasn't it here then?"

"Lots of criminals wait to get rid of the evidence," said the officer. "They stuff it in their garbage cans a week after. Morons, most of them."

"Quiet, Officer Bates." Brady cleared his throat. "Get your shoes, Zo. I'll wait outside."

"I can't go in my robe!" Zo protested. "I need to get dressed."

"You have five minutes."

Zo fled inside, running up the stairs and nearly tripping over George, who was waiting on the landing. What about the tick? What about his vet appointment? She pushed away the worry. She was getting arrested. The vet appointment would definitely need to happen later.

George followed her into the bedroom, jumping on the dresser. He tucked his orange paws under his body. His chest puffed out like a lion's mane. *Think of my health.* He relayed the concern with the flick of his eyes. *I nearly missed my bath tonight.*

"Ha!" said Zo, throwing on a Beatles t-shirt. "I'm going to jail. J-A-I-L. I might waste away in a cell for the rest of my days. Then who would take care of you?"

He closed his eyes. Her welfare didn't concern him.

She pulled on jogging pants and tied her hair into a short ponytail. Grabbing her purse, she thought about stopping to brush her teeth, but then popped a piece of gum in her mouth instead. Brady wasn't the type of person to be kept waiting. If she didn't want to be hauled off in handcuffs, she needed to hurry.

Brady was waiting for her by his police cruiser. Bates and another officer were still combing the area for clues. Someone had obviously planted the evidence at her house. Couldn't Brady see that? It had to be the man in the hat near her store. He must have dumped the evidence near the garbage, arousing enough suspicion for someone to call the anonymous tip line. Safely tucked in the back of his squad car, Zo told Brady the idea.

"The man in the hat. Isn't that from a child's cartoon?"

She huffed a breath. He wasn't convinced and kept checking the rearview mirror, as if she might pull open the door any moment. Like a criminal.

"You described the man as *lumbering*," said Brady. "Unless you were using one of your fancy journalist words to impress me, that doesn't sound like a man fleeing the scene of a crime."

True, but George was spooked. That was enough to cause alarm. She wasn't going to bring it up, however. She didn't want to mention *George* in the same sentence as *the man with the hat*. Brady was right; both names came from a child's cartoon. "The man was large. He couldn't move quickly. That doesn't mean he didn't want to."

That earned her another look.

"Think about it," Zo said. "Why did the tool show up just now? Why wasn't it found the night of Marianne's murder? Someone put it there."

"Save it for your statement, Ms. Jones." Brady turned into the station. "We haven't confirmed it's the murder weapon."

But they would. She was certain of it. Where would that leave her? Marianne was found near the store—by Zo. If the weapon was, too, she would face arrest. That's why Brady was collecting her statement at the station. He wanted everything to be official in case it went to trial.

Brady helped her out of the backseat.

"What about Marianne's missing purse?" Zo asked. "You said it might have been a robbery gone bad." The last-ditch effort was just as desperate as it sounded.

He held open the door to the station. "That was before I found a tire iron with blood on it at your store. This way."

By the time she finished giving her statement, the sky was no longer black. It was periwinkle, the color it turned right before dawn. As far as she was concerned, it might as well have been bright yellow. There was no way she would be able to sleep, even if she could, which she couldn't. First, she was too upset about Brady Merrigan hauling her down to the station. After all they'd been through in the last year, how could he think she'd harm Marianne? She knew he was just doing his job, but the implication stung. Second, she had to open Happy Camper in a few hours. Sleep would have to wait.

She unlocked the door to her house. What she needed was a strong cup of coffee—many cups of strong coffee. Much had to be done, including clearing her name, and it could only be achieved with an alert mind. Flipping open her laptop, Zo waited for the pot of java to brew. She also turned on the TV, wondering if last night's commotion would be covered on the news. Jake had to be the one who placed the weapon at her store. He was the only person who came to mind. He was large, like the man in the hat. Plus he had the most to gain from Marianne's death. But why now?

The start of the morning news program told her why: Justin Castle. His special report was being plugged—again. She returned to the kitchen and poured a mug of coffee. Jake was following Justin's program. He'd told her as much when she and Max were at his house. Planting evidence at Happy Camper would compound her guilt, and the cops would have no choice but to arrest her. All roads would lead back to her and away from him. It was a splendid way for him to ditch the evidence and incriminate someone else.

She held her mug, allowing the brew to awaken her senses before taking a sip. If she was to get anything done, she needed to focus on the things she *could* control, like her column. Harriet Hobbs wouldn't allow a little thing like a murder investigation to get between her and a deadline. She needed the article tomorrow, no exceptions.

After a few swallows, Zo opened her document and added Spirits & Spirits' event to the article. At least one person had received their Christmas wish: Duncan. He would be playing his guitar after all. Scrolling down the page, Zo realized it was still short. *Dang.* She was missing the police station's fundraiser. The last person she wanted to see again was Brady Merrigan. She'd just spent the last hour with him under not-so-nice circumstances. But there was nothing else to do but talk to him. She couldn't finish her column until she did.

Chapter Twenty-Seven

After a shower with lots of pumpkin latte bodywash, Zo opened Happy Camper. Today was Thankful Thursday, and she'd needed the seasonal scent to brighten her mood. The entire town would be shopping for deals. Downtown vendors put out their best bargains in what amounted to a Crazy Days sale before the cold weather set in. It was their way of saying thank you to shoppers who spent their dollars downtown. With the lure of shopping online, from the comfort of their couches, shoppers were encouraged to spend and save locally.

Zo had an assortment of gifts on sale, including her fall items, which everybody loved. Signs like HAPPY FALL Y'ALL and STOP AND SMELL THE PUMPKIN SPICE would go quickly, especially at thirty percent off. Harley would be in after her morning class, thank goodness. She said she didn't have an afternoon lab, but Zo wondered. She hoped she wasn't skipping out on it because of the event. The store would only get busier as the holidays approached. She didn't want Harley cutting class just to help out.

Hattie Fines was her first customer, which was a surprise. The library held a used book sale today. She should have been happily ensconced in well-worn books. Zo questioned her about it.

"Two words," answered Hattie. "Agnes Butterfield."

Zo carried a miniature haystack to a table of merchandise. "The new library employee?"

"That's the one." Hattie slipped her glasses on her nose, and her eyes magnified to twice their size. They were round and light blue like faded tea saucers. "She's turned the library into my own Puritanical Hades."

Zo set down the merchandise. "I'm sure that's overstating it."

"But I'm not here to talk about her." She handed Zo a piece of paper. "She's the last person I want to talk about," she added under her breath.

Zo examined the printout. "What's this?"

"You said you wanted to find your birth mother." Hattie gestured to the sheet. "This might help you out. It's a list of plays that performed around the time you were given away."

Hattie had been there for her in so many ways through the years: librarian, mentor, friend. Zo would never forget the time she'd helped her obtain her first library card. Zo was sixteen and Hattie had waived the parental consent. It shouldn't surprise her that she'd go out of her way to help her again. This time was different, though. Zo wasn't sure Hattie wanted her to pursue this mystery. Still, here she was, giving her information that might help her. Zo gave her an impulsive hug. "Thank you, Hattie!"

"Don't thank me yet," said Hattie into Zo's shoulder. "It may be nothing."

"Even if it isn't, it's the thought that counts. It's a great idea." She explained Nikki's offer to look through old playbills. "Nikki said the theater is a mess right now from the renovation, and I'm sure hundreds of papers are in the box. This will save me so much time. That is, if I'm not in jail."

Hattie frowned, and Zo told her about last night's trouble.

"Leave it up to Chief Merrigan to haul you down to the station," grumbled Hattie. "He didn't need to do that. He didn't the night you found Marianne."

"I think he wants it to be official. In case..." Rearranging a flowerpot on the sale table, Zo let the idea trail off. "I'm going to talk to Max today. He'll know what it means."

"You talk to him quite a bit these days." She sneaked a glance in Zo's direction.

Zo noticed. "That's because he's always coming in here to bug me about a sticker or license or something."

"I don't think so."

Zo crossed her arms, trying to keep the smile from her face. "I suppose you're going to tell me what you think."

"I think you're falling for him."

Avoiding Hattie's stare, Zo hung a Happy Camper birdhouse on a hook. She hated to put them on clearance, but with winter on the way, fewer people would be buying them. Winter was the perfect time to care for the birds, but customers didn't always see it that way.

"I think it started after he saved George," added Hattie.

"You're right about one thing," Zo agreed. "He's my hero for saving George. And he did it again last night." She told Hattie about the tick. She didn't tell her about the kiss.

"And speak of the devil, here he comes." Hattie nodded to Max, who was walking in the store, along with a passel of customers. He stood out as the only man in the group.

Zo might have forgotten all about the sale if she stared at Max long enough. The only thing on her mind right now was last night's kiss. Until Hattie cleared her throat. Then Zo dusted off her hands and tried to look busy. She rearranged more merchandise.

"You already moved that," said Hattie with a grin. "I liked it better over there."

"How's the book sale going at the library?" asked Zo, changing the topic. "Shouldn't you be overseeing it?"

Hattie's one-word answer was "Yes."

"Good morning, ladies," greeted Max. "How's George today?"

"Much better," said Zo.

"And you?" asked Max.

"She's not that great," Hattie informed him. "She was arrested last night."

Zo hushed her. Customers were approaching. "Not arrested. Brady took me down to the station to give a statement." She lowered her voice. "They found the murder weapon outside Happy Camper."

"You're kidding me. I can't believe Merrigan didn't tell me." He shook his head. "Actually, I can. I'm not surprised at all. This is why I'm the town's tick remover."

"There are worse things," said Hattie. "Just be happy we live in a city with so little crime—or used to. The less you see of Chief Merrigan, the better."

"Besides, town tick remover is an important job." Zo squeezed his arm. "I can't tell you how much better George feels. He's back to all his old tricks." Her impromptu affection couldn't be helped. Anytime she considered what Max did for George, she wanted to give the ranger a hug. It was a natural reaction.

"I'm glad to hear George's feeling better," said Max. "Not so glad about you being hauled down to the station. Any ideas who planted the weapon?"

Zo was pleased they were on the same page. At least one law enforcement officer was on her side. "A man in a baseball cap was outside my house not long before the police came. It might have been Jake Morgan. He's the same size as the man I saw."

Max looked as if he was running the scenario in his mind. His eyes were thoughtful, focused on a point in the distance.

Just then, Cunningham entered the store. "What was all the commotion last night? I saw the police cars."

Zo put a finger to her lips. She didn't want her trouble with the police announced to one and all at the sale.

Cunningham stopped in front of them. His white hair was combed in a handsome wave, and he wore a dark navy sweater with a brown button at the round collar. His scruffy eyebrows were another matter. "Hattie Fines. What a lovely surprise. Red becomes you."

Hattie smoothed her red fall jacket. Now it was Zo's turn to smirk. Cunningham had been chasing after Hattie for a while now, but she wasn't his only pursuit. Zo did think she was his favorite, however.

"And how about me?" Max smiled. "How do I look?"

"You always look good in green," claimed Cunningham. "I thought Zo might be in stripes this morning. What happened?"

Zo filled him in.

"Brady can't go arresting anyone he pleases. Someone needs to show those Merrigans once and for all that they don't run this town." Cunningham pointed a finger at Zo. "And you're just the gal to do it."

"First of all, I wasn't arrested, and second, how do you propose I do that?" asked Zo.

"Find the killer, and solve the murder," proclaimed Hattie. "Just like last time."

"Hello?" Max interrupted. "I was there, too."

"You need to take George to the vet," said Hattie. "Look around." She motioned to the customers filling the streets. "Zo is going to be swamped with the sale."

Max rolled his eyes.

"Don't underestimate the power of your work, Max." Cunningham cleared his throat. His voice turned professorial. "John Muir once said 'The clearest way into the Universe is through a forest wilderness.'"

"I love that," said Zo.

Cunningham pointed to her merchandise. "Maybe you could put it on one of your birdhouses."

"But seriously, can you take George to the vet?" Zo asked Max. "Harley won't be in for a couple hours, and I need to keep the store open for the sale."

Max checked his waterproof watch. It also had a compass on it and other gauges that helped him navigate the forest. "I have thirty minutes. I can see if Dr. Iron Cloud will give him a quick look."

"Would you? That would be wonderful." She turned to Hattie. "Can you watch the store for a sec while we get George?"

"I'll keep her company," Cunningham added.

Zo bet he would. She led the way while Max called the vet, who said Max could bring George right over for a quick peek. When he ended the call, she said, "I can't thank you enough for doing this." She grabbed George's carrier from her laundry room. "I'll pay you back, I promise."

"How are you going to do that?" he asked.

She put the carrier on the kitchen table, scrunching up her nose. "A Happy Camper gift card?"

"I was thinking of something a little more personal."

The comment caught her by surprise.

"That came out wrong." His cheeks flushed, making him look incredibly wholesome and handsome.

"I knew what you meant," she said with a smile. Putting her hand on his jaw, she gave him the briefest of kisses. It was meant to be a joke, a payment for taking George to the vet, but electricity danced on her lips even as she put George into the carrier. She was playing with fire and knew it. She'd better stop before she got burned.

She handed him the crate. George growled.

Max tucked the jar with the tick in his jacket pocket. "I'll bring George back safe and sound."

"I know you will," said Zo. "Thanks again."

Thirty minutes later, he returned George with a clean bill of health—and a report of his bad behavior. A fellow forest ranger had brought in a stray German shepherd with a hurt paw, but George wouldn't cooperate long enough for Max to look into the situation.

Zo wrapped up a customer's candle as she listened. She was offering free holiday wrap for the sale, and customers loved all the colorful options. Zo's favorite was the one that said Happy Christmas! in blue-and-white letters. "But the dog is going to be okay?"

Max put his finger in the middle of the tie while she did up the bow. "I'm going to check back later. George didn't exactly give me a chance to ask."

George was hiding behind a stack of books on the counter, planning a sneak attack on the ribbon. He wanted to put the finishing touch on the holiday packages—kitty-cat style.

"Uh-oh," moaned Zo. "He didn't like the dog?"

"By the giant hiss he let out, I would say no," said Max. "George is not a fan of dogs."

"Huh." Zo shrugged. "He never hisses."

"It wasn't pretty."

George pounced on the ribbon, still wrapped around Max's hand.

Zo laughed. "I don't think he appreciates the criticism."

"I'm sorry, George," Max apologized. "You're a very handsome cat."

George was happy with the compliment. At least he let go of the package, anyway.

Max left, and the store got busier. By the time Harley arrived, Zo was swamped with gift-wrapping requests that had backed up over the last hour. While free gift wrap was a great idea, it was also time consuming. Zo told customers to pick up their packages when they were finished shopping downtown, and she had a feeling several would be back any minute.

While Harley rang up merchandise, Zo caught up on wrapping. When the last bow was tied, she asked Harley if she needed food. Zo was starving, but Harley said she'd eaten.

"Do you mind if I pop out for lunch?"

Harley glanced up, her blue eyes almost violet in her retro Prince t-shirt. "You own the store. You can do whatever you want."

"You know what I mean," said Zo, tucking away a roll of paper. "Will you be okay here by yourself?"

Harley shooed her toward the door. "Go, I'll be fine. If I need anything, I'll call."

"I won't be long," said Zo. Grabbing her jacket and backpack, she hurried outside. Across the street, Buffalo Bill's had pulled pork sandwiches, chips, and a drink for five dollars. That *was* something to be thankful for. Buffalo Bill's was a bar and grill with good food and live music. Usually, more customers came at night than in the afternoon, but not today. Today, people were lined up on the patio, where the smoker had been cooking the meats for hours, wafting the delicious scent into air.

Zo joined the throng of people waiting in line. That's when she noticed Jake Morgan, drinking a beer at a table. An empty paper basket sat in front of him. Even with him seated, she knew he was the same size as the man she saw last night. He wasn't wearing a hat, though. In fact, she'd never seen him wear a hat. Of course, a hat was the easiest disguise without going to much effort.

She ordered her lunch. If Jake planted the weapon at her house last night, she would know it. She'd be able to tell by his reaction. She took her sandwich to the table. He was definitely surprised to see her. Nervous? She couldn't say—yet.

"Is anybody sitting here?" she asked.

"Go ahead," said Jake. "I'm finished."

She took a seat. "I don't want to intrude."

He sipped his beer and went back to reading his phone. If he was bothered by her presence, he didn't show it.

"I thought you should know, the police might have found the weapon that killed Marianne." Zo ate a chip, studying his reaction. "They're testing it now."

He looked up from his phone. "What are you talking about?"

Finally, she had his attention. "Marianne was hit in the head the night she died. The police think they found the weapon that hit her."

He flicked the whiskers on his chin with the back of his grease-stained hand. His beard was at least three days old or older. "Where?"

"You really don't know?" Zo couldn't tell.

"Would I be asking if I did?" Jake's cheeks colored.

He had a hot temper. Zo didn't want to test how hot. She'd seen the way he'd blown up at Nikki. She didn't want to be his next target. "Not far from my store."

"Well, that figures." Jake squinted. If he had a pickax, he would have looked like an old-fashioned miner. A dark smudge crossed his cheek. He must have been working on his car again. "Justin Castle says you're a sneaky one."

Zo was pretty sure Justin hadn't said that, but it was implied all the same. "I had nothing to do with her death. I liked her, and she liked me. Why would I kill her?"

"That's what Justin's going to tell us tomorrow." He swigged the rest of his beer and stood. "Until then, stay away from me—and stay away from my daughter, too."

Zo remained silent. With him looming over her, she didn't want to make him any angrier than he was.

"You got that?" He pointed a finger at her.

She nodded, but what she was really thinking as he walked away was how he asked where the weapon was found but not what the weapon was. It was possible he already knew the answer to the question.

Chapter Twenty-Eight

Zo contemplated her conversation with Jake as she rang up a sale at Happy Camper. He didn't want her talking to his daughter, Emily, but Zo decided that's just who she needed to see. Emily was a bright young woman with insights into her mother. She'd already tipped off Zo about the meeting with the lawyer. What other information might she have?

Zo considered the possibilities as she waited for the customer to write out a check, an orange paper covered in pumpkins. If checks came in holiday themes, Zo might have to take up the outmoded form of paying more often. She paused before placing the check in the drawer. Something was familiar about it. Not the check, exactly. She couldn't put her finger on it. Then she remembered. *Marianne wrote a check for merchandise the day of her book signing.*

Customers rarely used checks, which made the transaction easy to remember. Zo might be able to match the number with her check registry, on paper or online. That would tell her to whom the check was written. She really did need to see Emily after all.

"Is there something wrong?" the customer asked.

Zo realized she was still holding the woman's check in her hand. "No, sorry. These are just the cutest checks I've ever seen. Would you like free gift wrapping?"

"No thanks," the woman said with a smile. "This is an early gift for me."

Zo wrapped the mug in tissue paper and placed it in a brown paper Happy Camper bag. Her mind was still on Marianne's checkbook. Had it been in her purse the night it was stolen? There was only one way to find out. Go to Marianne's house. The proof Zo needed to clear herself might be as easy as a short walk up the hill. Her heart fluttered at the notion.

Zo handed the customer her purchase and surveyed the store. Traffic had tapered off, the afternoon lull hitting. Customers would return after work, but Zo would be back by then. While pulling up Marianne's address on her phone, she told Harley she was going out for a while. Then she grabbed her coat and left.

Marianne's place was a half-mile from Happy Camper. Scanning the directions, Zo realized it made sense that her body was found near the store. Marianne might have been walking to or from her house when she was killed. Unfortunately, Brady Merrigan didn't see the connection, especially after the murder weapon turned up at Happy Camper.

Propelled by the cold and perhaps a little fear, Zo picked up her pace. She needed to figure out the murderer before Justin's program aired tomorrow, and she was running out of time. As a journalist, she'd never missed a deadline. She'd cut it close, but time was a respected commodity in the business, and she'd never lost sight of the finish line. She needed to make sure she reached it before Justin Castle did.

Marianne's house was a small white ranch. High on a hill, it had a neat view of the town below. White with blue shutters, it was much plainer than the woman herself. It had a single-car garage and a tidy front stoop, free from clutter or decorations. The single ornament was the witch sign she'd purchased at her book signing. When Zo saw it, she stopped short of knocking, remembering the author she admired. The book had spoken to her own experiences. Marianne had persevered through so much: a poor childhood, little schooling, and a bad divorce. Now Zo would persevere to find her killer.

She squared her shoulders and knocked. She hoped Emily was home. Zo hadn't called ahead because she wanted the element of surprise on her side. Jake might've put a bug in her ear, warning her about Zo. She might decline to talk to her. With any luck, he hadn't mentioned the incident at Buffalo Bill's yet—but he would, given a few more hours. If Zo had one chance, this was it. She couldn't blow it.

Hearing soft footsteps approach, she took a deep breath and smiled.

Emily pulled open the door, her face surprised but not unhappily. Good. Her dad hadn't talked to her yet. "Hey Zo."

"Hi, I hope I'm not bothering you," said Zo. "I know how busy you must be."

"Actually, I wouldn't mind a break." Dressed in a polo and jeans, Emily stepped to the side to let her in. She didn't have the same style as her mother—or demeanor. She acted middle-aged. But Zo knew what it meant to grow up early and felt a flood of empathy for the girl. She understood how it felt to have responsibility thrust on one's shoulders. She respected Emily. Even amidst tragedy, the young woman was holding it together.

The living room was nothing more than a plain rectangle with a window, but the kitchen was wallpapered and inviting. Zo followed Emily's cue and took a seat in the dining room. Papers were spread over most of the small oak table, and Emily gathered them together so that Zo had a clear place to sit.

"Sorry for the mess." Emily stuffed the papers into a nearby bin. "It's been…well, you know how it's been."

"Don't apologize," said Zo. "I'm surprised you're keeping it together as well as you are."

"You do what you have to do, I guess."

Zo noticed the dark circles, the chapped lips, the frizzy hair. Emily was doing what she had to, but at what cost? She had a feeling Emily had been strong a long time, the steady person her mom needed in her life. "How are you doing?"

Emily folded her hands on the table. Like her hair, they were dry and neglected. "Honestly, not that great. Mom's death has been overwhelming, and the idea that someone murdered her makes it that much worse."

Zo voiced her innocence in case Emily had been watching or intended to watch Justin Castle's special report. "I didn't have anything to do with her death. I hope you know that."

She shook off the suggestion. "I didn't think you did for a second. Do you have any ideas who did?"

"I've been asking myself the same thing," Zo admitted. "That's why I'm here. Do you mind if I ask you some questions?"

"Not at all," said Emily.

"At the book signing, Alex laughed at your mom," recalled Zo. "They didn't seem to get along. Did they?"

"Nope. Mom thought he was a spoiled brat."

That pretty much describes it. "That had to be difficult for her and Roberto. Did they fight about him?"

Emily tucked her hair behind her ears, making her plain pale face look plainer. "Mom wasn't a judgmental person. She didn't blame Roberto for Alex's bad attitude. She did blame him for this college thing, though. They fought about that."

"Alex says he's already been accepted to college," said Zo. "How can that be?"

"With a huge donation to the university," Emily claimed. "That's how. Mom called it a bribe. When she found the check, she was furious. She worked her way up from nothing, so did Roberto, and Mom didn't believe in free rides."

Checks again. Zo wondered if it had anything to do with the one in Marianne's hand the night of her death. But the check was hers, not Roberto's. Still, it was an interesting coincidence. "Did she confront him?"

"Yes," said Emily. "Roberto claimed it was a donation to the water polo team, but Mom knew better. Roberto bought Alex's way into college, plain and simple."

Just as Cunningham had said.

"I understood why he did it," continued Emily. "He wanted to give Alex an advantage he didn't have. He wasn't trying to cheat the system. He was just trying to be a good dad."

"Did you tell your mom that?"

"Are you kidding?" laughed Emily. "She would have put a curse on me or something. And she was right, of course. It's better to earn your way than take handouts. I would feel crummy about getting into college with a bribe."

Zo admired her integrity. Marianne had done a good job of raising her daughter. Maybe she wanted Roberto to raise Alex the same way. Had she insisted Roberto take back the money, or that Alex come clean with the university? If so, both of them had motives for murder.

"You mentioned a check." Zo scanned the scattered papers on the table. "The night of her murder, your mom had a ripped check in her hand, just the corner, but it was enough to give me the numbers. She wrote a check for some merchandise at Happy Camper. Maybe we could find who she wrote the check to by looking at her check register?"

"That's a really good idea." Emily stood and walked to a three-tier bin on the counter. "Mom always kept her checkbook with the bills. She still paid them by snail mail." She thumbed through statements. "Huh, some of these are due. I didn't think to pay them."

"You can't think of everything," said Zo. "Has your dad been helping out?"

"He's called a few of Mom's relatives." She searched another bin. "I love my dad, but he's not the best in these situations. Plus they didn't get along—at all."

"Nikki mentioned the divorce was recently finalized."

Emily nodded. "They should have divorced years ago. They fought all the time."

"Why didn't they?" asked Zo.

Emily looked up from the bin. "Me." She rolled her eyes. "Don't you love how parents think they're saving you from something when they're really not? They just make things worse."

Zo smiled. "Not exactly, but I can imagine."

"First, Mom wanted to get me through junior high and then it was high school. The divorce was finalized the day I started Black Mountain College. Coincidence? I don't think so."

"Did your parents ever fight, physically?" Zo approached the subject as carefully as possible. Emily loved her dad, bad temper or not. But if he killed Marianne, she might be in danger, too.

"Never," said Emily. "Dad might have a bad attitude but he's kind of... lazy. I don't think he'd hurt a fly."

"Nikki got a restraining order against him," Zo prodded. "She felt threatened."

Emily stopped looking for the checkbook. "They never got along. Nikki wanted Mom to leave Dad a long time ago. She knew if Mom could get away from him, she would do big things. Dad thought Nikki was using Mom. He isn't exactly a fan of the theater—or writing. He hated that Mom shared the story of their divorce in the book."

Zo remembered the chapter vividly. "Hated it enough to...retaliate against her?"

"No." Emily leaned against the wall as if the question weighed heavily on her. Maybe she'd wondered about it herself. She blinked back tears. Obviously the idea of her father killing her mother was too much to handle.

Her response put a stop to Zo's other questions. Emily couldn't entertain the idea of her dad being a murderer. Fortunately, Zo could.

Emily flicked away a tear. "The checkbook's not here. It must have been in her purse."

An envelope fell out of the bin. Zo thought it was odd, and Emily did, too. She stood blinking at the envelope on the floor for several seconds before she bent over to grab it.

"It's a bank statement," said Emily. It was several pages thick.

"A bank statement..." Zo repeated, chewing her lip. "Genius! A bank statement will show us who cashed the check."

"What's the check number?" asked Emily, clearing her throat.

Zo pulled out her phone and checked the number. "3544."

Emily's index finger scrolled through page after page. "3541, 3542, 3543...3545." She glanced up. "It's not here. It wasn't cashed."

"Are you sure?"

Emily handed Zo the statements. "Look for yourself."

She thumbed through them, confirming Emily's declaration. Another roadblock on the road to justice. And here she believed it was ghostly intervention. It must have been a fluke. She set the papers down on the table. "I'm going to find whoever did this, with or without the check."

"I wish I could be more helpful," said Emily. "The truth is, I can't imagine anyone wanting my mom dead. She was my best friend, and now she's... gone. I wish I would have told her."

Zo touched her arm. "You've been incredibly helpful, and if anyone knew how you felt, it was your mom. I promise." She straightened the bank statements and returned them to Emily.

Emily nodded, her spirits seeming to lift a little. "Will you keep me posted?"

"I will."

Emily shut the door, and Zo began the descent down the hill back to her store. She didn't get far before she saw Max, with a German shepherd monopolizing the front seat of his old pickup truck. She waved, and he pulled over to the curb.

Zo made a detour toward the truck, a mint-green-and-white relic from the 1960s. She loved its matching mint-green hubcaps. "Is this the dog you were telling me about? He's beautiful." The dog had tall inquisitive ears and a tan and black face with deep dark eyes. A bandage covered one leg.

"She," Max corrected. "She's a girl."

"Can I pet her?" asked Zo.

"Sure," said Max.

Zo held out her hand, and the German shepherd gave it a lick. "Did you adopt her?"

"No, I'm just hanging on to her until her owner shows up," explained Max. "Doc doesn't have room in the office for a big girl like her."

Zo didn't see a collar. "Do you have any idea who the owner is?"

"I put out an alert at all the ranger stations," Max scratched the dog's neck. "I'm sure they'll come looking for her. She had a laceration on her leg, not big, but it could have become infected without treatment. They must be worried."

The dog sat up taller. Zo noticed her head touched the ceiling. "It looks like she can put weight on her leg. That's good."

Max laughed. "She can do more than that. She bounded into the truck like a jackrabbit."

That would be one big jackrabbit. The dog had to be a hundred pounds.

"Where are you coming from?" asked Max.

"Emily's house." Zo told him about the checkbook.

"It was a good idea," said Max. "Too bad it didn't turn out." His phone rang, and he glanced at the number. "Hold on. It's Brady."

Zo waited anxiously while Max took the call.

"Are you sure?" Max asked Brady.

This couldn't be good. She focused on the kind eyes of the German shepherd. Dogs had a way of making everything seem okay, even if they weren't.

"All right," said Max. "Thanks for the call." He hit the end button. "That was Brady."

"I know. What did he say?"

"The blood on the tire iron was a positive match," said Max. "It was the weapon used to kill Marianne."

Zo shouldn't have been surprised by Max's news, but she was. It was confirmation that someone had battered Marianne that fateful night and dumped the evidence at Happy Camper. It was a dangerous move. Sure, it linked Zo to the murder. However, it also provided the police with a weapon. The killer must be confident it couldn't be traced back to them.

She considered the man outside Happy Camper last night. He must have planted the evidence. Ergo, he must be the murderer. She needed to find him—like ten minutes ago. He was her only hope of not being charged with a crime. If he kept the weapon, he also kept Marianne's purse. If Zo could find the duplicate check, she could clear her name. The only person who came to mind was Jake. Like the man outside Happy Camper, he was good-sized. The problem was she knew what Jake looked like. The man last night didn't remind her of him, but that was the idea behind the hat. It was a disguise and kept his face hidden.

The other possibilities were Roberto and Alex. Neither of them was small, but they were muscular. She shook her head. No matter how hard she tried, she couldn't make any of the suspects fit the scenario. What was she missing?

"Zo, did you hear me?" Max said. His large dog underscored the question with a short bark.

She jumped. "Yes, no. I didn't hear you. I was too busy figuring out how the heck I'm going to get out of this jam."

"You're not going to *do* anything except get into this truck," said Max. "There's a bus behind me that can't get through."

One of the travel agencies that hosted bus tours was trying to turn around on the side street. "What about King Kong here?" asked Zo.

Max grinned and put his arm around the German shepherd, gently pulling her toward the middle of the seat. "There's room."

She hopped in. The dog's panting filled the silence all the way to the store.

Chapter Twenty-Nine

When Zo returned to Happy Camper, Harley was having a difficult conversation with a customer who thought an item was on sale. Unfortunately, it was not. Harley was a whiz with numbers but could be shy with people. The opposite held true for Zo. She loved chatting with customers. It was one of the reasons she enjoyed writing her Happy Camper column. The piece gave her the opportunity to talk to people in the community. Which reminded her, she still needed to talk to Brady Merrigan about the station's plans for the holidays. With the new evidence against her, she wondered how fun that *wouldn't* be.

She brushed aside the worry and joined Harley and the customer's conversation. "Is it a gift?"

"Yes, it's for my mother." The woman's voice softened. "She's a huge cat lover." The merchandise was a sign that read, COFFEE, CATS, AND KINDNESS: IT'S ALL THE WORLD REALLY NEEDS.

"I'm sure you've met George the cat, then," said Zo.

The customer shook her head, and Zo led her to the bookcase, where George was shelved above the A and B section. He stretched out as Zo approached.

"My mom would love him." She smiled. "Can I snap a picture?"

"Of course," agreed Zo. "George is very photogenic." George took the opportunity to cover his face with one fluffy orange paw. He loved proving her wrong, but she didn't care. She liked his aloofness and was glad he was feeling like his old self again.

"Adorable," the woman cooed, handing Zo the merchandise and snapping a picture. "You can go ahead and wrap this up—even if it isn't half-off."

She followed Zo to the register. "If there's anyone who deserves the perfect gift, it's Mom, right?"

Zo's eyes fell to the printout of plays Hattie had given her. Within the stack may be the key to her birth mom's identity. Murder or not, Zo deserved to grant herself permission to look. "You're absolutely right."

After Zo wrapped the purchase and bid the customer goodbye, Harley approached the counter. "There goes another happy camper."

"How about you?" said Zo. "You must need a dinner break. Why don't you go early? You've had a busy afternoon, and I can handle this."

"Sure." Harley grabbed her wallet from beneath the counter. "Honey Buns has their buns half-off for Crazy Days."

"Yum," said Zo. "Take your time." Honey Buns' saucer-size rolls were meals in themselves. Drenched in natural honey or huckleberry jam, the large fluffy pastries were perfect for an early supper.

While Harley was gone, Zo straightened the rest of the wrapping supplies. From the looks of the messy counter, it must have been a busy afternoon. She glanced at George, still asleep on the bookshelf. Or George had been busy. After the bookshelf, his favorite bed was a piece of wrapping paper.

Harley reappeared with a soft drink and satisfied smile. Zo took it to mean the bun was delicious. When Zo inquired, her reply was "heaven."

Stuffing the list of plays into her backpack, she bid Harley goodbye. She needed to finish her column and that meant a detour to the police station. Next stop, the theater. She wasn't going to let another day go by without perusing the old playbills. Tomorrow the playhouse would begin its weekend shows, and another three days would pass. She wasn't about to let that happen without at least spending a few minutes looking through the storage room.

The walk—and column—were welcome reprieves from thinking about Marianne's murder. She gazed at the azure sky, which was fading quickly. The days were getting shorter. Dusk loomed at the edge of the forest, waiting to cloak the sun like a black cape. Gold lights began to flicker from store windows, and smoke puffed from crooked chimneys. Under the footbridge, the creek babbled below. Zo took a breath of frosty air. The fall was picture perfect.

She stood in front of the police station, surprised by her quick arrival. It was as if her legs knew what to do. They were on assignment even if her brain was elsewhere. Her "Spirit of the Season" column was one of her favorite pieces. No one could get cranky talking about holiday charities, even Chief Merrigan.

She gave the woman at the desk her name and asked if he was there. After a quick call, the woman confirmed he was and buzzed Zo in. Brady met her in the hallway, his cowboy hat titled to one side, revealing more of his jet-black hair than usual. Maybe he was on his way out.

"To what do I owe this unexpected pleasure?" asked Brady.

"My column is due tomorrow," Zo explained. "I never got your response. What's the station doing for its charity drive?"

"And here I thought I was going to get out of work a little early." Brady gestured to his office, a large room surrounded by smaller cubicles. "Come this way."

The décor hadn't changed since the last time she was here. Bison prints, horns, and a geographic map of the state made her feel as if she'd entered the Wild West as she crossed the threshold. She would have sworn she smelled cowhide. It must have been his leather chair, though it didn't look new. Zo had to wonder how much of it was her imagination, which had a tendency to add its own details.

She took out a notepad and pencil from her backpack and plopped down in the chair across from his desk. Poised to jot down his answer, she asked, "What did you come up with?"

He rubbed his jaw. "This murder investigation has eaten up a lot of my time—all of it."

Tell me about it. It had taken over her day job. But it *was* his day job. It had to be hard concentrating on anything else. "Do you have any new leads in the case?"

"Nice try, Zo." Brady let out a chuckle. "You know I can't discuss the case with a civilian."

She crossed her foot over her knee. "I think I'm a bit more than a civilian. Marianne was found near my store and so was the murder weapon. If the case isn't solved by seven p.m. tomorrow night, I'm going to be primetime news."

Brady tapped his desk. "That Justin Castle is a bugger."

"Thank you," said Zo. "It's nice to hear you and I agree on one thing."

He smiled. "If I find anything that clears your name, he'll be the first to hear it. I promise you that."

"I appreciate it." She felt the wall between them shift an inkling and returned his smile. "I'm guessing you don't have any ideas for your charity drive."

"Oh I have ideas," said Brady. "I just don't know if they're any good."

"Maybe you want to run them by me," Zo suggested. "I'll give you an honest opinion."

"I don't doubt that." Brady looked out the window, then back at her. He must have decided it was okay to discuss them because he continued. "We did the coat drive last year, and the food bank the year before."

Zo nodded. "Right. So you want to do something different?"

"Yes, something new."

"Any idea what that might be?" Zo would be here all night if he didn't spit it out, and she wanted to get to the theater while it was still open.

"I have one, but I don't know how it would work."

"Maybe we can figure it out together," Zo tried. Really, Brady was being downright shy.

"Formula," he sputtered. "For babies. I'd like to see about donating formula to babies."

"That's a great idea," said Zo. "Where did you see that?"

His brow furrowed. "What do you mean? I didn't see it anywhere. I came up with it myself."

Zo was pleasantly surprised. She'd never seen the softer side of Brady Merrigan, but here it was, in the form of baby formula. The holidays really did bring out the best in people.

"Seems like it wasn't long ago that you were left here, in our care," said Brady. "We didn't have anything for you to eat except the bottle in your carrier. I was young. And I'm not too proud to admit I was afraid."

Zo sat up in her chair. "Wait. You're telling me you were here when I was dropped off?"

"Of course I was." Brady laced his fingers. "I've been with the station thirty-five years. I was just a kid then. A rookie, and scared as heck, too. You wouldn't quit crying. Even then you had a set of lungs and knew how to use them."

Zo could hardly believe her ears. Picturing the scenario in her mind, she smiled. Poor Brady Merrigan. She couldn't see him dealing with a baby. "What did you do?"

"Well, I gave you the bottle, for starters, but I didn't want to. I could see it was the only one you had, and I was worried you'd start crying again when it was gone." He stopped, clearly remembering. "Actually, though, you went to sleep."

She leaned back in her chair. "Huh. I never knew."

"I guess I should have told you."

"It's okay," said Zo. "I never thought to ask. Did you ever have any idea who dropped me off?"

He shook his head. "We never did. Nobody saw her—or him. It was Christmas time. Cold and frosty. The roads were slick, and the station was a ghost town. Every officer we had was out helping with accidents and the storm. That's when you decided to make your entrance. It was as if you were delivered by a phantom."

Phantom. His comment reminded Zo of the Opera House's current production. Actors and actresses were masters of disguise. Maybe her mom disguised herself the night she dropped her off. Maybe that's why no one saw her. "A phantom or an actress."

Brady leaned over his desk. "What do you mean? What makes you say that?"

In the heat of the moment, Zo almost spit it out. Then she checked herself. Only her close friends knew about the necklace. Though she and Brady chipped away at a barrier tonight, she wasn't prepared to share anything else. "It's nothing. Let's get back to the formula drive before you have to leave."

For the next ten minutes, they talked about the details of the fundraiser. By the time they were finished, Zo had a page full of notes and a newfound respect for Brady. He must have felt likewise. When she stood to leave, he held out his hand.

"Thanks for your help with this, Zo."

"No problem."

He walked her to his office door, and she scurried down the hallway, a new enthusiasm in her step. Their conversation brought the nagging questions surrounding her birth to the forefront of her mind. She had a lead on her natural mother yet she hadn't followed it. Why? Was she afraid of what she might find? Did a part of her not want to know? She opened the door to the late afternoon, shaking off the doubt that always surrounded this part of her life. She wouldn't be satisfied until she knew the answers, no matter what those answers were. Life was a series of stories. She deserved to know how hers began.

Chapter Thirty

The opera house didn't have a performance tonight, so Zo hoped she could catch Nikki before she left for the day. It didn't even need to be Nikki. Chances were, someone would be around to let her in, and Nikki said she could dig through the old playbills anytime. Still, Zo wanted to get there as soon as possible, before the doors were locked for the evening.

She walked double-time toward Main Street, noting the new clouds blotting out the remaining drops of daylight. Steel-gray, they would bring a quick, cold rain. The wind, too, indicated a storm. A wind whistled through the street, sending shivers up her back, and she scampered toward the opera house, where the lights shone bright white.

Once inside, she smoothed her hair, which had been ruffled by the wind. She checked the lobby for someone to help her. It was empty. So was the will-call booth and concessions stand. From the inside of the auditorium, she heard a clang. Maybe that was Nikki. She ducked inside the theater, hoping she wasn't too late. "Hello?"

A construction worker met her at the bottom of the stairs. Zo recognized him as the helpful person who found the necklace. With his long black braid and kind eyes, Chaska was a man not easily forgotten.

"Oh, hey." He was carrying a bucket of paint supplies. They were finished with the touch ups.

"Hi, Chaska. Is Nikki in?"

"I don't know." Chaska shrugged. "She was earlier." He scanned the auditorium. "I haven't seen her for a while."

"Oh." She had no idea where the playbills were stored or how to get to them. If Nikki had left for the day, Zo would have to come back tomorrow. She kicked herself for taking too long at the police station.

"Maybe I can help you?" Chaska offered.

"It looks like you're packing up for the day," said Zo. "I don't want to keep you."

"It's no problem."

"That's very generous of you," she said. "Thanks. All I need is for you to point me in the direction of the storage room. Nikki said I could go through the old playbills in there anytime."

Chaska set down the pail. "Storage room...I wonder if you mean the prop room?"

"Nikki said there's a bunch of junk in there from the remodel. She's still going through it."

"Oh, I know where you mean," said Chaska. "Come on. It's in the basement."

Zo followed him toward the stage, where they turned and went through a doorway and down a steep flight of steps. At the bottom of the stairwell, Chaska flipped on a light, which began to buzz. It didn't give off much illumination. From what Zo could see, though, there were a series of rooms. As they continued, she noted some of them held dusty props like vases and candlesticks while others stored racks of old costumes.

Chaska stopped in front of a room with file cabinets, boxes, and bags. "This has to be what she was talking about. A lot of this needs to be archived yet."

"I believe you're right," said Zo. "Thanks so much."

"Do you need anything else before I go?"

"No, you've been more than helpful," said Zo. "Have a good night."

"You, too."

His footsteps echoed as he climbed the concrete stairs. Zo instantly missed the company. She wasn't skittish, but it was downright spooky here. The masks, the costumes, the props—everything that brought the stage to life—looked strange and otherworldly. They, like her, were abandoned in the cement cellar, the buzz of a single lightbulb the only sound.

Shaking off her unease, she got to work, unlocking the file cabinet with the key that hung on the drawer. She didn't have time for childish fears. Inside were the usual folders and papers, business items. The theater camp had several tabs, organized by theme and year. Nothing about the plays themselves.

Zo skipped to another drawer, where she found information on the renovation, including donors' names, addresses, and amounts. She sneaked a quick peak under M for Marianne Morgan. Marianne donated on a monthly basis, not to mention a hefty sum for the renovation. When Zo and Emily were searching for the checkbook, she'd noticed the reoccurring payment on the bank statement. She only remembered it now.

Still, Zo found no playbills. She shuffled through some boxes on the floor. A few were marked; others were not. She passed over the ones that didn't relate to old productions, turning to the unmarked boxes in the corner. One held newspaper clippings. The clippings must have been displayed once because they had little holes in the corners. Zo spent some time poring over them, unable to resist the news from ages past.

Twenty minutes later, she realized the evening was slipping away from her. She dusted off the top of another box, looking for a label or marking. It was haphazardly closed, the corners folded into a cross.

Her heart flip-flopped when she saw a program on top. This could be the box Nikki was talking about. Digging deeper, she realized it was. She removed a slippery stack of playbills and placed it on the floor. Then she grabbed the printout Hattie gave her from her backpack. There were twelve productions listed, six from thirty-four years ago and six from thirty-three. Zo started with the list from thirty-three years ago, knowing that her mom had to have been wearing the necklace *after* she was born. *Cats*, *A Streetcar Named Desire*, *Into the Woods*, *A Raisin in the Sun*, *Oklahoma!*, *West Side Story*—those were the six playbills she needed to find.

Sifting through the stack, she found all but *A Streetcar Named Desire*. She started with *Cats*. Turning to the cast bios, she wasn't sure what she would find. Ideally a woman wearing a moon necklace. But she knew that would never happen. The headshots were taken well before the productions. They were also black and white. It was hard to tell hair color or eye color. Zo was relying on sheer intuition—and the short bios. Maybe the name would be a clue. Something that started with a Z.

Nothing jumped out at her, and she turned to the next program and the next until she came upon the bios from the cast members of *Into the Woods*, a production put on by a touring theater company. The young actress playing the witch caught her eye, and Zo snapped a quick picture with her phone. Light hair, feathery brows, a straight nose. Her similar appearance had to mean a connection. Zo scanned for her name: Elle Hart. She leaned back on her heels. It made perfect sense. The necklace had her own name on it! How could Zo have been so blind? Zoelle: the name was a combination of hers and her mom's.

Zo studied the picture. Elle lived in New York, where she'd recently graduated from the American Academy of Dramatic Arts. Though new to the theater, she'd received an award for her role as Emma in *Song & Dance*. It seemed to Zo that Elle was well on her way to stardom. She was educated, talented, and toured with a popular theater group. A baby was not in her plans, and Zo understood why.

Earlier, Zo spotted contracts in the file cabinet, and she rose to recheck them now. Maybe something existed from the troupe's time in Spirit Canyon? Zo wasn't sure how theater contracts worked, but maybe they listed troupe members' phone numbers or addresses. She thumbed through the paperwork, finding nothing on the touring group with *Into the Woods*.

She moved to the bottom drawer, and as she searched through old donations, hoping to find a paystub or ticket, she stopped on a large donation. It wasn't just the amount that had her startled; it was the contradiction. The construction crew was volunteering their time, yet many donations had been made to a renovation fund, including Marianne's. Where was the money going?

Zo shut the drawer. It was time to ask Nikki, who might also be able to help her with Elle Hart. If anyone knew how to track down an actor or actress, it would be the managing director.

She walked out of the room and down the narrow hallway, keenly aware of her solitude in the dark, damp basement. The dankness made her skin feel cool, and her arms prickled with gooseflesh. She took out her phone and turned on the flashlight. If nothing else, the modern illumination made her feel less alone.

The hallway grew brighter, propelling her forward. Zo squinted at her phone. Had the latest software update improved the flashlight? It seemed impossible, and yet the entire area was bathed in a glow that was hard to explain.

Forging on, Zo noticed the antique props from productions past in the side rooms. Coats, wigs, statues, purses. Zo stopped. She recognized one of those purses, didn't she?

She made an automatic detour. Her hand was shaking as she set down her phone on the prop table. Unlike the other items, the purse looked newer and, much to her surprise, was heavy. Inside she found a brush, a mirror, a wallet. Zo took out the leather billfold, undoing the buckle with twitching fingers. It was just as she thought. *Marianne's checkbook.* This was her purse, and the good news was she used duplicate checks.

Zo fumbled through the duplicates: 3542, 3543...3544. She found the copy of the ripped check, and it was written to Nikki Ainsworth. Theater Donation was scribbled in the memo line. Quickly, Zo took a picture of it and sent it to Max. Because of the lack of a signal in the basement, the message hung. She stared at the blue bar, wondering what to do. Should she take the checkbook, the wallet, or the entire purse? She decided on none of them. More evidence in her possession wasn't what she needed. Right now she needed to get the police to the theater, before Nikki returned. She checked her cell phone. Still no signal.

She crept out of the room, up the stairs, and found herself on the backstage of the theater. She must have taken a wrong turn. Twisting in the dark, she didn't recognize her surroundings. Curtains, ropes, and the *Phantom of the Opera* scenery added to the eerie feeling. Zo tamped down her desire to flee. Running headlong out of the auditorium wouldn't do anybody any good, least of all Marianne. If Zo was to get her justice, she needed to use her head, not her legs.

Taking a deep breath, she inched across the stage, holding out her hand for guidance. Running into something was a possibility, but she didn't want to use her phone flashlight, just in case Nikki returned. There was no way she was confronting her on her own.

Her hand brushed some kind of fabric, lace. Then satin. Zo was near a clothing rack. Something felt squishy, and she pinched the material. It felt like foam, a padded outfit. Squinting, she realized it was a suit used to make actors appear larger. She stood blinking into the darkness. Why wasn't she moving? The costume interested her for some reason. What that reason was, she couldn't say.

Then it came to her. It was a disguise, just like the one used to conceal Marianne the night of her murder. Zo had mistaken Marianne for a real witch, a trick of the trade done by a theater professional like Nikki Ainsworth. Nikki had used a disguise again, when she wore the padded suit to Happy Camper to plant the murder weapon. That's why Zo didn't recognize her—and that's why Nikki moved so slowly. Nikki wasn't used to the extra weight of the suit. Combined with the hat, the disguise made Zo believe she was a man. Boy was she wrong.

Zo heard footsteps, and they weren't hers. They were tiny clicks—high heels. She clasped her hand over her mouth to keep from sucking in a breath. How would she get out of here now? *Stay calm*, she told herself. As a child, she'd been a master of slipping in and out of houses. If she could channel her inner-foster kid, she knew she'd get out just fine.

That was, until her phone started ringing. Katrina and the Waves' "Walking on Sunshine" reverberated through the auditorium, and the lights turned on seconds later. Zo pulled her phone out of her back pocket and silenced Max's call. But it was too late. Her location had been revealed.

Chapter Thirty-One

"Zo?" called Nikki. "Is that you?"

Zo had no choice. She stepped out from behind the curtain.

Nikki was approaching the stage with a confused look on her face. "What are you doing back there? Chaska said you were in the archives."

"I was," Zo said. "I must have taken a wrong turn."

Nikki considered her explanation. Maybe it was the knowledge that she'd killed another person that made her look so sinister. Zo hadn't seen it before, but Nikki's blue eyes weren't clear—they were cold-blooded. Zo wondered if they saw through her poor performance.

"Did you find what you were looking for?" asked Nikki.

"I did," said Zo. "I found a program with what I believe is a picture of my mother. *Into the Woods.* Believe it or not, she was the witch. Thanks again for letting me take a peek."

"Wonderful," Nikki gushed. "Let me see. I want to know if there's a resemblance." A reassuring smile was plastered to her lips, but Zo decided everything about her was fake. She was just too good of an actress for Zo to realize it before.

"Oh I didn't take the program," explained Zo. "I thought you might want to display it somewhere."

"Absolutely not," said Nikki. "You should have it. Let's go down and get it."

The idea of going anywhere with Nikki was terrifying, especially the dank theater cellar. "That's okay. I took a picture. I don't need it."

"Wonderful. May I?" She nodded toward the phone, still in Zo's hand.

Zo didn't have a choice but to show her. "Of course." She pulled up the photo of the program and flashed it at Nikki.

"I believe I know her." Nikki squinted at the picture.

Zo took a step forward, forgetting the danger. Nikki had been in theater for over a decade. If anyone knew something about her birth mother, it might be Nikki. "Really?"

Nikki reached for the phone. "She might have played Lady Macbeth a couple of years ago."

Zo watched her study the picture for several moments. Then she swiped to the next picture, which to Zo's horror, was Marianne's duplicate check.

"It looks as if you found something else in the basement," accused Nikki.

Zo shook her head no. Nikki's assertion was a ploy to get her phone. How could Zo have been so blind?

"Yes, but you did." Nikki pressed the trash can icon next to the picture, and the picture of the check was gone.

"Hey!" Zo exclaimed. "Give me my phone back."

"I don't think so," said Nikki. "I'm going to hold onto it for a while."

"Whatever. I'm leaving." She went to step past Nikki, but Nikki blocked her way.

"I know you used to be a journalist," said Nikki. "Don't you want to know why I have Marianne's purse in the basement?"

Zo wanted the truth, desperately, but it wasn't worth her life. If Nikki told her, she'd have to kill her to keep the information from getting to the police. "I think I have an idea."

"I'm not a bad person," insisted Nikki. "In fact, I'm a really *good* person. Do you know how many hours I've spent in this theater?" She motioned to the auditorium with her hand. "Painting scenes, coddling actors, organizing workshops, begging for money while not receiving a decent paycheck myself?" She didn't wait for Zo to answer. "Thirteen years. I revive the opera house single handedly, and what thanks do I get? Marianne calling me out. You snooping around the basement, after all I've done for you. I'm done with being used."

"Think of all the enjoyment you've brought to audiences who've seen the productions," tried Zo. "Not to mention the joy to the town itself. That's worth more than money."

"Ha!" said Nikki. "You're either too young or too naïve. People have to get paid—in dollar amounts."

"Which is why you deposited the donations into your own account, to make up for your poor salary."

"I didn't take anything I didn't earn." Nikki picked up a bronze candlestick from a table near the wings. "I deserved it."

"But Marianne didn't deserve to die." Zo watched Nikki carefully. "She was your friend."

"*Was*," repeated Nikki. "Until she 'reclaimed her power from me.' That night, I returned her latest donation—her largest donation, too. I told her I'd stop all future deductions, but it wasn't enough. She said she was turning me in to the theater board."

"That's when you killed her," said Zo.

Nikki didn't blink. "I couldn't see the theater destroyed. It's my life. I did what I had to do, and I'd do it again. I took the check. I took the purse. I thought I had all the evidence. How did you know?"

"Marianne told me."

Nikki smiled, a slow bone-chilling grin. Her eyes narrowed to slits. "I don't believe in ghosts."

A moment passed, an excruciating second of silence. Zo didn't know what to do or how to get out of there. One thing was certain: if she stood still, she would get nowhere but killed. Nikki had said as much.

Quickly, Zo turned to run in the opposite direction, and something heavy hit her between the shoulder blades. It was the candlestick. She fell to the stage floor. She yelped in pain as she tried to turn to a standing position. Her ankle was sprained from the fall.

Over her shoulder she could see Nikki coming toward her, her face twisted into a grimace. She wasn't afraid to kill for what she wanted. There was nothing Zo could do but defend herself. She wasn't running anywhere soon. She sat up, ready to do battle. That's when she heard a noise on the catwalk. A rush of wind, air flitting by. The ropes swayed, but no one appeared.

Without warning, the iconic gold and white chandelier from *Phantom of the Opera* fell from the ceiling. In a dramatic swoop, it hit Nikki, and she was on the floor, her legs pinned into place by the heavy fixture. She let out a yelp.

"Zo!" yelled Max, running up the aisle. The large German shepherd was at his side, moving fast despite a bandaged leg. "Are you okay?"

Zo scrambled to her feet, falling in the process. Her ankle was worse than her back. "I'm okay," she hollered. The dog came to her aid, standing like a guard over her. "It's Nikki. She killed Marianne and tried to kill me."

Max went to Nikki, placing her in handcuffs before she could flee, though with the chandelier restraining her, escape was improbable. Police officers surrounded them seconds later, and the next few minutes were a blur of uniforms, including firefighters and paramedics.

Zo assured a medic she was fine, but he wrapped the ankle anyway, telling her to make certain she got it checked out by a doctor tomorrow at the latest. But she had more important things on her mind than a sore ankle. Clearing Happy Camper of wrongdoing, for starters.

When the medic finished, Max approached her. He patted the German shepherd's large head. "Good girl." He checked Zo's bandage. "How's the ankle?"

"I'm fine," she said. "Really. It's just a sprain." She nodded toward the pooch. "I see you got a partner now."

"No one claimed her, so I did. I named her Scout."

Zo scratched the dog's perky ear. The name reminded her of Scout in *To Kill a Mockingbird*. "I like it."

"I saw your text," he explained. "A little too late, it would seem."

They watched the medics haul Nikki out of the theater. She was handcuffed to the stretcher, with Brady Merrigan following closely behind. "She was the false friend Marianne warned us about. I just wish I would have realized it sooner."

"How could you?" asked Max. "Nikki wasn't even on our radar."

"First the book passage, then the séance?" Zo let out a breath. "I should have put the clues together sooner."

Max helped her to a standing position. His warm hands felt good on her cool skin. "What about the séance?"

"A Halloween decoration fell off a clearance table," said Zo. "At the time, I didn't think anything of it. Now I realize Marianne was trying to give me a sign."

"What was the decoration?"

She rolled her eyes. "A mask."

"I wish I would have received your text sooner." He helped her down the steps. Scout trailed behind them. "You might have been hurt even worse than you are."

"I'm just glad you arrived when you did," said Zo. "Though I have to admit, I never imagined you'd drop a chandelier on her. That was a surprise."

"What are you talking about?" Max questioned. "I came from the lobby, remember? I didn't drop the chandelier."

That's right. Max ran up the aisle. He wasn't backstage. "If you didn't, who did?" asked Zo.

Their eyes left each other's, looking into the sea of empty red chairs surrounding them. The lights flickered, the same cue that directed patrons to return to their seats.

Max clasped her hand, and they continued down the aisle. "I think we have our answer."

Epilogue

Friday night, Zo and her friends situated themselves around the television set in her living room. Jules had brought wine, Max had brought pizza, and Duncan had brought his charming personality. It was almost seven o'clock, which meant Justin Castle's special report would be airing any second. Zo was on pins and needles, wondering what he would say now that the police had charged Nikki with Marianne's murder.

As she waited, she was glad to be surrounded by good company. She absorbed the cozy feeling, finishing the last bite of her cheesy pizza. She and Max were sitting on the floor, leaning against the couch, with a warm Sherpa blanket covering their toes. Jules and Duncan were discussing the Sips and Swings event, and George was front and center, on top of the TV, annoying but safe. His orange tail twitched back and forth, counting down the seconds to the program.

The commercial ended, and music announced the special report. Jules leaped up, wine glass in hand. "This is it! This is it!"

"Down, George," yelled Zo. When he didn't budge, she stood and picked him off the TV and placed him gently on the blanket. But she was too anxious to join him. What would Justin say? What *could* he say? The murderer had been caught. The store was cleared from wrongdoing. Still, this was Justin Castle. If a way existed to get attention, he would find it.

"Shh!" Max sat up straighter. "Here he comes."

Justin appeared on the screen wearing a gray suit and navy tie. The studio lights beamed off his shiny, dark hair. He reminded Zo of a Ken doll, waxy and new. "Tonight's special is one you've been waiting for, viewers, as have I. There has been a slight...change in programing, but the new topic is just as urgent and important. The killer in the case of Marianne

Morgan has been apprehended, but another dangerous, predator is on the loose in Spirit Canyon. Tonight, I'm going behind the scenes to bring you all the information on Spirit Canyon's unseen danger in the case of the Killer Rocky Mountain Goat."

Jules scrunched up her nose. "Did he just say mountain goat?"

Justin's professional voice droned on. "Stay tuned to find out how to protect yourself and your family from this beautiful but harmful animal."

Zo burst out laughing, and the others joined in. Justin wouldn't be talking about her, the store, or anyone else. In the quiet town of Spirit Canyon, he was down to reporting on woodland animals, and it pleased her to no end.

Duncan flicked off the television set, and Jules raised her wine glass. "To the mountain goat!"

Max stood. "To Zo!"

"Actually, to Marianne." Zo clinked their glasses. "And to good witches everywhere."

Acknowledgments

Thank you to my husband, Quintin, who not only makes me "cackle" but also came up with the name for Zo's Cackle Cakes. To my daughter Maisie, who helped me perfect the recipe. To my daughter Maddie, who taste tested each and every batch. To my mom, who continues to inspire and encourage me. To my dad, for sharing his joy of reading with me. I miss him. To my extended Honerman family, for all their support. To my dear friend Amy Cecil Holm, for her keen ear and careful eye. To my agent, Amanda Jain, my editor, Norma Perez-Hernandez, production editor Rebecca Cremonese, and the staff at Kensington, thank you for making my work better. Your dedication is very appreciated.

Zo Jones's Cackle Cakes

Ingredients for cupcakes:

1 C. flour
1/2 tsp. baking soda
1 1/2 tsp. baking powder
1/2 C. cocoa
1/8 tsp. salt
3 Tbsp. butter, softened
1 C. sugar
2 eggs
1/2 tsp. vanilla
3/4 C. buttermilk
Oreo cookies, Hershey kisses, and orange and purple sprinkles for decoration

Ingredients for vanilla frosting:

1/2 C. unsalted butter, softened
2 tsp. vanilla extract
2 C. confectioners' sugar
2 Tbsp. of milk
2-3 drops of green food coloring

Directions:
Preheat oven to 350 degrees. Line muffin tin with liners.
Mix flour, baking soda, baking powder, cocoa, and salt in one bowl.
In a larger bowl, cream butter, sugar, eggs, and vanilla.
Alternating with buttermilk, slowly add the dry ingredients to the wet ingredients.
Fill muffin cups about 2/3 full.
Bake 17-18 minutes, or until a toothpick comes out clean.

For frosting, cream together butter and vanilla. Mix in confectioners' sugar and milk.
Add two drops of green food coloring. (I use gel food coloring.)

To assemble the Cackle Cakes, wait for the cupcakes to cool. Then frost.

Take apart an Oreo cookie, using one chocolate wafer for the hat.

Put a dab of frosting in the middle, and then press on the candy kiss.

Decorate the hat with candy sprinkles and place it on the cupcake.

Printed in the United States
by Baker & Taylor Publisher Services